Madeline Boyd's Eyes Were Darting Over Those Assembled on the Shore, Trying to Guess Which Was Felton Cate, the Man to Whom She Would Be Indentured for Four Years.

She saw a tall man standing a little apart from the others who were meeting the ship. He stood back from the wharf, and leaned against a maple tree whose blood-red leaves left his face partially in shadow. She could see that his eyes were on her, staring as though she were some species he had never seen before.

The captain motioned to her. "We will go ashore now. I have your papers here, ready for your master."

A few minutes later she and the captain were off the wharf, when suddenly she began to reel and stagger. The tall man she had noticed from the ship reached out and caught her before she fell. As he held her, she could feel her heart beating wildly.

"You do not have your land legs yet," he said, laughing.

Madeline pulled herself away. "You must be Felton Cate."

"No madam," he replied. "Gavin Durant at your service."

Dear Reader,

We, the editors of Tapestry Romances, are committed to bringing you two outstanding original romantic historical novels each and every month.

From Kentucky in the 1850s to the court of Louis XIII, from the deck of a pirate ship within sight of Gibraltar to a mining camp high in the Sierra Nevadas, our heroines experience life and love, romance and adventure.

Our aim is to give you the kind of historical romances that you want to read. We would enjoy hearing your thoughts about this book and all future Tapestry Romances. Please write to us at the address below.

The Editors
Tapestry Romances
POCKET BOOKS
1230 Avenue of the Americas
Box TAP
New York, N.Y. 10020

Bound by Honor

Helen Tucker

A TAPESTRY BOOK
PUBLISHED BY POCKET BOOKS NEW YORK

Books by Helen Tucker

Ardent Vows
Bound by Honor

Published by TAPESTRY BOOKS

An *Original* publication of Tapestry Books

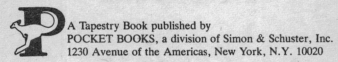

A Tapestry Book published by
POCKET BOOKS, a division of Simon & Schuster, Inc.
1230 Avenue of the Americas, New York, N.Y. 10020

ISBN: 0-671-49781-2

First Tapestry Books printing April, 1984

10 9 8 7 6 5 4 3 2 1

POCKET and colophon are registered trademarks
of Simon & Schuster, Inc.

TAPESTRY is a trademark of Simon & Schuster, Inc.

Printed in the U.S.A.

Chapter One

NOTHING HAD TURNED OUT THE WAY SHE HAD EXPECTED. Standing at the rail on the top deck of the *Sea Lion* and looking down at the swirling gray water, Madeline Boyd admitted that not even the ocean looked as she had imagined it would. She had thought the water would be vividly blue with perhaps a tinge of green here and there, but all she could see was gray, gray, gray. The gray billows reflected the gray sky. And as far as Madeline knew, it had been that way ever since the ship had sailed from Bristol harbor down the Bristol Channel and out into the Atlantic almost six weeks ago. For most of the six weeks she had been below in the long, oversized cabin she shared with nine other women and four children, too ill to know or care about the color of sky and sea.

Madeline had begun the voyage with a mixture of hope and fear, but her fear of the unknown was not nearly as great as the horror of what she knew her life would become unless she left England.

She turned her back to the water and looked across the deck. At the stern, near the captain's quarters, she spotted Jessie, her newfound and faithful friend who had tended her during her long, debilitating illness.

1

Jessie waved, said something to her two children that sent them scurrying down the ladderlike steps to the deck below, then slowly made her way to the bow to join Madeline. There was a roll to the ship today, but at least it wasn't pitching the way it had been before when Madeline developed the deathly seasickness that had almost become pneumonia. She was convinced that had it not been for Jessie's care, she would have died, and the thought of her body being thrown over the side of the ship, abandoned to the merciless gray Atlantic, made her shudder uncontrollably.

"Dear Lord, you're not getting the chills again, are you?" Jessie put her hand on Madeline's shoulder. "I told you not to stay up here too long. The air is chilly and damp and you're still weaker than you know."

Madeline smiled. "I know just how weak I am. But I am not having a chill. I was thinking of something . . . unpleasant."

"I'm glad that is all it is," Jessie said. "I don't think either of us could stand it if you got sick again."

"Amen to that," Madeline agreed. "Jessie, I don't know what I would have done without . . ."

"Don't start that again. You have thanked me quite enough for what little I did." Jessie gave an embarrassed laugh, then changed the subject. "Look over there by the third gun. See that sailor? He has been staring at you ever since you came topside. And so have those other two near the first mast. They can't take their eyes off you, and I'm afraid if they don't get back to their duties we won't set foot on land for another six weeks."

"I've hardly been up here at all since we left Bristol, so they probably think I'm a new passenger," Madeline laughed. "They're wondering how I could have boarded in the middle of the ocean."

"What they're thinking," Jessie said, "is that you're the prettiest thing their seagoing eyes ever beheld."

Now it was Madeline's turn to be embarrassed. Compliments always did that to her. She was not blind to the fact that she was attractive—with her silver blonde hair and steel gray eyes—but her beauty was not of her making and, therefore, undeserving of praise. One cannot help the attributes one is born with, she thought. It is the qualities one acquires—like kindness, consideration of others, generosity—that should be complimented. That was what her father had taught her ever since she was old enough to understand so that she would not be vain about her beauty.

Madeline was tall and reedy. She had a wide, generous mouth, which some said denoted good nature, and dimples when she smiled, which was often . . . until the past few months when life had become intolerable.

But she had promised herself not to think about that. She would think only of her new life in the new land.

"Will your husband be at the dock to meet the ship?" she asked Jessie.

"Yes, even though there is no way of knowing when the ship will get there. Bath Town is small. I think Cyrus said there were less than thirty houses and a population of less than a hundred, so when the word goes out that a ship is coming down river, everyone rushes to the wharf."

Jessie told Madeline that Cyrus Roland was a blacksmith and lived right in Bath Town in a house he had built himself. He had left England two years ago, not because his business wasn't providing a living for his family but because he wanted, just one time in his life before he was too old, to answer the siren call of adventure. He had promised that as soon as he was well established he would send for Jessie and the two children.

"I wonder if he'll think . . . that I look old now," Jessie murmured as though talking to herself. She was thirty-six years old and her dark hair had no hint of gray and her hazel eyes were clear with only the tiniest crinkles at the corners when she smiled, but she was thickening in the middle and, looking at her, one would know the first bloom of youth had vanished. To Madeline, whose twentieth birthday was still some months away, Jessie would have seemed more like a contemporary of her mother's, had her mother been alive.

"He's probably wondering if you'll think *he* has changed," Madeline said.

"I am, and he most likely has," Jessie said. "But what about the man you are to marry—your betrothed?" she asked. "How long has it been since he left England?"

Madeline turned back to the rail and looked again at the gray sea. The day she had come aboard ship and met Jessie, who had the bunk next to hers, it had seemed easier—certainly more logical—to say that she was going to Bath Town to marry rather than tell her her real reason for leaving home. *That* was something she had vowed never to tell anyone. Now, with the possibility of sighting land in less than a fortnight, she wondered if she shouldn't tell Jessie at least a very small part of the truth, that part which she certainly would find out anyway as soon as the ship docked.

"Jessie, I am not going to Bath Town to marry." She

hesitated, wondering if she should give some reason for having misled the woman who had become her close friend. "I am going as a servant, an indentured servant. It was the only way I could get money for my passage and be assured of shelter and a livelihood once I was there."

Jessie's mouth dropped open and her hazel eyes widened. "I . . . that is, you . . ." she stuttered. She was silent for a moment, then said, "What you are doing takes a lot of courage."

Much less courage than staying where I was, Madeline thought. "I apologize for not having told you the truth in the beginning," she said, "but I was afraid you would think me . . . that you would have a low opinion of someone who . . ." Her words trailed off as she remembered the two men in the London office where she had signed the papers of indenture.

That afternoon seemed more of a dream than reality now. It had been unusually cold for June. A fine mist was falling and a bit of fog rolled across London from the Thames. She had had another violent argument with her guardian and had rushed out of the house on Wigmore Street without cloak or bonnet. Her only thought had been to get as far away from Rufus Delong as possible. She took no notice of where she was going, while a jumble of thoughts raced through her mind. She knew she could not continue to live with her guardian and do the degrading things he demanded of her. Her father, had he known he had left her in the care of that depraved man, would have come back from the grave to rescue her.

But it was not possible, of course. How could she get away from him? She had asked herself that question dozens of times in the past six months. She could leave London, perhaps take a position somewhere as a governess, or even a domestic if necessary, but if she remained in England, he would find her and bring her back. He had told her as much.

She walked for what seemed a long time, then suddenly, noticing her environs for the first time, she stopped. She had left the residential area and was approaching the seedy business district near the river. She was about to flee in the opposite direction when she saw a large board with notices posted on it hanging from the side of a tavern. It was the top notice that caught her eye.

ADVERTISEMENT FOR SETTLEMENT
OF THE CAROLINAS

If there be any among you desiring to make a new life for yourself, then look you to the Carolinas where land is plentiful under a sunny sky, where no man is molested or called in question for matters of religion, where with a few servants and a small stock, a great estate may be raised. Be assured of hearty welcome as a settler.

If there be any among you desirous of becoming such settler but be without passage, then hie you to Master Conway at the Green House to the left of Black Friar's Bridge.

Signed by the true and absolute Lords Proprietor of the Carolinas.

Madeline read the notice three times, then almost involuntarily began walking in the direction of Black Friar's Bridge. When she reached the bridge, she began looking for a tavern with the name Green House, for she was sure that was what it was. Instead she saw a small stone house, large enough to contain only one room, its stone walls colored green from algae. She went to the door and pulled the bell cord, almost cringing as a man's voice yelled, "Come in, for God's sake, it's open!"

She went inside only to hear the same voice grumbling, "No one has rung the bell in ten years and . . ." The voice hushed as soon as its owner looked up and saw the beautiful girl standing before him.

The room was small and contained a desk, some chairs, and several boxes filled with what appeared to be some kind of official documents. There were two men in the room. The one who had bade her enter was a squat little man who seemed as broad as he was high. His bald head shone in the lantern light of the windowless room. Behind him, sitting near a keg in the corner, the second man, also bald but with beard and mustache, was staring at her as though he never had before set his eyes upon a female of the species.

She could think of nothing to say as she stood just inside the door staring back at them.

"You must have the wrong address, dearie," said the man nearest her. "Bessie's place is a ways down the street, halfway between here and London Bridge."

"She don't look like one who'd work for Bessie," the man in the corner said, leaving his seat and standing beside his colleague. Both continued to stare at her, hardly blinking.

Madeline found her voice. "I am looking for Master Conway."

"Well, you found him."

Madeline continued. "I saw a notice that said any one who wanted to go to the Carolinas should come here." This room, these men, were almost enough to make her change her mind, but she thought of Rufus again and went a step farther into the room.

"We don't sell you passage here," the man named Conway said. "We just help those with no money to get there."

"I have no money and I need help in getting there." She tried to keep her voice steady.

"What about your family, or husband?" Conway asked. The way he looked at her made Madeline know that it must be unheard of for a girl to come alone to this office.

"I am going alone," she told them, "and I have no money for the passage."

Conway began to laugh. "She has nary a feather to fly with," he said to the other man, then turned back to Madeline. "You running away from a mean husband or a tyrant of a father?"

"I-I am not running away from anyone." Unused to lying, she was afraid they could tell by her face that she was. "I have no relatives, no husband." That much, at least, was true. "That is why I want to try a new life in a new country. The notice said that one desirous of settling in Carolina but who had no money for passage should come here."

The men looked at each other, then one whispered something to the other.

"If you want to become an indentured servant your passage will be paid by the person in Carolina you're indentured to."

"What does that mean, 'indentured'?" she asked.

"It means that you will, in a way, be owned by this person for four years. You will work during that time to pay for your upkeep and to pay back any expense put out on your behalf. After four years, you will be given some money and you will be free then to go where you choose, having paid off your debt."

"But that's slavery!" She was momentarily appalled. But then thinking of the circumstances of her present life, she began to nod in agreement. Conway went on. "Not quite. In four years you'll be free of all obligation." After four more years with Rufus she would be . . . well, it was doubtful that she could survive four more years like the last six months. She still heard the words he had shouted after her as she left the house: "Leave if you want, my girl, but you'll come back. If you don't, I'll find you. No matter how far you go, you'll be brought back to me because, legally, you belong to me until you are of age. And since you have no money of your own, you will still be dependent upon me." His wild laughter had followed her into the street.

Belonging to a total stranger, as a servant, for the next four years could be no worse . . . and might even be much better. Certainly Rufus would not cross the Atlantic looking for her, even if he found out where she had gone.

"I would like to go," she said. "I am willing to be an indentured servant."

"I don't know." Conway scratched his bald pate. "People who want servants usually want a man or a couple. Tell you the truth, dearie, we never had a lone woman come in here before wanting to indenture herself. You sure you don't have yourself a mite of trouble somewhere, like with the law?"

"I'm sure!" she snapped. "Will you or won't you arrange passage for me?"

"No need to get testy about it," he said. "Mackey, look in the second box over by the table. I think I put some of the new letters in there."

The second man lumbered the few steps to the box, picked up the top handful of papers and put them on the desk.

"He can't read," Conway said by way of explanation. His eyes went to the papers. "Here," he said after a minute or two. "Here's one. Fellow named Felton Cate wants either a manservant or a couple provided the woman is a good cook and seamstress." He looked up. "You a good cook and seamstress?"

Madeline, who was a passable cook but who had never sewed a stitch in her life, nodded.

"We send him a woman without a man, he's going to raise all hell, then we don't get our commission," Mackey said.

Conway looked Madeline up and down and her face reddened under his gaze.

His look turned into a leer and Conway smiled for the first time. "I don't think Mr. Felton Cate will be too unhappy," he said. "All right, dearie, I'll fix up the papers of indenture. Why don't you sit down and rest yourself a bit?"

Madeline sat down in a chair beside the desk. She watched Conway scribble with his quill pen. He looked up at her several times. Once, he spoke. "It's customary for an indentured man to be given fifty acres of land at the end of the indenture, but I don't think you'd know what to do with land if you had it."

"I will accept the equivalent in money," she said.

Finally, he handed her the paper for her signature.

This Indenture, on the Twenty-ninth Day of June in the Year of Our Lord 1710. Whereas I —————————————— of London will put myself as servant in the household of Felton Cate of Bath Town, in the colony of the Carolina of the North from the above date for four years to give good and faithful service in the best manner I can, and be given for faithful service, meat, drink, competent lodging, apparel and all things fitting my condition.

At the end of period of servitude shall be granted some payment in place of usual acreage, according to custom of the country.

She stared at the paper for a long time. Was she making the right decision? Should she not wait until the heat of her anger at Rufus cooled? She had heard many stories about the Colonies and the hardship of life there, and she had also heard about those murderous savages, the Indians. But the land was becoming more and more settled all the time, and the latest reports were that the Indians, the untamed ones, were retreating to the interior, far from the coastal colonies.

"You don't know how to read, do you?" Conway asked in a superior tone. "I will show you where to make your mark."

"Of course I can read!" She took the pen from him and signed the paper quickly. "When do I leave?"

Mackey gave a high pitched laugh. "In a bit of a hurry, are you?" He looked meaningfully at Conway. "Anyway, she signed it."

Conway got up and went to another box beside the door. He shuffled through some papers, then said, "Next boat for Carolina is the *Sea Lion,* leaving Bristol August fifteenth. You got money for the coach to Bristol or you want me to add that to your debt to Mr. Cate?"

"Add it, I suppose."

"And what about the money for Mackey or me?" he asked.

"What do you mean?"

"We don't just give you money and trust you to show up for the sailing, dearie. One of us must go with you to Bristol to make sure you get on the boat, and we'll have to have money for the return to London also."

"You have my word that I will be on the *Sea Lion* when she sails from Bristol," Madeline said. The longer she stayed with these two, the more they disgusted her.

"We need more than your word . . ." Conway began, but Mackey interrupted with, "I think she will, at that. She's mighty anxious to get away from something."

Conway gave her another of those long, searching looks, then said, "We'll meet you at the public house near the turnpike at the end of Oxford Street on the thirteenth of August. That's where you'll get the coach for Bristol. We'll give you your passage then."

She nodded and left, returning to the house on Wigmore Street in only a slightly better frame of mind than when she had left it.

* * *

Now, standing beside Jessie on the *Sea Lion,* she wondered for the millionth time if she had done the right thing. Right or wrong, she had done the *only* thing.

Jessie was looking at her, curiosity scarcely veiled in her hazel eyes.

"It didn't take courage to do what I did," Madeline said. "I needed . . . that is, I wanted to get away." Suddenly she wanted to tell Jessie more, thinking that if she told at least part of the story, it would not prey on her mind so much. Then too, after all Jessie had done for her, she deserved to have her curiosity at least partially satisfied.

"But I cannot imagine your family letting you come alone," Jessie said.

"I have no family," Madeline said. "My mother died when I was a baby. My father was a physician in Bath and he took care of me as well as any mother could. But he died two years ago and named a distant cousin—too distant to be counted as kin, really—as my guardian." There was a catch in her voice as she said it. "Rufus Delong is his name and he lives in London. I have lived there with him for the past two years and it . . . it has not been pleasant. That is why I decided to go to the New World." She gave a little laugh. "Like your husband, I wanted adventure."

"I'm surprised your guardian would let you go," Jessie said.

"I didn't tell him I was going. I simply packed up all my belongings and left while he was out."

It had not been easy to get away. Although Rufus went out every morning, she was never sure at what time he would go, and it was necessary that she get to the turnpike by ten o'clock of the day she was to leave for Bristol. Luck was with her, however, and on the morning of the thirteenth, Rufus went out shortly after nine. Madeline rushed out as soon as he was gone from sight and secured a hackney carriage that took her back to the house to get her baggage and then to the public house at the turnpike. She had less than five minutes to spare, and Conway and Mackey were already pacing in front of the public house, worried expressions on their faces. They put her in the coach and as she rode out of London she thought what a strange farewell it was to a city she could have grown to like under different circumstances.

Madeline and the other coach passengers spent the night at Twelve Trees Inn at Marlborough. They arrived in Bristol late the next day, and Madeline hired a hackney carriage to take her straight to the port. The *Sea Lion* was docked beside the *Good Intent,* and there was a flurry of activity as men loaded supplies onto both ships.

Feeling extremely timid, she approached a man who seemed to be in charge of the loading of the *Sea Lion.* "Excuse me," she said, "but I am to be a passenger on this ship tomorrow and I wonder if I might spend tonight here. I have just arrived in Bristol and have nowhere to stay."

"You mean get aboard now?" he asked. "I suppose it will be all right, if you keep the door locked." He helped her take her baggage aboard and she was well aware that other men had stopped what they were doing to stare. She tried to ignore them while looking at the ship. The *Sea Lion* was much larger than she expected; indeed, it was the largest ship she had ever seen. Later, as she tossed about, too sick to raise her head from the bunk, she wondered if the ship was large enough to withstand even the smallest wave.

The *Sea Lion* was a one-hundred-fifty-foot-long, three-hundred-ton, three-masted square-rigger with three decks. In the stern of the top deck, near the helm, were the captain's quarters, and at the bow were the crew's quarters. In between the deck was open, and at the rail were six cannon on both port and starboard sides to be used, Madeline was told later, in case of attack by pirate ships. Also on either side was a lifeboat with four oars. If the ship goes down, she thought, more will be lost than saved. The lifeboats could not possibly hold more than a dozen people each.

Beneath the top deck was the main deck where the passengers were quartered. There was a long, dormitorylike room for the men and the boys and another for the women and children. There were also a few private cabins for those who could afford them. The lower deck and bilges were beneath the main deck and that was where the cargo was being loaded. The galley, with long tables for dining at one end, was midship on the main deck.

For that first night, Madeline was taken to one of the small, private cabins, but was told she would have to move the next day. She locked herself in at once, but she still felt uneasy as she lay awake listening to the movement and noise aboard ship as the loading continued through the night.

"I was terrified," she told Jessie, "and that was the first time I really regretted leaving London. I was afraid that one of the men might break down the door to my cabin and . . . But I kept telling myself that nothing would happen and that when morning came, I wouldn't be afraid any more, and I wasn't."

"You poor dear," Jessie said sympathetically. "Your guardian must be a monster for you to go through all that to get away from him."

Madeline nodded. That was one part of her life she did not want to tell to Jessie, or anyone, so she changed the subject quickly. "I think the fact that I am going to Bath Town is a good omen," she said. "I loved Bath so much when I was growing up there, and I wept for three weeks when I knew I had to move to London."

"But Bath Town was not named for our Bath," Jessie said. "Cyrus wrote me that it was named for the Earl of Bath."

"Well, anyway, I'll feel more at home there because of its name," Madeline said. Her body swayed as the ship plunged through a big wave, and she caught the rail for support. "You're right," she said. "I am still weak. I think I'll go below and lie down for a while before supper."

"I was afraid you'd overdo it," Jessie said. "Don't try to get up for supper. I'll bring you something from the galley."

"No, I want to go. You've waited on me enough for one voyage." She walked to the ladder-steps in the stern, holding onto the rail, and disappeared below.

Jessie shook her head sadly as she watched Madeline staggering as though drunk, trying to keep her balance. She also noticed the attention directed Madeline's way by every man on deck, sailors and passengers alike. The girl was too beautiful for her own good, and it was highly likely that her beauty could turn out to be a curse instead of a blessing. It probably had already, for why else would someone so lovely have indentured herself to go to a strange, wild new country where she knew absolutely no one?

Though she had tried not to show it, Jessie had been shocked by Madeline's story, more by what Madeline hadn't told than by what she had. It was obvious there was more to her leaving England than a guardian who was too strict.

Chapter Two

ONCE SHE BEGAN REGAINING HER STRENGTH, MADELINE seemed to recover unusually fast. The weakness left her body, and her dazed mental state changed to one of avid curiosity. She became more interested in the ship and in her fellow passengers, especially the women who shared her cabin. These were, after all, the people who would be her friends and neighbors in Bath Town. Heretofore, she had taken notice only of Jessie because it had been Jessie who had nursed her back to health. Now she found herself looking at Jessie's children as affectionately as a doting aunt and wanting to get to know them better. Conon was a gangling, brown-haired boy of eleven, and Carryl—called Carrie—a doll-like little girl of eight with honey-colored hair, china blue eyes, and a bit of baby fat still on her pudgy little body.

Madeline was the only unmarried woman on the ship. Four of the women in her cabin were going to Bath Town to join husbands who had preceded them, and five had husbands aboard ship who slept in the men's cabin. Carrie and three other little girls, one a babe of two, were in the women's cabin while Conon, who spent most of his time prowling the ship and observing the crew, slept in the men's cabin. There were a few women aboard who shared private cabins with their husbands.

When Madeline began to feel more like her normal self, she noticed her own appearance for the first time in weeks. Ghastly! she thought. She had never looked worse. Her hair, which fell midway between shoulders and waist, hung limply. If only she could wash it, but there had been no rain for more than a week and the rain barrels on the top deck were depleted. Indeed, even the supply of drinking water was now being rationed, lest it give out before land was sighted.

She braided her hair and coiled it around her head, then looked closely at her face. Her cheeks were a bit sunken, Lord knew how much weight she had lost during her illness. All she could remember now was Jessie standing over her saying, "But you must eat something. It's better if you do not have an empty stomach." So in order to stop the pleas, she had eaten and had promptly been even sicker.

Now, as the terrible first weeks of the voyage were beginning to fade in her mind, she was looking forward to what was ahead: the sighting of land, her new country, her new home . . . and what she hoped would be her new family, for she had resolved to do everything she could to make the Cate family like and accept her. A servant, yes—almost a slave—but had there not been servants who had worked for her father whom she had loved and looked upon as part of the family?

"I can tell you are much better," said a voice behind her.

Madeline turned to find another passenger, Elizabeth Milton, baby in arms, looking at her. "That's a lovely gown."

Madeline had rummaged through her trunk and brought out a lilac muslin to wear to supper. Though it was wrinkled, she was tired of the heavy cambrics and crepes she had worn during the past week that she had been up and about. "Thank you," she said. "I think it sometimes makes one feel better to dress up a bit."

"You have so many gowns," Elizabeth said wonderingly, peering down into Madeline's opened trunk. She fingered a delicate primrose gauze. "Your trousseau is elegant."

Madeline's smile and murmured thanks successfully hid the turmoil in her mind. She was going to have to tell the women she shared the cabin with, all of them, that she was not a bride-to-be but an indentured servant, because they would all find out as soon as she left the ship and went with the Cate family home.

But how could she explain the trunk full of clothing, as well as the two portmanteaux and a number of oversized reticules full of accessories like the hand-painted shawls from the East, silk scarves with gold and silver threads woven through them, Danish sandals, the daintiest of undergarments . . . Though she had not brought out any of the most elegant gowns, she knew that Jessie had gone through her belongings trying to find a clean nightgown for her while she was sick. The others in the cabin must have seen also.

It was logical that a woman on her way to marry would carry such a trousseau; it was completely illogical that an indentured woman would have such an array of expensive raiment. But she was not yet ready to give up her secret.

"I thought I would walk on deck before supper," she said. "One gets very little exercise aboard ship."

Elizabeth, looking rebuffed, merely nodded.

Madeline was glad to exchange the close, stale air of the cabin for the cool, salt air of the top deck. Today was the fourth of October, and she wondered what autumn was like in the new land. Soon, in a little more than a week, she would know. A thrill went through her as she stood at the rail, her eyes searching the vast length of water ahead of the ship, but she was not sure whether it was a tremor of fear or of anticipation.

"Have you heard the news, Miss Boyd?" The young voice beside her caused her to start and she looked into the excited face of Conon Roland.

"I've heard no news in weeks, Con," she said.

"I just heard it from Captain Buckwinder," he said, his excitement spilling over as though it were a tangible thing. "The wind has been just right for the past week and we've made better time than anyone expected. We'll see land within two days! It's true, the captain himself said so." He was fairly dancing about the deck.

"Yes, I heard him also." Jessie, with Carrie by the hand, joined Madeline. "Think of it, only two more days. I didn't realize how tired of this ship I had grown until I heard we were to leave it soon. Now I don't think I can wait another day, much less two."

Madeline smiled. "I can wait. I think the closer we get, the more nervous I become about my . . . situation."

"Don't worry about it, dear," Jessie said. "Cyrus and I will be right there in Bath Town, and if everything isn't all right, you just come to us."

"I do thank you, Jessie," she said appreciatively,

"but I doubt if I can leave the Cate home. After all, the indenture lasts four years. But," she added optimistically, "I am sure everything will be all right. I have a feeling I am going to love it in Carolina. I'd better, because I'll never cross the ocean again."

Jessie and both her children laughed. "I don't think we'll be in any hurry to go home for a visit either," she said. "But I must stop thinking of England as home."

"You look nice, Miss Boyd," Conon said, as though just noticing her for the first time.

"She's pretty, isn't she?" Carrie piped up.

"My children are not wanting in the upper story," Jessie said, agreeing with them. "You do look unusually beautiful, Madeline. I'm glad to see you taking enough interest to wear some of your pretty gowns. It is a sure sign that you have recovered."

"Thank you," Madeline murmured, and changed the subject immediately. "Jessie, tell me about Bath Town, everything your husband has written you."

Jessie looked slightly embarrassed. "I don't know very much about it. In fact, I think I've already told you just about everything Cyrus has said. He isn't much of a writer. He never had any schooling and he taught himself to write. He mostly just says that he's well and misses his family. He tells me about the house he's built. And sometimes he talks about politics. He said something in one of his last letters about there being two governors of the colony. I didn't understand what he was talking about, though."

"Right now it isn't the politics that interest me most, it's the people . . . and the land itself," Madeline said.

"Right now, from the rumbling of my stomach, it is supper that interests me most." Jessie put her arm through Madeline's. "It's almost time. Let's go see if we can hurry things along in the galley."

Land was sighted in a day and a half and the word went through the ship almost by the time the lookout in the crow's nest had finished shouting "Land ho!"

Madeline, who was alone in the cabin resting, heard running footsteps and unusual activity on the deck above her. Quickly, she left her bunk and went to the door. "What is it?" she asked a man who was scurrying up the ladder steps just outside her cabin.

"Land!" he cried. "Finally, land!"

"Madeline, over here," she heard Jessie's voice as she topped the ladder, but it was a minute or two before she could spot her friend in the squeeze. Jessie was standing near a rail with her children and Madeline pushed her way over to them. "I can't see anything," Carrie was complaining, while Conon was climbing up on one of the cannon in order to see above the heads of the adults. "There's nothing to see," he said disgustedly. "Nothing but water and sky."

"Look all around," his mother ordered. "There must be land *some*where or the call would not have gone out."

"It's not there," a man at the rail called to the sailor in the crow's nest. "You are seeing things."

The sailor pointed to his long spy glass, then pointed straight ahead and called "Land ho!" again.

Then from the bow someone called, "I can see it dead ahead. Just a dot on the horizon."

"Hallelujah, praise the Lord!" Jessie said, and Madeline saw two large tears course down her friend's face. She also felt like crying for entirely different reasons, but she knew if she started she would not be able to stop. She bit her bottom lip and grasped Jessie's hand.

"Quiet, everyone!" roared a voice from the crowd. "Quiet!"

"It's the captain," said the man standing beside Madeline. "He's left the first mate at the helm."

"Quiet!" The deep voice of Captain Buckwinder came again. "Let us give thanks for our safe crossing of the deep."

Immediately about three quarters of the people on the deck knelt and the others bowed their heads.

"Lord, we thank thee for bringing us in safety through the perils of the voyage and we ask thy further blessings on this ship, its crew and passengers, as we complete our journey. Amen."

The amen was echoed by all on board.

The captain then announced that they would anchor near Portsmouth and reach Bath Town the next day. Jessie looked stricken with disappointment, but for her own part, Madeline was glad to have one last night to prepare herself for what lay ahead, anxious though she was to leave the ship. Suppose she did not like the Cate family? Suppose they demanded more of her than she could do or give? What would she do then? No matter how unbearable the situation in which she found herself, she would have to endure it somehow for four years. For the first time since leaving England, she was more than merely apprehensive, she was *terrified*. Before land was sighted, her future lay murkily in the distance, so far in the distance that it seemed unreachable. But now she had caught up with the future.

She looked down at the water swirling below her. The color was a gray-green and the sky was the palest blue, dotted with tiny pearl gray clouds. The sky and sea had changed from monotonous gray to pastel colors, and the noon sun was warm on the deck. Surely these were all good signs. Even so, she began to tremble, and finally she went back below to the cabin to lie down on her bunk. She was still there two hours later when Elizabeth Milton brought the baby down to change her.

"Madeline, are you ill again?" Elizabeth asked in concern. "Do you know that land has been sighted? It was just a speck on the horizon at first, but now it's clearly visible." Her excitement was evident.

"I am all right, thank you," she answered. "I was up on deck and got a little tired from standing so long."

Elizabeth and her freshly diapered baby left to take their places again on the top deck, but Madeline remained where she was. From time to time she would hear a joyous cry from the top deck or hear feet above her which were unmistakeably dancing. Everyone was celebrating, so delighted to reach the destination. Everyone but her.

In an instant she was awake, though she had no idea what had awakened her. Around her she could hear the gentle snores and regular breathing of the others who shared the cabin. It was as dark as midnight and there was very little movement to the ship, just a soothing little rock. Was it possible that they had reached land after she had left Jessie up on deck? She got out of the bunk and went to the one porthole in the cabin, pulling aside the blanket which covered it at night. Outside the whole world was gray—water, sky, mist, and earth . . . yes, land! She could distinguish land, even see a tiny wharf or pier jutting out into the water and behind that the dark shadowy trees.

Her heaviness of the day before was gone entirely and she felt the embryo of excitement beginning to grow in her. In the thin gray light from the uncovered porthole, she looked at Jessie's bunk. It was empty, but Carrie slept peacefully in the bunk on the other side of it.

That was what had awakened her, then. Jessie had arisen, dressed, and gone above to the top deck again. For a moment she felt a sense of loss and grief because the lie she had first told her cabin-mates—that she was going to the Colonies to marry—had not been true. She could imagine now how she would feel, how Jessie felt, about seeing in the next few hours someone whom she loved very much and had not seen for a long, long time.

Madeline dressed quickly in a dark blue traveling suit, the one she had worn when she left London for Bristol, and went to the upper deck to join Jessie. Still apprehensive, she realized that the terrible fear that had assaulted her yesterday had given way to hope, hope and optimistic expectations.

In the mist, she did not see Jessie at once, but then she spotted her beside one of the cannon on the port side.

"Are you expecting your husband to meet the ship in a row boat?" she greeted her friend.

Jessie started, then laughed when she saw Madeline. "We are still a distance from Bath Town," she said. "But I simply cannot sleep and had to come up here to see what is going on. The pilot from Portsmouth Island is on the ship now, and the crew is weighing anchor." Even in the dim light Madeline could see Jessie's eyes alive with excitement. "We should be underway again at once. I got a chance to talk to Captain Buckwinder when I first came out and he told me where we will be going."

"To Bath Town, I thought," Madeline said.

"Yes, but it seems to be a circuitous route," Jessie said. "Over there," she pointed, "is Portsmouth Island and straight across is Ocracoke Island. We will go through Ocracoke Inlet to the Pamlico Sound and up the Pamlico River."

"How long will it take?" Madeline asked.

"He said we should get to Bath Town by afternoon, probably late afternoon." Jessie's chin trembled slightly as though about to cry . . . or laugh.

"Oh, Jessie, I am so happy for you!" Impulsively Madeline hugged Jessie. "How good it must be to know you will be met when we finally dock, that you will be home even though it is a new country."

Jessie looked at the girl fondly. "You will be met also," she said. "I am sure someone from the Cate family will be on hand to greet you and take you to your new home. Probably Mr. Cate himself and Mrs. Cate as well."

Madeline nodded. "You are right, I am sure, but still . . ."

"Don't be nervous, Madeline," Jessie said comfortingly. "I know your life will be different now, I feel it in my bones. You are going to be happier than you ever dreamed."

Madeline smiled. "It would have to be a bad situation indeed if I was not happier than before."

"Will you let your guardian know where you are once you are settled?" Jessie asked.

"Never!" Madeline shuddered. "And if he should ever find me, I don't know what I would do."

Jessie looked at her questioningly, but said nothing. She would not intrude on the girl's privacy. Then, noticing the pink glow in the eastern sky, she exclaimed, "Look, oh look!"

Madeline turned in the direction to which Jessie was pointing and gasped. Never had she seen a sunrise so glorious. She had never imagined so much color, such rich hues taking over the sky so quickly.

"It's a good omen," Jessie said softly. "I just know it is."

"Yes." Madeline sighed as though she had been holding her breath for days. "Yes, it is. It has to be."

The two women, along with most of the other passengers, stayed on deck all day, leaving only at noon to go to the galley. They watched the *Sea Lion* slowly leave Portsmouth Island behind, and then plow through Pamlico Sound.

"A good swimmer could beat this tub by three hours," Jessie complained.

But Madeline, who again had a stomach full of butterflies, murmured, "We'll get there soon enough."

By midafternoon they had exchanged Pamlico Sound for the Pamlico River and land was sighted again. Indeed, as the ship made its way up the river, there was land on both sides and Madeline drew in her breath, both startled and delighted at the beauty of autumn in Carolina. There were all shades of red and gold on the many varieties of trees.

"We must be nearly there," Jessie said, then turned from the rail as a thought struck her. "Oh, I must go see to the packing, be sure that Con and Carrie are ready. Children," she called to the two who were only a few feet from the rail, "come, we must get ready to leave the ship."

The two cheered and willingly followed Jessie below. Madeline continued to stand at the rail. She had finished her packing the night before. And she had been told by the captain that she and the others who were indentured would be the last to leave the ship when it docked.

It was another hour and a half before the ship made a slight turn into what appeared to be a bay and by that time Jessie and the children were again waiting impatiently on deck beside Madeline.

"Look!" Madeline pointed skyward. "Isn't that smoke?"

"Yes, it must be. It is!" Jessie cried.

"We're there, we're there!" the children chanted together.

Simultaneously, they saw the wharf ahead and heard the cry from the bow, "Bath Town ahead! Bath Town!" It was only a minute or two after that they heard another cry go up, this one from shore, "Ship's in! *Sea Lion* approaching! Ship's in!"

"We're early," Jessie said. "At least five or six days before we expected to get here. What if Cyrus is not here to meet us?"

"Where else would he be?" Madeline asked. "Of course he will be here."

"He could be out hunting," Jessie said. "He wrote that he goes hunting every two or three weeks." Her hands gripped the rail until her knuckles were white.

Madeline could see a street—a path, really—just up

from the river, lined by crude log cabins. She could see people streaming from the houses down to the landing. Was one of those houses the Felton Cate home? Were he and his family already at the wharf waiting for her? From the shore came loud cheers, echoed by all on board, including the crew as they worked.

"There he is!" Jessie screamed and began to wave both arms wildly. "Cyrus! Cyrus!"

The children followed her gaze but remained silent, neither recognizing any man in the crowd whom they had called father.

Madeline's eyes were darting over those assembled on the shore, trying to guess which was Felton Cate. From this distance, most of the men looked alike, bearded and wearing clothing made from animal hides. Some of them had long black hair down to their shoulders and beyond. Oh, have mercy! she thought suddenly. Those with the long black hair were the savages, the Indians, but they were dressed almost identically to the other men.

"Listen, Madeline," Jessie turned to her, "once we are docked, I may lose you in the push to get off the ship, so I want to tell you now that if you need me—or us—all you have to do is let me know. And if things don't work out for you, then come to us. I mean it . . ."

"Oh, Jessie." Madeline threw her arms around her friend. "I can never thank you enough for what you've done already and I . . ." she broke, afraid she would begin to cry in earnest. Then she said, "We'll see a great deal of each other." She gave a little laugh. "After all, Bath Town doesn't appear to be large enough for either of us to get lost."

At that moment they both nearly fell to the deck as the ship slid to the wharf, shook slightly, and came to a sudden stop. They caught at the rail for support and watched as a long, wide plank was put in place, connecting the hold on the bottom deck to the wharf.

Jessie, unable to contain herself any longer, grabbed a child with each hand and headed for the hold.

Madeline, with tears in her eyes, watched as the first passengers crossed the plank and joined friends and families waiting on the shore. She was alone on the top deck now except for seven men who stood nearby looking down with interest at the goings-on on shore. They were the others who were indentured, Madeline knew. The captain would escort them off the ship and present their papers to the people to whom they were indentured.

It was a few minutes before Madeline saw Jessie and Con and Carrie leave the ship. As soon as they appeared at the head of the plank, a tall, slightly stooped man with dark, graying hair and a short beard the same color, bolted across the wharf calling, "Jessie!"

"Cyrus!" Jessie dropped the portmanteau in her hands and enveloped herself in the bearhug of her husband.

Madeline lowered her eyes. It wasn't envy she felt, but happiness for her friend.

Her eyes scanned the crowd again and she saw for the first time a man standing a little apart from the rest of the group. He stood back from the wharf, where the grass began, leaning against a maple tree whose blood-red leaves left his face partially in shadow. Even so, she could see that his eyes were on her, staring as though she were some alien species he had never seen before. Could this be Felton Cate? she wondered.

He was extremely tall—she could tell that even from this distance—and he had sandy hair with a reddish glint. Unlike the other men, he was clean-shaven, and he wore dark brown trousers made of what appeared to be homespun cloth rather than animal hide. His white cotton blouse was open at the neck. As she watched, he stepped out from the shadow of the tree as though to see her better, for he never once took his eyes from her face. He looked to be in his late twenties, possibly thirty.

Could that be Felton Cate? She asked herself again. She had pictured Cate as a much older man.

She would know in a moment, for Captain Buck-winder had appeared on the top deck and motioned to her and to the seven men. "We will go ashore now," he said. "I have your papers here, ready for your master." The word made Madeline cringe.

She looked one more time at the sandy-haired man on shore and a shiver, or thrill, went through her. Then she followed the captain down through the hold to the wharf.

While the townspeople were rushing madly down to the dock, one man alone appeared almost disinterested. Slowly, he ambled down Water Street, watching the crowd with no visible excitement of his own. To him, the *Sea Lion* was only another ship coming in. True, it would bring supplies, maybe even some furniture he had ordered from England, possibly news or even a letter, but really nothing to make him carry on wildly as though the final trumpet had sounded and judgment was on the way.

He stopped short of the wharf under a tree and leaned against the trunk, watching passengers and cargo being unloaded. The reflection of sun on the water had caused him to squint his piercing blue eyes when his gaze fell on something equally dazzling. On the top deck of the ship, standing at the rail, was the most beautiful woman he had ever seen. His attention went to her at first because of the sunlight in her pale, almost silver, hair that seemed to sparkle like the water. From that moment on, his eyes never left her.

He saw her looking into the crowd as though expecting to see someone she knew and wondered why she did not go below like the other passengers to disembark.

For the briefest moment, their eyes met and he felt a tingling in his loins and a shortness of breath. He had seen beautiful women before, he had possessed beautiful women before, but he had never seen one who stirred him as this one did, and from this distance, too! Idiot! he told himself, she has either come here to meet her husband or he is with her aboard ship. The man knew that as far as he was concerned, she was unattainable, still he could not tear his eyes from her.

After all the passengers were off, he saw the captain approach the woman. She nodded and put on a dark blue bonnet that matched the gown and shawl she wore, then she disappeared from sight. What a shame to cover that glorious hair!

His curiosity stirred, he made his way through the

happy, chattering people, down the grassy slope to the landing. He was convinced now that she must be the captain's wife, why else would she have waited for him?

A few minutes later the lovely lady left the ship on the captain's arm. Behind them came seven more passengers. They must be the indentured servants, he thought. Perhaps while the captain was involved in the transfer of their papers he could arrange to meet the captain's wife. More than anything in the world, he wanted to stand beside that alluring woman, engage her in conversation.

The captain stopped when they were off the wharf, and opened the papers he had been carrying in his free hand and began to read off names. One by one men emerged from the already departing crowd, signed the papers and shook hands with their indentured servant.

The man continued to look at the beautiful woman, realizing now that they were only a few feet apart that she was hardly more than a girl. He also could not believe his good fortune, for she was walking straight toward him. Suddenly, she began to reel and stagger and flung her arms out in order to maintain her balance. He reached for her and caught her before she fell.

"Oh!" she cried, terror in her voice, "the earth is shaking so I cannot stand. It is rolling beneath my feet!"

"You do not have your land legs yet," he said, laughing. "It is not an earthquake." He held her close, savoring the moment, his breath almost stopping entirely as he looked into her steel gray eyes. Beneath the material of her gown, he could feel her heart beating wildly. It seemed only the most fleeting instant that he held her, yet it could have been an eternity.

She pulled away, then reached out to his arm to steady herself. "You must be Felton Cate?" she said simply.

"No, madam," he replied. "Gavin Durant at your service."

Chapter Three

MADELINE TURNED AND LOOKED BACK AT THE SHIP UN-
certainly. The crew, with the help of some Indians,
busily unloaded the cargo. The river water still sparkled
from the bright sunlight and the sky was a brilliant blue,
broken only by high scudding clouds. Her nose wrinkled with the welcome, pungent smell of evergreens.
Everything in this new Eden seemed perfect . . . then
she remembered her situation.

"Are you a relative of Cate's?" Gavin Durant asked.

"No, I am . . . I . . ." She struggled for an answer
and was saved by Captain Buckwinder who came up to
them at that moment, paper in hand.

"Where might I find Mr. Felton Cate?" he asked
Durant. "I must turn this paper of indenture over to
him."

Durant's mouth opened and he almost gaped as he
looked from the paper in the captain's hand to Madeline. "Cate left this morning to go hunting," he said
finally. "He probably will not be back for another day
or two. You see, no one expected the ship in for at least
a week, and we take turns hunting for food. It was
Cate's turn to supply the meat."

Madeline, still holding to Durant's arm because the

ground seemed to be rolling worse than the ocean, said to the captain, "What am I to do now?"

Durant, not quite comprehending the situation, stared at Madeline. It seemed impossible that this lovely creature was indentured—and to Felton Cate, at that.

"I will have to turn this over to someone in authority in Bath Town," Captain Buckwinder said, "someone who will see that it is put into Mr. Cate's hand the minute he returns."

Making an instant decision, Durant said, "I will be happy to take care of the matter for you, Captain. My name is Gavin Durant. I will see that Cate gets the . . . paper of indenture?"

The captain handed the paper to him reluctantly.

"Madeline Boyd," Durant read. He looked at Madeline. "*You* are Madeline Boyd? You are indentured to Cate for four years?"

Why did she suddenly feel shamed? She looked down at the ground which even now appeared to be moving under her feet. "Yes," she said softly, "I am."

"Do you swear that you will be responsible for seeing that Cate gets the paper . . . and Miss Boyd?" the captain asked.

"I am a Quaker and I do not swear to anything," Durant said. "I will give you my word."

The captain's craggy face entertained a small smile. "That's good enough, I reckon. All right, Miss Boyd, I leave you with Mr. Durant." He bowed and went back down to the landing to see to the unloading.

Durant turned to Madeline, looked for a moment at the hand still tightly gripping his arm, and said, "It will take a few hours, maybe even a day, before the earth stands still for you. I know because I have experienced the same thing every time I have crossed the ocean."

"How many times have you crossed?" she asked, curious about this man who had now assumed responsibility for her.

"Three. The first time when I came here four years ago, and then twice more when I went back to England for a visit a year ago."

Madeline sighed. "I do not think I would ever want to cross the ocean again."

Durant laughed and his whole face changed. With the laughter his mouth relaxed, giving his strong features an easygoing look. "You may change your mind," he said. "Do you have baggage?"

"Yes," she said. "A trunk and two portmanteaux."

He gave her an odd look and she knew he was surprised that anyone indentured would have so much baggage. "I came to stay, so I brought everything I own," was her inadequate explanation.

He nodded. "Wait here. I will have to borrow a cart to get it all out to my house. I only rode my horse into town."

"You do not live in Bath Town?" she asked, suddenly alarmed.

"I live a little over a mile from here," he said. "I wanted enough land to farm."

"Your wife will be very surprised at your bringing home an unexpected guest." His wife will be furious, not just surprised, she thought.

"I am not married," he said.

She blinked, then her gray eyes were wide in astonishment. "But . . . but I cannot go with you if you live

alone," she said, though something within her wanted
to go with this compelling stranger.

He laughed again. "I do not live alone. I have
a . . . a servant, an Indian girl, who lives in the house."

"Oh." Madeline did not know quite what to make of
this. Then she remembered having heard that some of
the settlers had made slaves of the Indians. "Is she a
slave?"

"I do not have slaves. I think it wrong for one human
being to own another. Tondah works for me and she is
free to go back to her tribe whenever she wishes." His
words were clipped, as though he were angry at her.
"Stay here until I return with a cart."

It was only after he had disappeared into one of the
cabins down Water Street that it suddenly occurred to
Madeline that she could have told Captain Buckwinder
to let Jessie's husband be responsible for her. That way
she would have remained among friends until Felton
Cate returned. But they had already left the wharf—
there was no one else in sight. Another thought
came to mind which she expressed the minute Gavin
Durant returned with his horse hitched to a borrowed
dray.

"Would it not be better to take me straight to Mr.
Cate's house and leave me with his family? You would
not have to put yourself out for me."

Durant gave her a long, hard look before he said,
"Cate has no family. Like me, he is unmarried."

Madeline gasped. "No family! Then why . . .
why . . ." She broke off, unable to express the many
emotions and questions going through her mind.

Was it possible the girl really did not know she had
indentured herself to a bachelor? Durant wondered.

Surely she must have had some idea of the circumstances she was coming to. And, for the hundredth time, he again wondered why so beautiful a girl had indentured herself at all. With her looks, she could have married royalty.

They rode in silence for a while, Madeline having no idea how to express all the uncertainties, the returned apprehension, that gnawed at her, Durant too polite to ask the many questions that plagued him. They were soon out of Bath Town which, as far as Madeline could determine, consisted of Water Street, which had cabins and one or two frame houses on either side, and another "street," little more than a path, which intersected Water Street near the river landing. Once they left the town they were in dense woods, riding on a path of pine straw.

Finally, when the silence began to be embarrassing—to her at least—she asked, "Why did the Indians at the wharf stare at me so? Surely they are used to seeing white women by now."

Wondering why she would have noticed the Indians, in particular, staring when every man at the landing, including him, had gaped at her, he answered, "They probably have never seen anyone with hair as light as yours." He hesitated a minute, then added, "Nor have I."

This answer seemed to satisfy her for she asked no more questions. His mind, however, was asking a few: What would she think of the rude log cabin to which he was taking her? What kind of house had she come from in England? (She was richly dressed and had brought enough baggage, no doubt filled with clothing, to last most of a lifetime, and yet she had come as an indentured servant—little better than a slave—and to Felton Cate, of all people.)

It seemed a long time before they reached a clearing. Madeline looked at the man sitting beside her holding the reins and he gave her a smile, a funny, crooked sort of smile that, for no reason she could think of, touched her heart. Her apprehension vanished and she relaxed. Gavin Durant would take care of her; he would not let anything happen to her. She felt that instinctively. She looked at him again, his long, lean torso, hardened from whatever hard work he did on his farm; his face, deeply tanned from his hours in the Carolina sun; those eyes, so startlingly, piercingly blue in the tan face, and the blondish red hair, curling slightly around his face and on his neck. She remembered her father saying, "You can usually tell what a man is by his face." If that was true, then she took Gavin Durant for a good man for it was a good face at which she looked: too rugged to be handsome, but with features which belied the coarse, hard world in which he had chosen to live.

"That's my house ahead." He pointed to a small log cabin in the clearing. "I put it up myself," he added, and she detected a touch of pride in his voice.

She did not know what to say. She supposed, as log cabins went, it was all right, but it was not what she had expected. Not what she had expected? She wasn't sure exactly *what* she had expected in this strange new country, therefore she had no basis for comparison with what she had thought she would find and what was actually there.

As they drew closer, she had a better look at his cabin home. The roof was made of clapboards, long shingles that had been split by hand. No nails had been used. The clapboards were held in place by rows of poles fastened at the ends with wooden pins. The spaces between the logs were chinked with mud, and even the chimney was made of wood.

Standing in front of the cabin was a girl clad, like the Indians Madeline had seen in town, in pants made of animal hide, and a bright orange blouse made of some indeterminate material. The girl had long, straight black hair and across her forehead and around her head was a wide orange band. She looked as though she were waiting for something or someone but was puzzled by what she saw.

Durant gave a little wave, but the girl did not respond. She continued to stand as still as a statue. Not until the dray was right in front of the cabin did she finally bestir herself to take the reins while Durant alit. "I did not expect you to return this way," she said in perfect English, gesturing toward the dray.

"Nor did I," he said with a laugh. "Tondah, this is Miss Boyd, just off the ship from England. She will stay here for a day or two."

Madeline had not the slightest notion how she should greet Durant's "servant." Looking at the comely Indian girl, she had an idea that the girl's serving duties went further than keeping house and cooking. "I am glad to meet you, Tondah," she said finally.

The girl nodded, a slight frown on her face, as she watched Durant unload the trunk and portmanteaux from the dray. "Come in." He gestured toward the door, which Tondah opened, and Madeline went inside. There was one big room divided by a rope on which hung a brightly colored blanket that was used to partition the room into two smaller ones. The fireplace was huge and over it hung a large iron pot and a kettle. In front of the fireplace was a table with two chairs. They even eat together, Madeline thought, and wondered why it bothered her to think of Durant breaking bread with the lovely Indian girl. Beyond the table were three other chairs, large wooden ones carved out of tree trunks, covered with cushions. In the corner, beyond the dividing blanket, was a large bed, also wooden, and a bureau of a finer wood. Near the bed sat the necessary chair, a hole cut in the seat and a chamber pot beneath.

Durant, his muscles straining, set the trunk down beside the bed, then brought in the portmanteaux. "Tondah, prepare a bath for Miss Boyd. I have a feeling she will appreciate a real bathtub after weeks aboard ship." He looked at Madeline. "I have to return the cart. I will be back shortly, and then we will see what kind of feast Tondah has prepared."

He was no sooner out the door than Tondah was dragging a large round tub from what turned out to be a second room in the cabin. Madeline had thought the door led outside, a back door, but she saw that there was another room there. From where she stood, she could see a cotlike bed, a small bureau, and a straight chair. There was room for nothing else.

"Is this where you stay?" Madeline smiled at the girl.

"Yes." The one word was almost like a rebuke. "Take off your clothing. I prepare bath now."

Tondah filled the tub with a mixture of hot water from the kettle and pot on the fire and cool water from a bucket. Then she gave Madeline an unwieldly piece of soap. She put a long piece of cotton material across one of the chairs and said, "Drying cloth." Then she proceeded to look Madeline up and down as she removed her clothes and stepped into the tub.

The steady gaze caused Madeline to feel self-conscious; she was unused to an audience while she bathed. But the moment she stepped into the tub she forgot everything but the wonderful feeling of being able to bathe in a tub again. With her knees raised, there was room to lie back and luxuriate in the warm water. Never had a bath seemed so welcome, almost miraculous.

"How long have you worked for Mr. Durant?" she asked the still-staring girl.

Tondah shrugged and said nothing.

Had she breeched some etiquette rule unknown to her? Madeline wondered. No, she thought not. The girl simply did not like her, probably even considered her an interloper.

After she had soaped herself she asked Tondah for more water, "I want to wash my hair."

Tondah did as she was bade and stared even harder as Madeline washed her pale silvery hair. Then, as Madeline finally had had enough of the marvelous tub and reached for the "drying cloth," Tondah moved silently out of the room into the tiny second room and closed the door.

All the way into Bath Town and all the way back home, Gavin Durant thought about the impulsive—no, foolish—thing he had done in taking the indentured girl home with him. The truth was, he had never had (or used) much will power when it came to beautiful women. His idea always had been that the way to get rid of temptation was to yield to it, and never before had he had such a temptation as Madeline Boyd thrust at him. From the moment he had first seen her at the rail of the *Sea Lion* while the ship was docking, he had known that somehow he was going to possess that woman, and the thought that she probably either had a husband with her on the ship or was coming to Bath Town to join her husband did not stop him from imagining how she would be when brought to bed.

Gavin unhitched the cart beside the shed behind Wesley Martin's cabin on Water Street and was mounting his horse to ride back home when Wesley appeared at the back door.

"Gavin, come in," he called. "We must talk."

"Sorry, I can't now. I must get back. Thanks for the use of the dray."

Wesley Martin walked over to Gavin. "Word came this afternoon. A letter from the ship. As we suspected, the Lords Proprietor *are* sending another governor."

Gavin hesitated. This portended no good in a situation that was already bad, not to mention muddled. To have the Colonies governed by eight men in London who never had seen the land they purported to govern did not make for Utopia. But Gavin thought of the girl waiting at his cabin and said, "I really have to get back, Wes. Could we talk tomorrow?"

"How about I go out to your place in the morning?"

"Fine. I will see you then." Gavin put his heel into the horse's flanks and rode down Water Street at a brisk trot, his mind definitely not on politics, rotten or otherwise. He was thinking again about the enigma of the girl who waited for him. She looked like quality, spoke like a lady, and had the manner and bearing of the highborn. Yet she had crossed the ocean, coming to a place where she apparently knew not one soul, and had indentured herself to Felton Cate, a man Gavin never liked. To be fair—and he tried always to be—he had no real reason to dislike the man, but there was something about him Gavin found . . . well, a bit shady. He had never known Cate to do an overtly dishonest thing, yet the man gave the impression that he would not hesitate if being dishonest was to his advantage. Cate, Gavin knew, had been married when he left England three years ago, but his wife had not survived the voyage. From the time he arrived on Carolina soil, the man had looked lustfully at every other man's wife, thus arousing the ire of most of the colonists. It was not surprising that he had sent for an indentured woman; the surprise was the one who had come. It could mean only that she was running away from something: a vile reputation, jealous lovers, possibly even a husband who had threatened her. Certainly, if everything in her life was as it should be, she would not now be waiting in his cabin.

He knew why he himself was here and realized that that colored his thinking. Sir William Durant, his father, had grown more than a little tired of and embarrassed by the exploits of his second son, Gavin. How many times had Gavin heard him say, "You are a disgrace to the family name. Thank God you are not the one who will inherit the title." To which Gavin had added his silent amen. His older brother, Frederick, was a replica of their father, therefore perfectly able to carry on in the manner expected of him. While, as Sir William said, Gavin merely "carried on" shamelessly. It made little difference to the old man that Gavin was graduated from Oxford with honors while Frederick dropped out after only two years. Nor did it matter that Gavin was much better with the land than his brother and lived at one of Sir William's country estates, the only one which really thrived. Gavin, acting as his own overseer, found to his surprise that he was interested in farming, interested in taking care of "his people" and in keeping up the property. What mattered was the gossip which drifted back to London from the estate: Sir William's younger son regularly had women brought from London for his pleasure; Sir William's younger son spent weekends in London in riotous debauchery; Sir William probably had an uncountable number of grandchildren spread from one end of England to the other, and probably even a few in Scotland.

The straw which broke the camel's back, or the gossip which finally succeeded in sending Gavin into exile, was told to Sir William shortly after Gavin's twenty-fifth birthday. One of the maids from Gavin's country house went to Sir William and declared herself to be with child by his son, Gavin. She asked for an enormous amount of money for herself and unborn baby as well as transportation to Scotland so she could go to her sister, who had married a Scotsman, for the birthing. At his wit's end, Sir William paid the buxom lass and sent her on her way. Then he sent for his son and (as Gavin liked to tell it) sent him on his way.

When Gavin was first told of the charge against him, he thought it extremely funny. Roxanna, his accuser, was probably the only maidservant at his house who had never given him a tumble or two. But telling his father that he had never laid a hand on the girl did him no good, for Sir William came back with, "It isn't a hand that gets a woman with child, as you very well know."

Then the matter no longer was funny, for Sir William sentenced his son to three years of exile, banishing him to the Colonies to "learn to be a gentleman." The most amusing thing of all to Gavin was that, among the settlers in Carolina, there was little opportunity and less reason for a man to be a gentleman.

It was an excruciatingly unhappy Gavin, however, who sailed from England and an even more unhappy one who first set foot on land. So far was this new world from the old one he knew and enjoyed to the fullest that he felt like an entirely new person who had been reborn on the dark side of the moon.

It took him exactly six months to adapt to his new life. For a while he slept in a corner of Wesley Martin's cabin, but this proved more frustrating than satisfactory. He was bothered during the night by the crying of the Martins' baby and even more bothered by the sound of Wes and his wife making love. Then the idea came to him that there was no reason why he couldn't build a cabin of his own out from Bath Town and do what he knew best and liked best—farm. With only a few instructions from Wes as to how to go about it, he managed to have the cabin erected before his first winter in Carolina began, and in the spring he started what turned out to be prosperous crops of cotton and tobacco, with a small vegetable garden to keep his larder filled.

At the end of three years, he received a letter from Sir William recalling him to the fold. Gavin went back to England, but only to visit his father, mother, brother, sister-in-law, and the three children which Frederick had begat in three years. To the astonishment of all, he could hardly wait to return to Carolina.

So he knew something about the reasons why people left good homes to come to the wilderness.

Which brought him back to his original question: Was Madeline Boyd the lady she appeared to be, or was she a woman of easy virtue, good for a tumble in his bed tonight? Just the thought made his body hot and rigid, made his manhood swell with the raw want of her.

By the time his cabin was in sight, his mind was made up; he would have the girl tonight. There was not the slightest doubt left in his mind that her appearance was deceiving; no real lady would come three thousand miles across water to live with a man she had never seen before, no real lady would have need of indenturing herself or would even consider such an action.

The thought of possessing her was only part of his joy. It gave him no little satisfaction to know that he would have her before Felton Cate did.

In the greatest haste, he put his horse in the single stall behind the cabin, poured some grain into the trough, then went inside the cabin.

The scene that greeted him as he opened the door caused him to suck in his breath, his eyes riveted to the tub. Madeline had just stood up and was reaching for the cloth on the back of the chair, her full body exposed to him. His eyes took all of her in at once: the creamy shoulders, the round fullness of the pink-tipped breasts, the hips which cradled the pale triangular bush, the long, shapely legs. He stood immobile, breathless, transfixed by her loveliness.

For a moment it was as though the scene were frozen

in time. Neither moved. Then Madeline clutched the long cloth around her and stepped out of the tub, her face red and angry.

"Sir, if you were a gentleman you would have knocked before entering."

"At my own home?" he asked, amusement showing in his vivid blue eyes.

Madeline went to the bed section of the room and jerked the blanket across the rope, obliterating his view of her. He heard her open the trunk and knew that she was dressing.

She was furious, but mostly at herself. She should have realized that she had been dawdling too long in the tub, that he would be returning shortly, but it had been so good to bathe in a real tub again that she had not thought about the time.

She looked through the gowns in the trunk, took out a sprigged muslim from which she tried to shake the wrinkles. As she dressed, she did not ask herself why she was putting on one of her finest gowns for she did not want her mind to dwell on what the answer to that question implied. She heard the sound of movement on the other side of the blanket and knew that Tondah had come back into the room. Then she heard the girl say, "We eat now," and Gavin replied, "I will set the table."

As domestic as though they were married, Madeline thought. But they were not, for Gavin had told her he was unmarried. She brushed her hair for a long time to dry it, but decided to let it hang loosely on her shoulders rather than put it up.

When she again pulled the blanket aside and rejoined Gavin, she could not help but notice her effect upon him. In the process of setting a candle in the middle of the small rude wooden table, he straightened and stared at her much as he had when he had seen her for the first time. Again his breath seemed to stop and his eyes could not take in enough of her. He felt as though some herculean hand had grasped his insides and was squeezing them unmercifully. She was so beautiful that it was actually physically painful.

"You look . . . different," was all he managed to say, and then berated himself, for "different" was not what he had meant. At least, it was not *all* that he meant.

"I feel different," she said quickly. "Thank you for letting me use the tub . . . and I am sorry that I screamed at you. It was not your fault."

He nodded and finished setting the table. From the huge fireplace, Tondah sullenly went about dishing a savory stew from an iron pot into two bowls. She did not look at Madeline at all, but her eyes went frequently to Gavin. This was not lost on Madeline. Tondah will be delighted when Felton Cate returns from his hunting expedition and I leave here, she thought.

The table was set for two, indeed was not large enough for three, and Madeline wondered if Tondah and Gavin usually ate together. But of course they did, she reasoned. Gavin emphatically had stated that the girl was not his slave, and he treated her as though they had been long married.

"Do you think Mr. Cate will return tomorrow?" she asked as he seated her.

"Possibly, or the next day."

"I am sorry to impose upon you this way."

"I do not consider it an imposition," he said tersely,

and she thought he must be angrier at her than she had thought because of her outburst. Or was it because she was ignoring the Indian girl and he considered her rude?

She turned to Tondah who was standing quietly beside the fireplace, her eyes welded on Gavin. "The stew is delicious, the best I have ever eaten." And it was, tender, flavorful chunks of meat with tiny potatoes in gravy. "What kind is it?"

"Venison," Gavin said when Tondah made no reply.

"And the bread," Madeline continued, determined to make the girl speak to her, "I have never seen any like it before."

"It is made from ground corn," Gavin said, putting another pone on her plate.

Madeline gave up. It was obvious that the girl had no intention of speaking to her as long as she remained here. She turned to Gavin. "Do you know Mr. Cate very well? What is he like?"

"I know him, but not well," Gavin said. "I can tell you little about him except that he has a house on the other side of Bath Town."

"He doesn't live right in the town?"

"No, he lives further inland, a mile or two, I think."

She was more than disappointed. She had looked forward to seeing Jessie and the others from the ship often, but if she lived out in the countryside . . . Then another thought struck her which she voiced before thinking it through. "But I cannot live alone, out in the woods like that with a . . . stranger."

"Would it be all right to live in Bath Town with a stranger?" Gavin asked, a curious expression on his face.

"I-I really hadn't thought about that." She felt he must think her utterly lacking in sense. Of course it would not be all right; it would be all wrong, as wrong as it was for her to come home with *this* stranger, but under the circumstances, she had had little choice in the matter. At least she and Gavin had a sort of chaperone in Tondah, and certainly Gavin had known that when he had suggested bringing her to his cabin. For some reason, she felt safe with him.

They continued to eat in silence while she pondered this. Then she happened to look toward the window beside the fireplace and she gasped, putting her hand over her mouth to stifle the scream which rose in her throat. In the fading light outside, she saw the outline and then the features of a savage face. It was a man with shoulder-length black hair, an orange band, similar to the one Tondah wore, around his head, with a long red feather at the back of the band. The expression on his face was fierce, murderous.

Gavin's eyes followed her terrified gaze to the window and he said calmly, "Tondah, Walking Bear is outside. Why don't you take the rest of the stew out to him and the two of you can eat together."

The girl picked up the pot and went outside.

"You know him?" Madeline asked, astounded.

Gavin laughed. "Don't be afraid. He is from the nearby village of Tuscarora Indians. His English name, from the Indian, is Bear Who Walks Upright, shortened to Walking Bear. He is a friend of Tondah's, wants to marry her, in fact. Or did want to."

"Then why doesn't he?" she asked.

"Tondah does not want to marry him," he said. "She came here to work for me about a year and a half ago and decided she likes white man's ways—that is, civilization—better than Indian ways and she refused to rejoin the tribe."

I am sure of that, Madeline thought, and was equally sure she knew why Tondah preferred to stay.

"Also, Walking Bear's father is Chief Hancock, the mightiest chief in this part of the country, and he would not sanction the marriage after Tondah left the tribal home. So Walking Bear slips away occasionally and comes here to see her."

The words were like icy water poured over Madeline. Even among the savages, those were the morals that prevailed. Tondah's reputation was ruined because she lived with Gavin. Her own would be also, except for the fact that Tondah was there. But what about Felton Cate?

"Do you know if Mr. Cate has servants, or slaves?" she asked.

"No, I know little about the man or how he lives," Gavin answered. He wondered if she worried about the amount of work she would have to do while indentured to him. Then, once more, his blood began to boil at the thought of this magnificent creature having to go to Felton Cate in *any* capacity, much less as an indentured servant. He got up from the table so Madeline would not see the distressed look on his face. "I imagine you are very tired," he said. "Do not feel you must sit and make polite conversation with me if you would rather retire."

When he said it, Madeline realized that she was totally exhausted. She had felt terribly fatigued by the time she had come to the cabin, but the bath and the food had revived her somewhat. But now she wanted nothing so much as to close her eyes and sleep endlessly.

"Where am I to sleep?" she asked suddenly, looking toward the bed, the only bed.

"You will sleep there," he said.

"And you?"

"I will make a pallet before the fireplace," he said.

"I can sleep on the pallet," she said. "I do not like to take your bed. Besides, I am so tired, I probably could sleep on the floor, even without a pallet."

"No," he said firmly, "you will have the bed."

She did not argue. "Thank you. Thank you for everything. You have been most kind." She pulled the blanket across the rope and almost fell toward the bed.

It was a rope bed, made of wood but with a rope across the frame. There were two mattresses over the rope, the bottom one filled with corn shucks, the top one with feathers. Madeline undressed quickly, put on her nightdress and got into bed. It was more comfortable than she would have imagined. She sank down into the feathers, knowing she was too tired to think, to worry . . . or even to dream . . .

Gavin stood by the fireplace, staring idly at the black kettle. He wished he had offered her a cup of tea, anything to keep her with him for a few minutes longer. He smiled suddenly. That kettle had been one of the few things he had brought from England and sometimes, looking at it, he was reminded of the way he had lived during what he now thought of as his callow youth. The difference in his life then and his life now was so great that the former seemed to have been lived by another person. He could hardly remember what it had been like, the revelry, the routs, the young women of varying stations in life with whom he had flirted.

He wondered if that was the kind of life Miss Madeline Boyd had left behind. Her life certainly could not have been pristine pure or she would not now be indentured to a strange man a world away from that other world. He heard the light crackle of the corn shucks in the bottom mattress as she got into bed, *his* bed, and for a moment he was almost overcome by desire for her. He stared for what seemed like a long time at the blanket separating them until he heard her steady breathing on the other side and knew that she was asleep. She probably was exhausted emotionally as well as physically; no matter what her past, coming to a new country in a new situation among nothing but strangers could not be easy for her.

Quietly, he went to the blanket and pulled it aside. In the moonlight he made out her head on the pillow, the long hair gleaming like silver in the thin, wispy rays of light coming through the window. In a way, she seemed childlike to him, yet in another way she was all woman.

Again, he felt almost suffocated by desire. He wanted nothing in the world so much as to get into bed beside her, take her in his arms . . .

Stop it! he chastised himself. You will not take her, or take advantage of her . . . at least not until you know for sure about her past and what brought her here to Carolina.

He made no further move toward the bed, but he continued to stare at the sleeping figure like a starving man eyeing a table laden with food.

* * *

. . . was it a dream? . . . it must be . . . and yet . . .

It was almost as though she were pulled from sleep by some strange invisible force. She opened her eyes only slightly, peeping out from tiny slits, and saw the shadow in the moonlight. She stopped herself just as she was about to scream when she realized that he was standing perfectly still, making no move to come closer to the bed. She continued to pretend to be asleep, hoping he would go away without bothering her, yet she had the strangest feeling just knowing he was there looking at her. A sort of tingle went up her spine and she wondered how long she would be able to feign sleep.

Time passed with painful slowness. She had no idea how long he had been standing there as still as a piece of furniture in the room. She could not even hear him breathing. Then suddenly, there was the sound of a door opening and the blanket was pushed aside once more. Tondah, her face glowing eerily in the light of the candle she held in her hand, went to the foot of the bed. She said not a word, but glared first at Gavin and then at the now wide-eyed girl in the bed. That scene, also, seemed frozen in time until, finally, Gavin sighed, turned his back to the bed and said to the Indian girl, "Go back to bed, Tondah . . . and I will do the same."

As Tondah went back to her room, Gavin looked once more toward Madeline, murmured, "I hope you sleep well," then pulled the blanket back across the rope.

Madeline lay awake for a long time, even after she knew that Gavin was asleep on the pallet on the other side of the blanket. Her initial fury had vanished, but she felt a little frightened—as though she had somehow been violated by his secret watching—and also somewhat frustrated. To think that she had felt safe with him! More frightening even than finding Gavin beside the bed had been the look of sheer hatred on Tondah's face. Yet could she blame the girl? First she, Madeline, had usurped her place at Gavin's table and then she had taken his bed.

Most of all, however, it was the feeling of frustration that bothered her. Why had she acted so uncharacteristically?

She could have spoken to Gavin sharply, demanding that he go back to the other side of the room and leave her alone, and he probably would have done it. Had she actually enjoyed having him there, looking at her as she slept? Had something in her, some strange new longing, wanted him to do more than look?

No, of course not! In her extreme fatigue, she was confusing the past with the present, thinking about those things she had promised herself she would forget.

Resolutely, she turned her face toward the wall, closed her eyes, and tried to go to sleep.

Chapter Four

IT SEEMED THAT THE NIGHT WOULD EXTEND THROUGH eternity and then some. No matter how she tried, she could not get to sleep and finally decided that the reason was she was trying too hard. She wanted to thrash from side to side in the bed, but she forced herself to lie still, not wanting to wake Gavin.

The past was too much with her. The more she tried not to think about her reason for coming to Carolina, the more she thought about it. Awaking and finding Gavin beside the bed had brought it all back to her in a rush, like a mountain waterfall, endlessly cascading.

Dear God! Her new life in this country had to be different; she could not, *would not,* take up here where she had left off there. She had never even come close to feeling anything except revulsion toward all the men who had tried to make love to her. Yet tonight, she had felt something of a thrill just from having Gavin stand silently beside her and look down at her vulnerable form. If Rufus could have known about that . . . A small sob escaped her throat. If only she could go back in her life, back to the time of her father's death, and do everything differently. That was when it had all started to go wrong.

She and her father had lived in a large, rambling

house in Bath that had required four servants to take care of the various phases of housekeeping. Clarence Boyd was one of the leading physicians in Bath. His reputation had been spread to London by the ladies who went to Bath regularly to "take the waters," and he was never without more patients than he could manage to see during laboratory hours. His laboratory was in the house, three rooms into which Madeline had learned from infancy she was not to go. There was scarcely a night that the good doctor did not extend his bedtime in order to treat some patient who could not wait until morning.

After her father's death, there was no doubt in Madeline's mind that he had worked himself to death. He was so busy treating the ailments of others that he had no time to give thought to the Biblical command: physician, heal thyself. Sometime between seeing his last patient late one night and the next morning when the maidservant went to clean the laboratory, his great heart had stopped, just too tired to carry on. The maid had found him lying on the floor of the examining room, looking as though he were just too weary to climb the stairs to his bedchamber and had decided to take a nap where he was.

Madeline was inconsolable. For days she wept bitterly until there were no tears left and then, languid, not caring from hour to hour about anything, she simply sat. Sometimes she stayed in her bedchamber, sometimes she sat in the green saloon while friends, making sympathy calls, enumerated the virtues of her father and offered advice as to what she should do now.

The advice was unnecessary; she knew what she would do now for her father's solicitor had brought her the will to read the day after the funeral. Her father had left her all his earthly goods, for there were no other close relatives, and the will concluded with the sentence: "Should I be deceased while my daughter Madeline is underage, she is to become the ward of my distant cousin, Rufus Delong of London, until her twenty-fourth birthday or until she marries, whichever event transpires first."

All Madeline knew about her new guardian, whom she had never seen, was that he was about ten years younger than her father and that her father had spent a week in the Delong home in London when he was a young man and had been much impressed with Rufus who, at the time, was a precocious boy of fifteen and showed great promise of becoming a highly respected and prominent man.

When she actually saw him a week after the funeral (he came to help her close and dispose of the house), she had no vivid first impression of him. He was very tall, almost emaciated looking, and had a long face, the length accentuated by a receding hair line. He had sparse brown hair and a little brown mustache. His eyes, the same color brown as his hair and mustache, seemed never to change expression. At all times he appeared to be squinting, staring at something just beyond sight in the distance.

Madeline knew that she had to return to London with him, and that added further heartbreak to her recent loss. She did not want to leave Bath and her friends there no matter how wonderful a picture of London Delong painted (who told her on first meeting that he was to be called Rufus, never Cousin Rufus).

Six months short of her eighteenth birthday, Madeline knew that she would have to obey Rufus in all things for the next six and a half years (unless she married, and that was not even a faint possibility at the time), and that he would have complete control of her finances (not inconsiderable, but not meager either, for Clarence Boyd had been as prosperous as any physician, more so than most) and of every phase of her life. He was, after all, her legal guardian and nothing could change that.

Tearfully, she said goodbye to Bath and left for London in the new carriage harnessed to the new team which Rufus had bought—with her money—to transport her belongings to her new home. The new home was as distant from what she expected as heaven from hell. Rufus had told her he was an innkeeper, but he was nothing of the kind. He was a tavern keeper and he lived in five very small rooms above the tavern, located between Fleet Street and the river.

There was no hiding her dismay as she looked at the front of The Toast and the Tankard. Her father's death had brought her to this: her home was to be a tavern!

She looked at Rufus and for the first time she wondered what he had felt at becoming the guardian of a seventeen-year-old girl he had never seen before. She asked him, point blank, before they went inside.

He shrugged. "I think it won't be too bad . . . for either of us," was all he said.

When he showed her to her room, a small bedchamber that he had used to store kegs of ale and Lord only knew what else, she was as numb as a sleepwalker. "You can do what you want to pretty it up some," he said, "and—oh, yes, I forgot to tell you, you will not be expected to work in the tavern. Your father's solicitor and I talked it over and we agreed that, if you want to, you should go on with your book learning."

Thank God for small favors, she thought. At least she would not become a tavern wench.

"Though why a girl who has your . . . attributes . . . should think it necessary to cram her head full of unnecessary things is beyond me," he went on.

Madeline knew then that she would never understand her guardian. He had the speech of a gentleman, he had come from a family of some substance and yet, for his life's work, he was a tavern keeper. Also, in spite of *his* attributes, she had the terrible feeling that, hidden beneath his seeming concern for her comfort, there was a baser side to him. Exactly what it was, she could not guess, for in two years he never made advances to her (she learned fairly soon after her arrival in London that he had a mistress, the discontented wife of a peer), and he left Madeline alone for the most part to pursue whatever she deemed worth pursuing at the time.

She spent her time reading almost everything she could get her hands on, and learning the art of cooking. Rufus ate most of his meals downstairs in the tavern or else out in some secluded place with his mistress, so she had only herself to cook for. She had no friends, no opportunity to make them, for the men and the few women who came to the tavern, whose loud voices came up to her room through the floorboards, did not interest her. Had it not been for books, the works of Shakespeare and Marlowe and Bunyan, the poetry of Milton, Donne, and Dryden, she would have been

ready to commit herself to Bedlam at any time. At first
she wondered how long she could go on living like that,
then lethargy set in, and she settled into the jejune
routine. Rufus remained more or less a stranger to her
for they saw each other only occasionally in passing.

Her life continued in this way for almost two years,
then suddenly Rufus did not make himself so scarce any
more. At least three or four nights a week he would
leave the tavern and come upstairs to eat supper with
her, claiming that she was a better cook than Chauncey
who "just throws food together downstairs." At first
Madeline liked the company at mealtime, but as the
days, then weeks, passed she began to feel uncomfortable with Rufus. Those squinting brown eyes of his
seemed to be trying to look inside of her, see things
never seen by anyone. Also, he was often not entirely
sober when he came abovestairs to their apartment.
Though never reeking drunk, he often had a slightly
glazed look in his eyes, and sometimes his speech
slurred just a little.

However, on the night he told her about his ideas
that would change their lives, he was entirely sober.

"I would like your permission," he said without
preamble, "to use your inheritance to make a better life
for you."

She had just finished putting their supper—a pungent
stew—on the table in the miniscule dining parlor and
sat down across from him at the table. "What do you
mean?"

"I want to sell the tavern, get out of this neighbor-
hood," he said. "With the money I get from the sale,
plus your inheritance, I can buy a house in a more
elegant section of town and we will be able to live quite

comfortably without my having to spend my days like a common laborer."

The idea of a complete change in lifestyle so startled her that for a minute she only stared at him.

"You are getting on in years," he said bluntly. "You're a looker, but you'll never find a husband around here. I think we'd better go elsewhere before you're in your caps and it's too late . . . for either of us."

She hadn't realized how much she had hated the life she was leading until that moment. Impulsively, she pushed her chair back, rushed around the small table, and kissed him resoundingly on the cheek. "Oh, Rufus, can we? Can we really move away from here?"

He gave the closest thing to a smile she had ever seen from him and said, "Very soon. Very soon now."

Apparently Rufus had been looking into the matter some time before he mentioned it to her for within a week he sold the tavern and moved them both into a house on Wigmore Street.

"We won't be living among the nobility," he told her, "but it's close enough."

"Close enough for what?" she asked.

He gave a laugh that sounded rusty from disuse and said, "Close enough for our purposes."

They had been in the new house scarcely six weeks before she found out what "our purposes" were.

He told her one night as they sat in the small saloon of the house, she reading, he pouring over some figures he had written in a book.

"Madeline, we have to have some money. There is nothing left."

She gasped. "But . . . but, it is not to be believed,

Rufus. You said you got a good price for the tavern, and there is all that money my father left me, plus the sale of our house in Bath."

"It was not enough," he told her. "It takes more to buy less now. Besides, what didn't go into the buying and furnishing of this house has gone on your back."

Which was true. For some reason she could not understand at the time, he had furnished the house lavishly, recklessly spending money on the most expensive furniture, draperies, tapestries, and carpets to be found in London. And then, that done, he had taken her on shopping expeditions to the most fashionable modistes and had bought her a new wardrobe from the skin out of clothing the likes of which Madeline had never seen before, not even in the upper circles of Bath society. There were gowns of every conceivable material and make, some she was sure she would never get to wear since she had not, since coming to London, received a single invitation.

"I can take back most of the new wardrobe," she told him, "except for those gowns that were made especially for me."

"That won't be necessary," he told her. "I have a better idea."

By the time he had finished telling her his idea, all the color had drained from her face and she was shaking visibly.

"I won't do it," she said when she could calm herself enough to say anything. "I will not, under *any* circumstances become a whore."

"And I would not, under any circumstances, have you become a whore," he said. "Apparently you did not understand. Let me tell you again."

He went through his entire plan again and ended by saying, "I have made the acquaintance of someone on the edge of the court. He lost to me at cards the other day and he owes me a favor because I did not take his money."

"I won't do it, Rufus."

"Shut up and listen to me." He scowled at her. "Unless you *really* want to take up whoring for a livelihood, you'll do exactly as I say. I am not exaggerating when I tell you there is no money left. There is not enough to pay the grocer through next week! Now, here is the plan. This man I spoke of, Reginald Vine, is invited to a large do at Kensington Palace and you will go with him, but you'll stay with him only long enough to get in the door. It will be a dull affair, you can count on that. Brandyfaced Nan and Prince George will both be nodding before the refreshment tables are brought out, but you will not be there to impress royalty. You are to set about using your charm and your beauty, and you are truly beautiful, my girl. Even though I may not have mentioned it before, I am not blind. *Ravishingly* beautiful. You are to attract a man, a married man. Be very sure that he is married, wealthy, and vulnerable to gossip. And you are to get him to bring you home with the promise that he will get his reward when you get here. Tell him your escort has taken ill and deserted you.

"Go straight to your bedchamber and close the door. Let him embrace you and then begin to remove your clothing . . ."

"No, Rufus, no! I will *not!*"

". . . and then I shall come barging in," he said as though there had been no interruption, "and accuse him either of trying to rape my wife or of having an affair with her, whichever seems most appropriate at the time." He gave a short laugh. "I can hardly wait to see the face on the first one. He'll beg for mercy and be only too happy to be sheared like a sheep. When he finds out I mean neither to kill him nor tattle to his wife, he'll gladly part with half his holdings."

"The first one!" she caught on the phrase. "You mean there to be others, I suppose."

"Many others. We shall have a steady income, and a big one. After all, I have made quite an investment—this house, your wardrobe—and I expect it to pay off."

"How often do you think you'll be able to manage an invitation to Kensington Palace?" she asked sarcastically.

"Not often," he admitted, "but we won't need the palace. It won't take London long to discover you, my beauty, and you will not want for invitations."

"Just how many invitations do you think I'll get, once it is known how the evening ends?"

"It won't be known," he said. "Not one of the men who brings you home is going to tell what happened to him. After all, he will be paying us so that it won't be known."

"Rufus, you are the basest, most depraved man I have ever met," she all but screamed at him. "You are no better than a pimp!"

"Tsk, tsk! Where did a nice young girl like you learn about pimps?" His eyes squinted at her for a minute, then he said, "Anyway, you can hardly call me a pimp when you will remain with your virtue intact."

No amount of arguing or pleading—and not even tears, which she had never shed in front of him before—could make him change his mind. She went with Reginald Vine, a man about Rufus's age, but with a round face and short, stocky build, to Kensington Palace the following night. Her gown was pale blue gauze over a navy silk underskirt. The bodice was cut lower than she thought decent, clearly revealing the top of her small, firm breasts. Had she actually been a lightskirt, she could not have felt more like one.

As soon as they were inside the palace, her escort said, "Rufus said I was only to get you inside . . . and I see someone over there I must speak to." He left her and she did not see him again.

She did not want for company, however. Two men, coming from the opposite directions, reached her simultaneously, each requesting the honor of taking her to the reception hall. Feeling as though *she* were the sheep about to be sheared, she nodded to both of them and, with one on either side, made her debut into London society.

Because of her extreme distaste for what she was doing, as well as her nervousness, the night did not remain entirely clear in her memory. After it was over, she remembered nothing at all about Kensington Palace, only that she spent several hours in a large place with which she was not familiar. She remembered nothing about the people to whom she was introduced, only that there were many of them, a sea of faces staring at her and, she was sure, knowing instantly the rig she was running and condemning her for it.

One of the men who had first rushed to her side was soon put off by the other and it was this one—a middle-aged man with large brown cocker-spaniel eyes in a round face, receding brown hair, and unusually small, pudgy hands—who stuck to her like a leech the rest of the evening, trying (but not entirely succeeding) to discourage any other males who wanted to make the acquaintance of the beauteous new woman. Through the haze of timidity and fright, Madeline was aware of several things: that her escort introduced her as his cousin to several people, that he was married and his wife was in Sussex visiting her family. He was exactly the type Rufus wanted her to bring home.

With knees shaking so she could scarcely stand, she told him at the end of the evening that her original escort seemed to have vanished and, as though on cue, he offered to take her home. When they arrived at the house on Wigmore Street, she would have given years of her life to have been able to thank him and send him on his way, but she knew she had no choice. She invited him in. Since the hour was very late, she knew he could put only one interpretation on the invitation. Inside the house, she did not even pause in the saloon, but headed straight abovestairs to her bedchamber. The man, of course, followed her. She looked back once and noticed the slight smile that curved his sensual lips.

Inside her bedchamber, not a word was spoken as she lit one of the lamps. Nor did either of them speak as he crossed the room immediately and took her in his arms, kissing first her cheek and then her lips. "I knew we would get along the minute I saw you tonight," he whispered then.

For a moment, she was unresisting, and then she stiffened. This was going to be even worse than she imagined. Where was Rufus? Why did he not carry out his part of this disgusting, unfunny farce?

"Let me help you," the man said, taking her shawl

from her shoulders, then kissing her neck. It was all she could do to keep from cringing.

It was at that moment that the door was flung open and Rufus stormed into the room demanding, "Madam, what is the meaning of this?"

As much in relief as in repugnance, Madeline sank into the nearest chair, her legs refusing to hold her any longer. Rufus had the man by the neckcloth and was half-choking, half-pulling him out of the room. "Trying to seduce my wife, eh?" he said. "We'll just see about that."

Then they were out of the room and the door closed. Madeline heard their loud voices from belowstairs where Rufus continued his charade, but she could not—nor did she want to—hear what was said. A few minutes later, a laughing Rufus again opened her door and told her they could live for several months on the blunt that sadder-but-wiser man had parted with.

"Then I won't have to do this again any time soon," Madeline said.

"Not for a night or two," Rufus told her. "We certainly are not going to wait until we are in dire straits before we replenish the larder."

That was the beginning. Rufus had not misjudged the beauty of his ward nor her ability to attract males of all ages. After her appearance at Kensington Palace, she did not want for invitations, but Rufus very carefully screened them, letting her accept only those that he thought advantageous to his scheme. From then on, Madeline was sent out once a month, sometimes more often, and expected to bring home what Rufus referred to as "a new pigeon for plucking."

At first Madeline thought that, after several times, it

would get to be mechanical, that she could, with hardly any thought at all, go through the motions, get it over with, and not think about it until she had to repeat the performance. She told herself that she was an actress in a play with a long run and she would have to keep doing the same scenes over and over until the play closed.

It didn't work. No matter what she told herself, she still felt the same dread, the same fear, at the beginning of every performance and the same nausea and self-loathing when it was done.

It was when the "pigeon plucking" had been going on for six months that Madeline finally called a halt to it, though she did not tell Rufus. Her last performance (though she did not know at the time it was to be her last) was at Rufus's suggestion that she visit the tavern he had formerly owned. "The clientele is the best," he said. "It always was—if not the best people, the best pocketbooks." She refused, saying that would make her no better than a tavern wench and that no respectable man would tumble into her clutches that way. Rufus was adamant, and so just after dark, he dropped her off at the tavern.

It was the longest night of her life as well as the most uncomfortable. Several men made advances to her in the tavern, but by then she was somewhat expert in picking out just the right pigeon and none of those was. As the night wore on, she was sure the right man would not appear and that the new tavern owner might even try to have her arrested by one of the constables who passed at regular intervals. She would have left, but she had no way to get home other than to walk through the dark streets, which she would not do. Finally, desperate, she noticed a very presentable-looking man sitting in a corner alone. He was better dressed than most of the others, had a thin, aristocratic face, and was one of the few in the room who had not, at some time during the evening, tried to put his hands on her. She went over to him and asked if he would be good enough to go outside and find a hackney carriage for her. He gave her an inquisitive look, then rose at once. "Of course, madam."

Outside he looked at her again in the light of the lantern hanging over the door. "My gig is just around the corner," he said. "May I drive you home?"

Unsure what to do, she hesitated.

"My name is Robert Crawley," he said, "and I am in London on business. I know very few people here, and I would be delighted to see that you get home safely."

Finally she nodded, taking his arm and going with him to the gig. It probably was just as safe to go with him as with some hackney driver she'd never set eyes on before.

Crawley proved to be quite nice, she thought. He chatted amiably after she gave him directions for getting to Wigmore Street. He told her about his home and family in Kent, his loneliness when he had to come to London, and how much he hated spending evenings in taverns, but that it was better than staying in an inn all evening by himself. "At least I can see and hear others around me having a good time," he said.

He asked her no questions and she volunteered no information other than that her name was Madeline Boyd. She realized, somewhat belatedly, that the reason he asked her nothing was because he thought he already knew. After all, how much knowledge of the human race was necessary to figure out why a young woman, unaccompanied, was spending an evening in a tavern making up to the men?

At the house he helped her alight from the gig and walked with her to the door. She could tell he was surprised at the section of town as well as the house itself. It was not what he had expected.

She paused a moment at the door, her first thought being to send him on his way with her thanks for bringing her home. Then a picture of Rufus's angry face appeared in her mind, along with the nasty words he would say to her if she let this pigeon get away. She knew he was waiting just behind the partially opened saloon door, listening for his cue.

"Will . . . will you come in?" she asked finally.

"Thank you, yes," he said as though expecting the invitation.

Madeline, as usual, started straight up the stairs. When she heard no footsteps following, she turned. Crawley was still standing at the foot of the stairway, looking up at her with a slight smile. "I was wondering," he said, "do you not offer a glass of wine first, or perhaps something stronger?"

Momentarily taken aback, she could only stare down at him, then recovering, she said, "There is a decanter in my . . . up here, I think."

He went with her to her bedchamber without further ado. Of course there was no decanter and she grumbled, "I suppose that silly maidservant forgot to leave it."

"It is late," he said, "so perhaps she thought you would not require it tonight."

She would not even presume to guess what he meant by that. Already she was wondering why Rufus did not burst into the room. Since Crawley made no motion toward removing her shawl, she did so herself. Still he did not approach her nor did Rufus enter. She supposed her guardian had his ear to the door and was waiting for a more propitious time. Her knees beginning to tremble, she crossed the room to Crawley. "I want to thank you again for seeing me safely home," she said, unable to think of anything else.

"My pleasure," he said. Slowly, almost gingerly, he reached out to her, his arms encircling her waist. She did not resist until his hands began to move across her breasts, and then she drew back. Where was Rufus? Why didn't he come in?

Crawley, his eyes narrowed to slits, his breath coming faster, grasped her again, whispering, "Don't pretend to be shy, little bird, I know you've flown this way before."

For an instant the humor of the situation almost caused her to laugh. He was calling her a bird while she was thinking of him as a pigeon. But then all the humor was gone as he took her lace blouse in both hands and ripped it straight down the front, then tore off the top of her chimse. Her scream was aborted by his mouth crashing down on hers in a biting kiss.

She tried to push him away but his arms were like iron bands around her body. While she squirmed in his grasp, he worked at her ruffled skirt, trying to push it and her underclothing down simultaneously. His eyes were small, beady and shining with lust now. He was not going to be deterred.

Finally, her mouth free, she screamed, "Rufus!"

In a matter of seconds, the door burst open and Rufus strode into the room. "What is the meaning of this, sir?" he roared. "I will kill you for attacking my wife!" He pulled a pistol from behind him, surprising Madeline almost as much as Crawley, who was by now frozen into immobility. "You reptile!" Rufus continued. "Stop looking at my wife like that! Madeline, clothe yourself!"

Rufus took Crawley by the arm, yanking him out of the room. Madeline, in tears by now, fell across the bed, too stunned with humiliation even to remove the remainder of her torn clothing and put on a wrapper. The usual loud voices came from below for a few minutes and then the front door was opened and closed and there was silence. Madeline got up and went to her door and locked it. She did not want to see Rufus's face again tonight nor hear his voice. The truth was, she never wanted to see him or hear him again. She had seen his face as he himself looked at her half-naked body and had seen as much lust there—even more, actually—as she had on the face of the pigeon.

That night, she knew, would be the last of it. Never again would she be a part of her guardian's criminal career. He could do anything he liked to her—beat her, kill her—she would not go out looking for men to cheat and rob again. That was what it was, pure and simple, robbery. She was just as much a robber as if she donned mask and went out on the highways and held up coach passengers.

She would not do it again. Tomorrow she would think of some way to stop it for good and all.

It had been the following morning that her violent argument with Rufus about ending their criminal activity had sent her running from the house and to the sign that had advertised for settlers in the Carolinas. Now, lying in Gavin Durant's rope bed, unable to sleep, the thought went through her mind again and again: Did I do the wrong thing in coming here?

She knew she had not done the wrong thing in leaving Rufus, but this was a strange new country, and the people, though English, seemed as strange as the land itself, as foreign as the savages who had inhabited the land before they came. The fierce, scowling face of Tondah came to mind, the staring Indians, silently appraising her as she had left the wharf. She had heard, and had believed, that the Indians had disappeared into the forests and thence to the interior wilds of the country.

And then there was Gavin himself who had stared down at her while she slept. She did not know what to make of it, nor of what she had felt, pretending to be asleep yet somehow *liking* the knowledge that he was looking at her. Even now, hearing him breathing on the other side of the room, separated from her by the hanging blanket, she was completely unsure whether he was her friend or . . . what? He had done her a favor by taking her in until Felton Cate returned, but should she continue to stay here?

She began to turn restlessly in the bed with the urgency of having decisions to make. Finally, near dawn, she began to grow sleepy, and the first red rays of sunrise were beginning to streak the sky when she finally slept.

There were voices. Was she dreaming or was someone talking on the other side of the blanket? Warily she opened her eyes to bright sunlight, and smelled the enticing aroma of coffee and the yeasty odor of bread. And she heard the voices clearly for they were only a few feet from her, Gavin and another man. Was it Felton Cate? She listened.

"Will it never end, Gavin?" the unfamiliar voice asked. "Those old men in England, the Lords Proprietor, have never set foot on these shores, yet they purport to run our business, our very lives, as though they know what they're doing."

There was a sigh, then Gavin said, "I don't know anything we can do about that, Wes. We've discussed it before, you and I. But what brings you out here this morning. Has something happened?"

It was not Felton Cate but, Madeline guessed, Wesley Martin, the man from whom Gavin had borrowed the dray to bring her to his cabin yesterday.

"Yes, no sooner do we get through one crisis than another is dropped on us."

"What now?" Gavin asked.

But his friend seemed in no hurry to relate whatever news he had brought. First he needed to get other complaints off his chest. "Things were just beginning to get back to something approaching normal," he said, "what with folks accepting Cary as governor."

"So?"

"With John Porter in the background, more or less, and Glover no longer trying to take over our government, it is a settled, known fact that Thomas Cary is our governor, our *only* governor."

"So?" Gavin repeated.

"It's going to start all over again, this two-governor business," Martin declared.

"But I thought . . ." Gavin began.

But Martin was now anxious to say his say. He interrupted. "There's a rumor—came on the ship yesterday—that the Lords Proprietor are sending still *another* man to be governor."

"That's ridiculous!" Gavin snapped.

"Tell *them*. I already know."

"Who're they sending?"

"I don't know that they are. As I said, it's just a rumor," Martin replied. "But you know how it is, the rumors we hear. They usually are true. I don't know who he is because the man who brought the news didn't hear any names."

The rumor had now turned into news.

"But the situation of having two governors had just been resolved when Cary was declared the governor," Gavin said. "Why would the Lords want to complicate the matter further?"

"You should be able to guess that, Gavin," Martin said. "Cary is a Quaker and the Lords want a governor who is Church of England."

Gavin made a noise, indicating disgust.

"Will you fight to keep Cary, if it comes to that?" Martin said. "After all, he is our neighbor, so to speak. Lives right here among us."

"No, I am a Quaker and Quakers do not bear arms against other men," Gavin said.

"Some do," Martin reminded him, "and Cary certainly will lead the fight."

"He is a Quaker-come-lately," Gavin said. "I will not fire a gun at another human being." Then he added softly, "Pray God it will not come to that."

"I'm afraid it will," Martin said ominously. "In fact, I predict it will."

There was a moment of silence, and then Gavin said, "For the good of everybody, it is best that the whites do not become embroiled in petty politics now because the Indians are getting restless."

"Where is that Indian woman that works for you?" Martin asked.

"She's outside," Gavin said. "We can talk freely."

"Well, I've been saying for a long time that an uprising was likely, but now I've changed my mind," Martin said. "The troublemakers among the Indians have left this area."

"Oh no," Gavin said, "they have merely stopped making trouble. But they will again, and this time it will be trouble such as none of us has seen before. They are not only getting more restless, but also more resentful all the time about their lands being taken. While we fight among ourselves over trivialities, they . . ." He broke off.

"But it isn't trivial, this business of governing ourselves," Martin said.

As though Martin had not spoken, Gavin continued as if talking to himself, thinking through the problem out loud. "They are beginning to feel that they are being crowded out of their own country by white men who never stop arriving on these shores. They have no idea what a surveyor is or what he does with his compass and chain; they only know that where the surveyor goes, some square-jawed white man with a gun and axe is going to make claim to the lands the Indians have worked, fought for, and lived on all their lives."

"You are right," Martin said, "but still I see no way to forestall trouble over the Cary mess."

"Let us hope," Gavin said fervently, "that this new rumor you have heard is just that—a rumor and nothing more."

"Amen to that."

A chair creaked and Madeline heard the two men get up and go outside, and then horse hooves as Martin left. Though the talk of Indian uprising had frightened her badly, the talk of political unrest had surprised her. The quietness of the cabin was soothing and she still felt tired from her long night of wakefulness. It was only a few minutes before she had drifted back to sleep again.

When she awoke the second time the room was even brighter, and through the window she could see the sun high in the sky. Midday. She turned over, facing the room, ready to get up, and inhaled sharply. Once again, Gavin was standing beside the bed staring at her.

Chapter Five

SHE STARED BACK AT HIM, HER STEEL GRAY EYES AS unblinking and ungiving as his piercing blue ones. What was he thinking as he looked at her prone form? Was he not quite sure about her morals? Was he wondering if it would be acceptable to her if he slipped into bed beside her? If that was the case, she would settle that issue in his mind at once.

"Would you mind going to the other side of the room and pulling the blanket back across the rope so I may get up and dress?" she asked, her tone as frosty as an English winter.

He continued to stare at her for a moment then, without a word, did as he was asked. Only after the blanket separated them once again did Madeline throw aside the covers and get up.

Why did he keep looking at her that way when she was asleep? The question repeated itself over and over in her mind, but only one answer came: he was trying to decide if she were a lady in the moral meaning of the word, or if she were a woman of tarnished reputation.

That thought caused her to stop in the midst of dressing and stare unseeingly toward the blanket. Actually, she was both. Morally, she could not be faulted on any point; no matter her past, her virtue was intact. Yet there were at least a dozen men in England who—if they could speak freely without ruining their own reputations—would have declared her reputation so besmirched and sullied that beside it tarnish would have appeared as gold.

This was something Gavin Durant and the other residents of the Bath Town area would never know. She would keep this knowledge locked up in the vault of her mind as safely as though her mind actually were a steel or iron box, impossible to get into without the key.

She continued dressing, looking through her trunk and choosing a rose-colored cambric gown, and hating it because it was part of the wardrobe Rufus had chosen for her before she knew why he was insisting that she have so many new gowns. But Rufus and the past were not foremost in her mind now. She kept seeing Gavin's face, his eyes as he looked at her. That look had left her both frightened, perplexed, and . . . yes, thrilled.

She had not understood her feelings about him last night, nor did she now. Dressed, finally, she sat on the side of the bed for a moment trying to decide what she should do. If Felton Cate returned from his hunting trip today, there was no dilemma; she would, of course, go to his house. But if he did not return? Should she spend another night here? Her better judgment told her it might be better for her to go to the Rolands. They would have had a day and night for reunion and celebration of the family's being together again; surely they would not mind so much putting her up for one night. Cate would certainly return by tomorrow.

She made up the bed, then pulled the blanket aside again and joined Gavin, who was sitting at the table.

"Breakfast was hours ago," he said, "but there's still some coffee."

"I smelled bread, or thought I did, earlier." She remembered the tempting yeasty odor.

"I'm afraid Tondah and I ate it. We decided you were going to sleep the day away."

"Oh." Ravenously hungry, she was keenly disappointed.

"It's almost time for the midday meal," he said. "I'll get Tondah to . . ."

"No, I wouldn't dream of disturbing her, whatever she's doing," Madeline said.

"You have to eat," he told her. "Maybe there's something already prepared. Tondah will know." He got up, went to the door, opened it, and called, "Tondah, would you come inside, please?"

Madeline liked the way he spoke to the Indian girl, not demanding or taking her for granted the way some men did their servants. But then, why shouldn't he treat her almost as an equal? She was. At least, she certainly was more than a servant. That had been made fairly clear last night when Tondah had also stared down at Madeline, the contempt in her dark eyes clear in the candlelight.

"May I prevail upon you to take me into Bath Town today?" she asked Gavin. "I appreciate your hospitality, but I think it better if I stay with the Rolands until Mr. Cate returns."

"Impossible," Gavin said. "You have to stay here. I signed a document saying I am responsible for you, so you will have to remain with me until I, personally, turn you over to Cate."

"Oh," was all she could think of to say as she considered this new aspect of her plight.

Gavin's blue eyes crinkled as an impish grin lit his face. What devilment, she wondered, went on behind that heretofore serious facade? She did not have time to ask, for Tondah came in at that moment.

"As you can see, Miss Boyd is up now," he said to the girl, "and she would like something to eat. If you could give us our midday meal now, even though it is a bit early . . ."

"If you say," Tondah said in a low voice, a scowl like a thunderhead crossing her face. "But she wait maybe."

"I am hungry also," Gavin said simply, and Tondah went instantly to the larder and began removing food.

Madeline watched the girl in fascination. She had never seen anyone who exerted so little control over hiding animosity. Today she seemed openly hostile rather than merely sullen; she did not care if Gavin and, indeed, the entire universe, knew that she wanted the unwelcome interloper as far away from the Durant cabin and its owner as possible. As she went about placing the food on the table—cold ham, dried fruit, and corn pone—she glanced from time to time at Madeline as though willing her to disappear into thin air, then checking to see if she had. For some reason she could not discern, Madeline found herself glaring back at Tondah with equal hostility. There was no doubt in her mind now, if there ever had been, that Tondah was Gavin's "woman" and would brook no competition from anyone, especially a newcomer who had no right to be there in the first place.

Competition. Madeline's thoughts suddenly tripped on the word. Why had she thought of herself as competition for Tondah? She most assuredly was not. No, it was Tondah's attitude that had brought the word to mind, not any idea of her own.

She ate distractedly, wishing Gavin would carry on some kind of conversation, either with her or with Tondah. The silence was oppressive. But he seemed as busy with thoughts as inexpressible as hers. It was when Tondah was clearing away the empty dishes that he finally said, "Would you like to go into Bath Town and familiarize yourself with the village? I will take you."

"Oh, yes," she said instantly, "I would. But from what I saw yesterday, I don't think it would take more than a few minutes to cover the whole of Bath Town."

He smiled and she realized that the impish look came to his face every time his lips curved upward. "Add a few minutes to the original few minutes if I introduce you to all the citizens."

"Some of the new citizens came with me on the ship," she said wistfully, longing to see the familiar faces. "I will not have to be introduced to them."

"Then you can introduce me," he said, getting up from the table. "I'll hitch up the cart while you get ready."

"It's close enough to walk," she said. "Only about a mile, isn't it?"

"A mile and a half," he said, "but I want to get some things at the store."

Gavin's horse was a roan stallion about eighteen hands high. Hitched to him, the small cart, similar to the dray Gavin had borrowed yesterday, scarcely looked large enough for the two of them. Madeline got in the cart, with Gavin's help, and sat directly behind him. It was early afternoon and the sun was still high in a cloudless sky. Madeline marveled again at the beauty of autumn in Carolina, the flaming red trees, the bright gold, the shining coppery look of some, and her nose crinkled at the pungent odor of evergreens. She had read years ago in a history book that when Sir Walter Raleigh reached this new world, he thought he had found Eden. She could well believe it now. Excitement began to rise in her as, once again, she felt like giving thanks for her arrival here. She had truly done the right thing in leaving England and coming to Eden.

"You are smiling," Gavin observed. He was half turned around in his seat looking at her.

"I was thinking how beautiful it is here," she said.

"Even more so now that you are here to decorate the place," he said matter-of-factly, then turned abruptly back to give his attention to driving the cart.

They did not speak again until they reached the little village.

For the past five years, since its founding in 1705, Bath Town had nestled on a point of land between Old Town Creek and Back Creek facing out on the bay which opened into the Pamlico River. However, for hundreds of years before it became a white man's town, an Indian village had stood in the same spot. The first whites to take an interest in the land were fur traders and explorers, but land speculators did not lag far behind. When the plague decimated the Indian ranks and removed the immediate threat to the white men, they began to take over the land, acre by acre.

The actual town itself had been laid out by John Lawson, one of the first settlers, Gavin told Madeline. The original plan called for seventy-one lots of one acre. In spite of the act of incorporation in 1705, Front Street, which paralleled Old Town Creek, was the only one to reach the required width of one hundred feet. Adjoining the north boundary of the town and fronting along Old Town Creek was the Bath Town Common, which was used as a park, pasture, and woodlot for the citizens of the town.

Only two years ago, there had been twelve houses in town and a population of fifty to sixty people, Madeline learned. The wood-frame houses and cabins straggled along Front Street only. Now, as Gavin pointed out, there were six streets in the town, though not all of them had houses, and livestock roamed freely. Madeline also noticed rooting hogs here and there, playing havoc with the lots.

"Where are the stores and businesses?" she asked Gavin as the cart went from street to street.

"The merchants have small stores in their homes," he told her, "and sometimes Indians bring furs in, which they exchange for cloth, trinkets, and guns and rum."

The tour, short of necessity since there was little to see, ended by the wharf where Madeline had arrived. "I did not see a church," she commented. "Are church services also held in the homes?"

"If there are services," he said. "There's no minister here . . . yet. From the beginning, the settlers have tried to get one here. Church of England, of course," he added offhandedly, "but so far, none has seen fit to come. Oh, we get the benefit of one occasionally who happens to be passing through on his way to one of the plantations, but it seems they do not want to take up residence here."

Madeline looked about her. "I thought it quite small yesterday, but compared with what you said it was two years ago, Bath Town appears to be growing rapidly."

"It would grow even faster if we could rule ourselves instead of being governed by those old men in England who know nothing about the land . . . or the people," Gavin said, bitterness in his tone.

Madeline gave him a long look. "That remark is almost treasonous. You had better be careful where and to whom you say things like that."

"I am," he said. "I only tell my opinion to the citizens of Bath County and environs, and all over England when I go back for a visit."

"I'm surprised you haven't been hanged," she said.

He laughed. "I am not important enough for my opinions to make a difference. Therefore, why bother to give me that importance by hanging me?"

"There's something to that, I suppose." She smiled, thinking she had never seen a more honest, open face than his, even with his impish grin.

"I forgot to tell you about that building over there." He pointed in the distance. "It is the public library, the only one in the Colonies."

Madeline expressed surprise, then suddenly straightened as she saw two familiar figures walking along Water Street.

"Jessie! Carrie!" she shrieked delightedly.

"Madeline!" Jessie answered, recognizing her friend. She set down the package she was carrying and ran toward Madeline, arms outstretched, and they hugged each other like friends who had been apart for years. Then Jessie looked toward Gavin, who was catching up to them. "This is Mr. Cate, I suppose," she said.

"Jessie Roland, may I present Gavin Durant?" Madeline said, amused at the astonishment on her friend's face. "Mr. Cate is out hunting and Mr. Durant is letting me stay at his house until Mr. Cate returns."

"Why, you could stay with us," Jessie said immediately. "We've room enough."

"Yes, yes," Carrie echoed. "Stay with us."

"Impossible," Gavin said, and explained the circumstances of his taking over the indenture papers temporarily.

"Cyrus could have signed for you just as well," Jessie said, "if only we'd known you didn't have a place to go."

"It's all right," Madeline assured her, unwilling to spoil any part of Jessie's happiness at the reunion with her long-absent husband. "Mr. Durant very kindly arranged to take me in and, as you can see, I am doing quite well."

"But, but . . ." Jessie's face showed plainly the questions she wanted to ask.

"I have a cabin a little way out from town, ma'am," Gavin said, "and an Indian girl who keeps house and cooks for me. She lives on the premises."

Jessie nodded, though this clearly was not explanation enough to satisfy her.

"How about you?" Madeline asked. "How did you find your husband, and how do you like your new home? I have been so anxious to hear."

"Cyrus is fine, couldn't be better," Jessie said. "He

and Con have gone to Cyrus's blacksmith shop now so Con can see it. We live in that house back there." She pointed to a wood-frame house around the corner on Front Street. "It's . . . different." She seemed to have trouble finding a word to describe her new circumstances. "But I think I'm going to like it. I like it already," she added hastily, "but some things are going to take some getting used to."

Madeline laughed. "I agree, but I like what I've seen so far very much. It's beautiful here." She looked down toward the sparkling water of the river, partially shaded on either side by the gold and crimson leaves.

"Where does Mr. Cate live?" Jessie asked.

Gavin pointed inland. "About a mile, or better, in that direction."

Jessie looked disappointed. "I thought it would be right here in town. I was hoping we might be neighbors."

"We'll see each other often, I promise," Madeline said.

"That's a fact," Gavin said. "Around here you see *every*body often."

Both women laughed. Then Jessie pointed to a cabin just beyond Water Street. "That's where the Miltons live," she said. "I saw Elizabeth this morning and she still hasn't recovered from the shock of seeing Indians yesterday when we arrived. She thought they had all gone inland."

"Surely none bothered her," Madeline said. She could imagine the skittish Elizabeth clutching her baby to her bosom as she walked past the savage, albeit civilized, red men.

"No, but she was sure they were going to," Jessie said. "She was clinging to her husband's arm as though she were an appendage."

"It is not likely the Indians would harm her," Gavin said, "though perhaps it's just as well for her to be a bit leery."

Madeline looked at Gavin. "Is there a possibility of danger?"

"I think not," he said. "Certainly not from the ones who watched the ship unload. Most of them work for the whites right here in town. Some are even slaves."

Jessie shuddered. "I'm glad Cyrus doesn't have any slaves, or even servants, if they are Indians."

"I shouldn't worry if I were you," Gavin said. "Most of the Indians are trustworthy."

"Most," Madeline said. "That implies that not all are." She was thinking of the scowling Tondah who had looked at her as though slitting her throat would have been a pleasure.

"Not all whites are trustworthy either," Gavin pointed out.

"Amen," Jessie said, and Madeline nodded agreement. Jessie picked up the package she had set down while greeting Madeline and said, "I guess we better get on home, Carrie. Your father and Con will be coming in soon and will expect us to be in the kitchen cooking up everything imaginable. Cyrus has already given me a list of all his favorites that he hasn't had since he left England," she said to Madeline. Then, indicating the package, "This is some buckskin I just bought for me and the children. Cyrus said to wear them everyday and save our good clothes for special occasions."

"I suppose I should do the same," Madeline said, knowing that she hadn't enough money left even to buy the rudest kind of clothes.

Jessie hugged her again, "Well, take care, and we'll see you very soon, I hope. Remember, if you need anything . . ."

"Thanks, Jessie. I'll see you again as soon as I'm settled at Mr. Cate's."

Gavin nodded. "Glad to have met you, ma'am."

"Yes," Jessie said, "and I'm glad you are taking care of our girl for us. Madeline is very special."

Gavin nodded again in agreement, but said nothing. They watched Jessie and Carrie until they went inside the house on Front Street, then Gavin helped Madeline back into the cart.

"Before we leave town," Madeline said, "would you mind driving me by the library? I want to remember exactly where it is in case I have time for reading once I'm settled."

"Of course," Gavin said, clucking to the horse.

He directed the horse from Water Street straight through what appeared to have been laid out as a "block" to the small wooden building in the center. "This is it," he said, "though I am not sure you will find reading material for diversion here."

"How does it happen that a town so small even has a library?" she asked.

"The library actually is five years older than the town," he told her. "In 1700, Thomas Bray, the Anglican founder of the Society for the Propagation of the Gospel in Foreign Parts, purchased the library with funds he had collected to establish libraries and support missionaries in the Colonies." He nodded toward the building. "It was supposed to have been two libraries, one parochial, designed to meet the needs of the minister of the parish, and the other a layman's library, but the two were combined soon after the books arrived."

"You called this a parish, yet there is no church, no minister," she commented.

"True, it is known as St. Thomas Parish, and if there is a church here, as some vow there will be very soon, it will be St. Thomas Church. I doubt there will be a church, though, until the residents are able to attract a minister. Those who have been here so far to look the place over have found living in Bath Town a difficult experience."

"I heard you say you are a Quaker," she said. "Do you have a church nearby?"

"There is no formal meeting house for miles," he said, "but some of us meet occasionally at the home of one of the Friends."

He flicked the reins lightly over the back of the stallion and the cart was moving again. "There is one more stop we should make before going back," he said.

"Oh, yes," she remembered, "you said you wanted to go to the store."

"For you," he said. "Cyrus had the right idea when he sent his wife out to get buckskins for herself and the children." Half turning in the seat, he eyed her gown. "Your clothes are mighty pretty, but a bit fancy for wear around here. You need something more . . . serviceable." It took him a few seconds to think of the word.

"I—I will buy some later," she said, not wanting to tell him she did not have the money for a new wardrobe now. "There's no need to take your time for something so trivial."

"I have nothing else to do right now, and it will be my pleasure to outfit you properly for your new life," he said.

"No," she said, "it would not be proper."

He turned all the way around in the seat and laughed heartily. "You are going to have to get over some of your notions of what is and what is not proper," he said. "You are in a new land now and people here worry about what is practical, not what is proper. I say the only practical thing is to get you some new clothing."

"Only if you will let me reimburse you later," she said stiffly.

"We will talk about that later," he hedged.

At the end of Water Street, he stopped the cart in front of a large log building that looked as though it were part family dwelling, part commercial enterprise.

"The Lester Mulligan family lives here," Gavin told her, "and the front half of the first story is a store."

A bell tinkled as they opened the door, and a woman came from the rear of the house. She was large with graying blond hair which was plaited around her head.

"Afternoon, Lucinda," Gavin said. "I brought you a customer. This is Miss Boyd, just off the ship yesterday, and she needs some clothes for everyday wear. While you're fixing her up, I'll go talk to Lester. He in the back?"

"No, he went with Felton Cate hunting," Mrs. Mulligan said. "It was his turn."

"Oh," Gavin said. "Any idea when they'll be back?"

"Tomorrow, or maybe the next day. Depends on how much game they bag in a day," she said.

Gavin nodded. "Well, I'll wait in the cart in that case. Don't hurry," he told Madeline, then turned to Mrs. Mulligan. "She'll need two or three outfits, buckskin if you have them."

The woman nodded, measuring Madeline with her eyes. "You're taller than most, but I think some buckskins came in just the day before yesterday that might fit you."

"Where did they come from?" Madeline asked curiously.

"Indians make them and bring them in from time to time, along with furs and a few other things we get calls for," Mrs. Mulligan said. "Now, let's see . . ."

She went to a shelf and began removing several of the yellowish gray buckskins. "Don't get as many calls for them as I used to," she said, "because a lot of the women make their own now. I guess you will too after you've been here a while." She handed two of the leathery skirts and blouses to Madeline and said, "You can step into the next room there and try these. I think they'll fit, but it's best to be sure."

They fit, but as Madeline looked at herself in a long mirror nailed to the side of a clothespress, she felt she was seeing a total stranger. The skirt was similar to the one Tondah had worn this morning, and though it had looked all right on the Indian girl, Madeline instantly decided that it was anything but flattering on *her*. But if Gavin said she should have it . . .

She sighed and took off the skirt and blouse and put it with the other. "They fit," she told Mrs. Mulligan as she went back to the other room.

The woman beamed. "Put them on Gavin's account, I suppose."

It was a statement, not a question, but Madeline felt herself reddening. She nodded, thankful that the woman had asked no questions about her "arrangements" now or why she had come to Bath Town. Although, of course, she would know—as would everyone—in only a matter of days.

She waited for the clothes to be wrapped, then realized they were not to be wrapped. "Thank you," she said, picking up her purchases and going outside.

Gavin smiled as she got into the cart. "Now you'll look more like one of us," he said.

"More like a savage, you mean," she said, adding, "though maybe if I look like them they won't scalp me."

"They are much too intrigued with that light hair of yours to remove it from your head," he said.

"Given the opportunity, Tondah would remove it in three seconds flat." She shuddered at the thought.

"Pay no attention to her seeming inhospitality," he told her. "Tondah's nose is a bit out of joint because she has been the only woman on the premises for so long."

I'll wager there's more out of joint than her nose, she thought, but she said nothing.

They had left the town now and were rumbling through the woods in the little cart along the now-familiar path. Madeline was beginning to feel, if not completely at home, at least more so since seeing Jessie and Carrie. Also, the landscape and scenery looked less alien, and even Gavin himself was beginning to seem like someone she had known a long time. Therefore, as he talked to her during the ride back to his cabin, telling her in more detail about life in Carolina, she answered quickly with her thoughts and observations without bothering to weigh each word as she would have with a stranger.

They were almost in sight of the cabin when she suddenly blurted the thought that had not been far from the forefront of her mind all day: "I wish I'd come here as Jessie and the other women did, as a free citizen, and not as an indentured servant."

Gavin was quiet for a minute, then he said, "Would I be presuming upon our acquaintance if I asked why you indentured yourself?"

"I had to," she said unhesitatingly, "to get passage to the Colonies."

"Why did you want to come here?"

"To get away from my guardian and unhappy memories," she said. "My guardian spent the money my father left me, so there was no other way to get passage but to indenture myself."

"That took a lot of courage," he said, admiration in his voice.

"No, not so much. It was easier than remaining in an intolerable situation."

Gavin asked no more questions, aware that Madeline would reveal more of her past if and when she wanted him to know. But he felt the most important question already had been answered: she was every bit the lady he had taken her for and not the lightskirt her indenture to a single man would imply. Obviously, she had not known Cate lived alone nor anything else about him.

He was very much aware of her presence behind him

in the cart and it was disconcerting. The thought of the beautiful girl living with and working for Cate made the hackles rise on the back of his neck. Although he did not know Cate very well, he thought he knew what Cate's reaction would be to Madeline and it caused him to clench his teeth. "If you have any trouble . . . that is, if things don't work out the way you expect at Cate's," he said, "let me know. Instantly."

He turned in his seat enough to see the worried little frown on her face. God, but she was something to behold! That pale hair shining in the sun like silver, those clear gray eyes looking at him with trust and friendship . . . "Madeline, I want to apologize." He changed the subject suddenly. "I had no right to stare at you while you were asleep last night . . . and this morning. I'm sorry. I—I just wanted to make sure you were all right."

The last was a lie, but he couldn't very well tell her, even while apologizing, that he had been staring at her trying to decide whether to get into bed with her. She might suspect that was the case, but if she knew for sure she would never trust him again. Right now, he wanted her trust; later, he would want more, much more, but nothing could be attained, now or later, if she thought him unreliable as a friend.

"I accept your apology," she said softly.

"I promise it won't happen again," he said as they came in sight of the cabin.

The shadows were lengthening when they returned to the cabin and Gavin had expected to see smoke curling upward as Tondah cooked a vegetable stew in the big iron pot over a fire behind the cabin. He had asked her before leaving to prepare the stew, a succulent Indian dish which she had cooked many times for him, and she had looked at him as though her command of English had suddenly deserted her. He had repeated the request and she had nodded.

He let Madeline out of the cart in front of the cabin, then drove to the rear to put away cart and horse. The pot was hanging over the iron tripod, but there was no fire under it, no sign of Tondah. He went into the cabin, expecting to see her there.

"Is Tondah in her room?" he asked Madeline, who was putting her new clothes into her trunk.

"I haven't seen her," Madeline said. "It is so quiet, I doubt if she is here."

"Next to stalking animals, Indians are the quietest creatures on earth," he said, "when they want to be."

He knocked at the door of Tondah's little room. "Tondah?"

When there was no answer, he sighed. "I suppose I am the cook tonight. Tondah's obviously gone out with Walking Bear."

"I'll cook if you will tell me what you want and show me where things are kept."

"It's easier to do it myself," he said, adding, "We'll have the stew I had planned for tomorrow. It has to cook for hours. I can't imagine why Tondah would wander off without starting the pot boiling."

"I can," Madeline said. "She doesn't like me."

"She doesn't dislike you," he assured her. "As I said, she's used to being the only woman here, and she may have a case of the sulks. She'll get over it."

Madeline put her hand uneasily on the top of her head. "I hope so." Then she laughed so he would know she was joking, though, to her, there was nothing really funny about the situation. Tondah obviously thought of her as a rival when there certainly was no reason . . .

No? She asked herself the question. Was there really no reason for the Indian girl to be jealous? Didn't she herself find Gavin nice, extremely kind to her and, yes, attractive? Another word insinuated itself into her mind: *desirable*.

She watched him as he busied himself emptying the larder to decide what they would eat. The reddish glint in his hair was more pronounced in the fading light, and though she could not see those piercing blue eyes with his back turned to her, she could imagine them as clearly as though he were looking at her. She would wager those eyes had proved the undoing of many a lass on both sides of the Atlantic. The broad shoulders, tapering off into narrow hips, had a look of power, as did the strong hands, brown from a long summer spent mostly outdoors. What would it be like to be taken in those arms, pressed against that powerful body, feel his lips upon hers?

She looked away from him, afraid he might suddenly turn and know exactly what she was thinking.

They ate supper companionably, like old friends who were in the habit of eating together often, neither feeling compelled to talk just for the purpose of making conversation. She cleaned up afterward, telling him she considered it her duty since he had prepared the meal. When the last dish had been washed and dried, she felt suddenly tired.

"I don't know why, having slept all morning, but I am quite fatigued," she said. She remembered as she said it that she had slept very little during the night.

"It may take you a day or two to get your full strength back," he said. "The voyage was tiring for you, then getting used to a new place. Your fatigue isn't hard to understand."

She went to the blanket, ready to pull it across the rope. "Thank you for everything you have done for me today. I shall never be able to repay you."

"Buckskins aren't that expensive," he said, "and besides . . ."

"I was not talking just about the buckskins," she said, pulling the blanket. "Goodnight."

"Sleep well," he said, his voice sounding curt. He had not meant the words to come out in such a clipped manner, but his mind had not been on sleep when he spoke. His frustration was beginning to show. He looked at the blanket longingly. He had given her his word that the blanket would be the same as a brick wall between them; he would not go on the other side. Yet in his whole life he had never wanted a woman so achingly. His want was like a sickness, weakening his whole body. But he would not go to her, for he had given his word.

On the other side of the blanket, Madeline was having conflicting thoughts of her own. She could not go to sleep easily, knowing Gavin was only a few feet away, but tonight she had no fear. She knew he would not come to watch her as she slept—and for the tiniest instant, she was sorry.

She turned over, looking toward the moonlit window, and opened her mouth to scream, then realized what she was seeing. The head in the window, reflected in the moonlight, was Tondah. Apparently the girl was peering in to see if Gavin had gone to bed with

Madeline. Drat that savage! Didn't she know enough about civilized ways to know that Madeline and Gavin were not going to meet and within twenty-four hours fall into bed together?

The fact that the thought had crossed her mind gave Madeline a twinge of guilt.

The head disappeared, then Madeline heard the door to Tondah's room open and close softly. She forced herself to stay awake to see if Gavin would go to Tondah's bed in the little back room, but when she finally fell asleep, she had heard no noise from Gavin except his regular breathing from the pallet on the other side of the blanket.

Chapter Six

FOR THE SECOND MORNING STRAIGHT, MADELINE DID NOT awaken until late and by the time she dressed and pulled the blanket back on the rope she had convinced herself that she was alone in the cabin. She had not heard a sound inside and only an occasional bird song from outside. However, Gavin was seated in the one easy chair in the room, reading. He put the book aside and stood up when she emerged. "I thought you were going to sleep half the day away again," he said.

"Didn't I?"

"Not quite, only half the morning." His eyes traveled appreciatively over her body. Not even the unfeminine buckskin skirt and blouse which she was wearing could hide her very womanly body or diminish her beauty. "Now you look more like us," he said approvingly. "You look as though you are a resident rather than a visitor."

"I will be glad when I feel more like a resident than a visitor," she said. "It shouldn't take long. Everyday the strangeness wears off a little more."

"I imagine Cate is back by now," he said. "The hunting usually is very good this time of year, so he would not have to spend extra days looking for game, especially with Lester Mulligan with him." He was quiet for a minute, then added, "I am reluctant to take you to him." He wanted to express his dislike and distrust of the man, but he refrained from doing so, not wanting to prejudice Madeline before she met him. Also, he had no concrete evidence that Cate was not to be trusted; it was more a feeling he had than a fact.

"Why are you reluctant?" she asked. "I should think I already have overstayed my welcome."

"Not by a mile . . . several miles." He grinned at her. "And I am reluctant to see you go because in the years I have lived here, you are my only visitor. Overnight visitor," he amended.

"And I can't thank you enough for taking me in," she said. "But if you think Cate has returned, then I should go immediately. He will hear that the ship came in the day before yesterday and he will think I wasn't on it. That could cause trouble."

"I suppose," Gavin admitted. "At least you will not leave before eating. Tondah!" he called. When the girl appeared from outside, he said, "We will both have our breakfast now."

Madeline was touched that he had waited for her, noting that it was more nearly time for the midday meal. But there was something gnawing at the back of her mind like a mouse worrying a piece of cheese. She had noticed the slight frown that appeared on Gavin's face every time Cate's name was mentioned.

From the little shed behind the cabin, Gavin brought out a wagon—much larger than the dog cart—and hitched the stallion to it, then loaded Madeline's trunk and two portmanteaux on it. As he helped her up to the seat, he noticed that she seemed a bit downcast and he wondered if it was because she was leaving him or because she was nervous about going to her new situation. He himself was more than downcast but he knew the reason. The thought of leaving her with Cate, returning to the empty cabin was enough to throw him into a fit of depression. No, he corrected himself, the cabin would not be empty. There was Tondah. But he resolved to check on Madeline often, to be sure Cate was treating her well (more specifically, not *mis*treating her in any way) and that she was happy. He climbed up on the seat beside her and they began the trip to Cate's cabin, a distance of about four miles. They spoke little en route, each deep in thought, though probably if those thoughts had been exchanged each would have found they were not far apart. Madeline looked out of the corner of her eye at Gavin from time to time and once, when she found him looking at her, she quickly lowered her eyes. She was determined not to let him know how much she dreaded going to Cate. Having had some indication of Gavin's feelings about the man had made her even more uncertain than she had been originally on learning that there was no Cate family, only one man.

Gavin was only one man, also without family, but she knew now she could trust him, that she was safe—and happier than she had been in months—with him. She knew nothing about Cate except that Gavin apparently did not like him and was obviously trying to hide that fact from her.

As they skirted Bath Town, Madeline strained for a sight of Jessie or a member of the Roland family or even one of the other passengers from the *Sea Lion*, but she saw no one she had ever seen before except, from a great distance, Wesley Martin, who was behind his house chopping wood.

By the time they neared Cate's house, her spirits were extremely low. Involuntarily, she sighed.

"It won't be so bad," Gavin said, "once you get used to Cate. He is a bit abrupt, I think. Not too well versed in some of the finer things of life, but you shouldn't have much trouble getting along with him." After a minute or two, he added, "If you do, forget the indenture. It isn't that important."

"I owe the man money," she said quietly. "And I have signed a legal and binding paper, so I can't just forget it."

"What I meant was," Gavin explained, "if life with Cate proves too unpleasant, don't let the paper stop you from coming to me. There may be some way to get you out of it."

"There's no way," she said, a tone of hopelessness creeping into her voice. "I have signed away the next four years of my life and there is nothing I can do about it." Then she gave him a forced smile. "At least the next four years couldn't possibly be as bad as the past six months have been."

He wanted to question her, find out what it was that had been so abhorrent to her that she would indenture herself, leave home, and come to a new land where she knew not one living soul, but the Cate cabin was in sight and he knew there would not be time for a satisfactory answer. "There it is," he pointed out. "Your new home."

Madeline sucked in her breath. In a small clearing just on the edge of dense woods was a cabin even smaller than Gavin's. It appeared to have only one room and she was about to say that she couldn't possibly stay when she remembered the rope-blanket division in Gavin's cabin. If necessary, a room divider could be devised.

A man came out the cabin door then, apparently having heard the approaching wagon. He stared at them until they were alongside, and when Gavin said, "Morning, Cate," he merely nodded and continued to look at them questioningly.

"This is Miss Madeline Boyd, Cate," Gavin introduced her, "and she is indentured to you." He paused for Cate to acknowledge the introduction, but the man could not take his eyes off Madeline or, apparently, utter a sound. It was plain for Gavin to see that Madeline clearly was not what Cate had expected. It became more and more apparent that all his leering precluded speaking.

Finally, he found his voice. Without preamble or apology for his lack of manners, he blurted, "Ship came in two days ago. How come she's been with you all this time?"

"I knew it was your week to go hunting, so I agreed to sign the captain's papers of temporary custody and see that Miss Boyd was taken care of until you returned."

"And I damn well bet you took care of her, all right," he muttered.

Madeline sat on the wagon seat as though she had turned to stone. She had recoiled at first sight of the man, but even more repugnant to her were his words, which were equally ugly. He was a large man, almost fat, with dark brown hair, brown eyes, and a mottled complexion. He appeared to be somewhere between thirty-five and forty years old, though he could have been older or younger, she decided. His facial expression, which had not changed at all since he had first come out of the cabin, indicated that either he was not happy with the world and all that dwelled therein or else he smelled a bad odor constantly.

"If you are dissatisfied and wish to break the agreement, I will be glad to take Miss Boyd back into Bath Town," Gavin said, his voice indicating how much pleasure it would give him to do just that. "She has friends there who will be glad to take her in."

"That so?" Cate all but snarled. "Then why didn't her friends sign for her and keep her until I got back? Never mind, just go on your way, Durant." He began to pull the trunk off the back of the wagon.

Gavin got down from the wagon and helped him. Reluctantly. It seemed that everything he had done so far today had been done with great reluctance, but taking Madeline's baggage from the wagon and leaving it, and her, with Felton Cate was next to impossible for him to do. He glanced up at her and knew that the stricken look on her face was matched by his own. However, as he helped her down from the wagon, her face was composed once more, as though she had resigned herself to staying here with Cate and was trying to make the best of it.

"As I said before, Durant, be on your way," Cate said. "I can manage very well by myself." This time, when he leered at Madeline, he actually smacked his lips.

Never in his life had Gavin wanted so much to fight a man. It would have made him supremely happy to ram his fist into Cate's face until the man's eyes bulged out and his teeth caved in. But he was a peaceable man and fighting was against his nature . . . and his religion. With whatever effort it took, he would have to remember that.

Madeline looked from one to the other of them like a prisoner waiting to see which would give her a reprieve. She had already developed such an intense dislike of Cate that her mind was completely rejecting the thought that she would have to share that tiny cabin— her whole life, in fact—with him for the next four years. Both the thought and the actuality of it were beyond endurance.

Gavin held out his arm to help her from the wagon and Cate, watching, said, "God's sake, man, is she a cripple or something? Can't she even climb down from a wagon by herself?"

"I am perfectly well." Madeline spoke for the first time. "Mr. Durant was just doing what any *gentleman* would in helping a lady down."

"Well, aren't we hoity-toity, though." The sarcasm in his voice was crushingly heavy. "Lady and gentleman, indeed. You've got some queer notions that you'd better get over in a hurry, my girl."

"That is a fact of which I am well aware, Mr. Cate," she said.

"Good. The sooner we understand each other, the better." Cate nodded in satisfaction, then looked at Gavin. "How many times do I have to tell you to be on your way, Durant? Do you want me to go get my musket and shoot you for a trespasser?"

Madeline gasped. "You might at least thank him for bringing me here."

"I might, huh? That is the least he could do after having the use of you for two days and nights."

"You wretched . . ." Gavin started toward Cate, then stopped suddenly. He stood still for a moment, then went to the wagon. As he passed Madeline, he whispered, "Remember, if you need me . . ."

"Save your sweet nothings for your redskin, squaw man," Cate snapped.

Gavin, his face even redder than his hair, his lips pressed together until they were just a hard line, leapt upon the wagon and slapped the reins over the horse's back. Without another word or a backward glance, he was heading back toward the wooded path.

I can't let him go like that, Madeline thought, suddenly in a panic. I can't let him leave me here with this rude, crude excuse for a human being.

She began to run after the wagon.

"Where do you think you're going, wench?" Cate caught up with her and held her by her arm.

"I—I . . . let me go," she demanded. "I forgot to thank him for bringing me here."

"I imagine you thanked him in advance," Cate said, "and in the way he most appreciated."

"I *will* thank him!" She snatched her arm out of his grasp and ran down the path calling, "Gavin! Gavin, wait! Stop, please."

He turned in the wagon seat, saw her, and stopped instantly.

She was out of breath when she caught up to the wagon. "Please, Gavin," she panted. "Please don't leave me here. I cannot stay with that man."

He shook his head miserably. "You have to, by law. I can't take you with me."

Tears spilled over in her eyes. She hung her head, hoping he would not see her total desperation.

"Look, Madeline, I will leave you here only for today," he said, aware that back at the cabin Cate was standing, hands on hips, looking at them. "I am going to find some way, any way possible, to get you out of the indenture. Before the day is over, I'll be back for you."

She nodded, unable to speak. She realized there was nothing he could do, no way he could take her away without breaking the law and getting them both in trouble. Her eyes brimming, she said, "Thank you," and added softly, "I will understand if you don't come back."

"I will be back," he repeated, "before the day is over. Somehow I'll find a way to get you out of this—legally."

She turned and walked slowly back toward the cabin and Cate. The saddest sound she had ever heard was the noise of Gavin's wagon jolting along the path, leaving her.

"I notice he didn't kiss you goodbye," Cate said when she reached him. "I guess he finally realizes you're my property now." He put his arm around her waist familiarly as they started toward the cabin door.

She pulled away from him, indignant. "Mr. Cate, you are to understand right now that I am not your property. I am indentured to you but you do not own me. I am your servant, not your concubine. You are to remember that at all times."

He laughed as though she had said something uproariously funny and pushed her inside the cabin.

There was one room, very small, and there was a

stench that caused her almost to gag. The furniture was crude but serviceable; several straight chairs, a small table, one bureau, and the one really nice piece, the bed. She thought the high, hardwood bed with the little trundle bed beneath it most likely had been brought from England. There was no linen on the bed, only a worn feather mattress and a soiled blanket. God willing, she would never have to sleep either in the bed or the trundle bed.

The place was filthy. Dust was everywhere and it was obvious the floor had not been swept for months. In the corner near the bed was an unemptied slop jar.

Cate was struggling to get her trunk through the door. "You might give me a hand and stop playing the lady," he told her. "Get it through your head right now that this wilderness is no place for ladies. Ladies don't survive long here."

I'm going to survive, she thought grimly, helping him pull the trunk into the room. I'm going to survive if it kills me.

He brought in the rest of her baggage, grumbling that she must have thought she was moving into a palace to have brought so much.

"Now," he said, putting down the second portmanteau, "I will expect to be thanked for that bit of work—and in a nicer way than you thanked Durant. But I don't want you to get the idea that life here is going to be nothing but pleasure, so you can put in a good day's work—or half-day—before we see how well we are going to suit each other." He was leering at her again and she supposed that leer was what passed for a smile in his mind.

"What would you like for me to do first?" she asked. "Clean the cabin?"

"Good a place to start as anywhere, I reckon."

It never entered Madeline's mind to unpack her trunk or bags. Somehow, some way, Gavin had to return for her before nightfall. She could not possibly stay here. For the first time since her arrival, she thought that staying in England would have been better. Not even Rufus or the men he forced upon her were as vile and depraved as Felton Cate. Thank God he had put her to work at once; it gave her something to do so she would not have to talk to Cate or look at him.

She found a broom in a corner and swept; she put water on to boil in the pot hanging from a hook in the fireplace and she scoured. She dusted and cleaned, and opened the door and the four windows and aired out the cabin. She washed out the one cabinet and larder and then washed all the dishes, most of which were caked with dried food. Never in her life had she imagined human beings could ever live like that. Even swine were cleaner.

All during the afternoon while she was working she was also listening for the sound of Gavin's wagon returning. But no such welcome sound was heard. She heard a grunt from Cate occasionally; he had gone outside and she had no idea what he was doing, but he obviously wanted her to know that he was remaining in the vicinity to watch her should she feel inclined to wander away.

At dusk, Madeline stopped her labors and looked out the window. She had not realized how late it was getting until the light began to fade. Where was Gavin? Why hadn't he returned as he said he would? Had he found that it was impossible to get her out of the indenture and didn't want to tell her the bad news? She had been afraid to hope anyway, knowing that when she had put her signature on that paper she had legally signed her life—the next four years, anyway—over to Felton Cate. Nothing could change that. But she had wanted so much for Gavin to come back for her and take her to Jessie in Bath Town or even to his clean, homey cabin again.

Cate came into the cabin, interrupting her thoughts. "If you're planning to eat supper you better stop all that turning around and start cooking," he said.

"What would you have me cook?" she asked, pointing to the larder. "The meat in there was spoiled and I threw it out."

"Damn you for a wastrel!" he roared. "What right you got to come in here and throw out my food?"

Unperturbed, she answered, "I did not think you wanted to die from food poisoning."

He peered in the cleaned out larder. "Cook eggs," he said. "The meat Mulligan and I brought back will be divided by tomorrow and I'll get my share."

She boiled eggs and made bread from cornmeal the way she had seen Tondah do. By the time she had put their supper on the table, it was almost dark. She knew now that Gavin was not coming back and she felt sick at the pit of her stomach at the thought of sitting across the table from Cate.

"You don't have to wait till I finish," he told her magnaminously. "I'll be broadminded and let you eat with me."

"I'm not hungry," she said. She went to the cabin door and sat down on the step outside. Staring toward

the path through the woods, tears once again welled
into her eyes. The stench was gone from the cabin now;
it was thoroughly clean, nothing like the sty she had
found. But there was no change whatever in the owner
of the cabin and Madeline knew exactly what would
happen to her if she had to spend the night with him.

Gavin was a stranger to despondency. He had always
been of a happy disposition, an easygoing nature that
had let him watch the troubles around him, even his
own, almost objectively. Very little—aside from cruelty, injustice, and boorish manners—ever disturbed
him, but as he drove away from Cate's cabin, leaving
Madeline behind crying, he was the closest he had ever
been to complete despair.

His every suspicion that Felton Cate was a clod and
not to be trusted too far had been confirmed. Worse
than that, the man was a scoundrel, the lowest and
basest of men. He had told Madeline that he would
return for her before nightfall and, a man of his word,
his despondency grew and grew from the fact that he
had no idea how to keep that promise.

He headed back toward Bath Town, his only idea
being to talk to some of his friends there, see if anyone
could come up with a legal way to get Madeline out of
Cate's clutches. The thought of her being alone with
that reptile overnight all but drove him wild. He knew
he had been quite taken with Madeline from the
moment he had espied her on the ship, but it wasn't
until he drove away from her that he realized just how
taken he was. She affected him as no other woman had,
both her beauty and her manner. His desire for her was
more than merely physical now; he wanted to be with

her, to get to know her well, to live with her and love
her.

By the time he reached Bath Town, his spirits were so
low that he felt he had descended into hell. He almost
paid no attention when he heard his name called as he
drove by Cyrus Roland's blacksmith shop. He stopped
the wagon and turned in his seat. "Afternoon, Cyrus,"
he said flatly. Then noticing Jessie with her husband, he
said, "Afternoon, ma'am."

Jessie, smiling, came up to the wagon, followed by
her husband. "Afternoon, Mr. Durant. Where is Madeline?"

"Call me Gavin," he said automatically. "I've just
taken Madeline to Felton Cate's."

Cyrus let out a whistle. "I wouldn't want a relative of
mine living out there." He looked fondly at his wife.

"Cyrus, maybe you can help me," Gavin said. "Do
you know anyway I can have her indenture papers
declared null and void?"

Cyrus shook his head. "Never heard of it being done.
Doubt if it's possible."

"That's what I was afraid of," Gavin said, "but I've
got to find a way. I can't leave Madeline there overnight."

Cyrus nodded understandingly and Jessie inhaled
sharply. "So that's the way it is, is it?" she said. "I was
hoping the poor girl would go to a decent family."

"Cate isn't decent, and there's no family," Gavin
said.

"Why don't you go talk to Wes Martin?" Cyrus
asked. "He's been reading law and I guess he's the
closest thing to a solicitor we've got around here.
Maybe he can come up with something."

"Maybe," Gavin said, "but I doubt it. I'll try anyway."

"Let us know if we can do anything," Jessie called as Gavin drove toward the Martin house.

Told that Wes had gone to Mulligan's store to help divide and distribute the meat brought in by Cate and Lester, Gavin went there. Several people were outside the store chatting, their share of the meat securely in hand. All nodded or spoke to Gavin as he went in.

Inside, Wes and Lester Mulligan were standing at a counter each nursing a small brandy snifter. Both greeted Gavin, good-humoredly saying they were reaping the rewards of dividing the meat for the village and environs.

"You want to reap with us?" Mulligan asked. "We might be talked into letting you even if you didn't shoot the deers, clean them, and cut them up for the citizenry."

Gavin shook his head.

"What's the matter with you, Gav?" Wes asked. "You look lower than a snake's belly."

"If I were any lower," Gavin said seriously, "you would have to elevate me to bury me."

Both men laughed until they realized that Gavin was not trying to be funny. "What's the matter?" Wes asked.

"Do either of you know any way to have an indenture paper declared null and void?"

There was a moment of silence, then both men shook their heads. "Far as I know," Mulligan said, "only death can do that."

"Death might be preferable to four years with Cate,"

Gavin said under his breath, then louder, "Wes, you've been reading the law, isn't there *any* way at all?"

Wes was thoughtful. Finally, he said, "I guess if you could prove that papers were improperly drawn, or if the signature was forged they wouldn't be valid."

Gavin shook his head. "It's nothing like that."

Lester Mulligan, who had put two and two together, grinned suddenly. "You're worried about that pretty little filly you brought in here yesterday, aren't you? My wife was telling me about her, then I heard from Cyrus that she's indentured to Felton Cate." The smile left his face as quickly as it had come. "Lord knows that ain't any life for *any* woman."

"I can't leave her out there with him," Gavin said miserably. "As sure as the sun will rise tomorrow morning, he'll spend the night raping her. He may not even wait until night." That thought drove him further into the depths.

"Tell you what," Wes said, "the governor will be at my house in another hour or so. Why don't you go home with me and talk to him? Maybe he can come up with something."

"Cary's here?" Gavin asked.

"Yep, he's been at his plantation seeing that all the crops were laid by and he's coming into Bath Town this afternoon to pick up some supplies," Wes said, adding, "and talk a little politics."

Gavin perked up. "I'll see him then." He still wasn't optimistic about finding a way out of the difficulty, but if there was a way, surely the governor would know.

Chapter Seven

Wes went to his house to be there when the governor arrived, and Gavin stayed at Mulligan's to buy some supplies which he needed. Several townspeople came in before he left and he found it almost impossible to get away. Though the people who lived right in Bath Town saw each other almost daily, they did not see those who lived outside very often, therefore, the conversations sometimes were of long duration.

Trying not to be rude, Gavin excused himself from one person only to be met by someone else as he inched his way to the door. Finally, beyond caring about rudeness, he muttered something about a crisis and rushed out. He hoped the only crisis was that which he felt building up in himself; with each passing minute he grew more frantic as his imagination became more active. In his mind he pictured in lurid, sickening detail what was happening at the Cate cabin and although he tried to remain outwardly calm, he was seething with fury inside. He had to get back to Madeline; he had to get back at once before . . .

But he couldn't go back yet. Common sense told him that to go back without being able to declare the indenture papers null and void would do Madeline no good whatever.

So, trying to compose himself, he left his wagon in front of the store and strode up the street to the Martin house. Mrs. Martin and one of the children were on the porch and Gavin knew that they were staying outside so as not to interfere with the political talk going on inside.

"Afternoon, Melissa," Gavin said. "The governor's here, I take it." He nodded toward the horse and buggy in the street.

"He got here a few minutes ago," she said. "Go on in."

In the front room, which probably looked more like a proper English salon than any other room in the colony, Wes sat opposite Governor Thomas Cary, who half-sat, half-sprawled in a big leather chair. Both men stood up when Gavin entered.

"Gavin!" The governor extended his hand. "I haven't seen you for a spell. Thought you might have gone home for a visit."

"Good to see you, Tom." Gavin shook his hand. "I consider this my home now."

Cary was of medium height and was dressed the way the rest of the colonists dressed on Sunday, in breeches and blouse and waistcoat and neckcloth, rather than in heavy trousers or buckskins. He had small but penetrating eyes which seemed to be taking in all of Gavin at once as though looking for changes since the last time they had met.

"We all do." The governor nodded appreciatively, as though Gavin had said exactly what he wanted to hear. "That's why these rumors that are constantly coming from England are so disturbing. Wes was just telling me the latest to make its way here."

"I told you yesterday, Gavin," Wes said, "the one that came on the *Sea Lion* about the Lords sending over another governor."

Cary sighed. "No sooner do we get it settled that *I* am the governor than someone wants to prove that I'm not."

"What will you do if it's true?" Wes asked, then said belatedly, "Sit down, Gavin. You can spare a minute or two before presenting your problem."

"If it's true," Cary said slowly, "I am going to do the only thing possible. I am going to get together as many men as I can and show those idiots once and for all time that they just can't come in here and force rulers on us as though we were children in need of chastisement."

"You mean you would fight?" Gavin asked. "Bear arms?"

"If necessary," Cary nodded, "though I hope to God it won't come to that."

"You are a Quaker," Gavin reminded him.

"I am also a governor who could be put out of office on a whim by people who know nothing about this colony except what they have heard second- or third-hand," Cary told him. "I would hope that you will be with me, Gavin, if I must make a stand."

"I am with you, Tom, and for you," Gavin said quietly, "but I will not take up arms against my fellow man."

"Glad I'm not a Quaker and have to make such decisions as that," Wes said.

"There is no decision to be made," Gavin said. "The decision was made, as far as my beliefs are concerned, at the beginning of time."

"You mean there are absolutely no circumstances under which you would fight?" Cary asked.

Gavin hesitated a moment. He was remembering his fury, only a few hours ago, at Felton Cate and his desire to smash the man's face in. "I can't say that," he said finally. "I can only hope that I will always be able to control whatever baser instincts might make me want to harm anyone."

"We'll see how you feel when the Lords Proprietor send someone here to replace me for no reason whatever except to show their power and authority," Cary said.

Wes, sensing that the discussion could become heated, said quickly, "Gavin, I believe you had a question you wanted to ask the governor."

"I do. Tom, do you know any way in the world to get indenture papers declared invalid?"

The governor's brows knitted together as he thought. "Why would you want to?"

"There is a young lady who indentured herself to Felton Cate thinking she was coming here to work for a family," Gavin said. "She found there was no family, and that the situation is intolerable. She wants to get out of the indenture."

"I remember Cate," Cary said. "If the paper was signed in good faith, and if he paid her passage and other expenses, I don't know of any way the indenture can be declared nonexistent. There is a way, however . . ."

"What?" Gavin asked instantly.

"If someone is willing to buy the indenture and Cate is willing to sell . . ."

"He'd never sell," Gavin said, but even as he spoke a modicum of hope formed inside him.

"Perhaps if he were paid more than he already has paid out for the young lady, he would."

"That's it!" Gavin cried. "He's a selfish bastard and maybe enough money would do it."

"Are you going to try to buy the indenture, Gavin?" Wes asked.

"I am, and right now." Gavin stood up, shook the governor's hand and started for the door.

"If you need any money," Wes called after him, "I could let you have a little. Very little, but it might make the difference."

"Thanks, Wes, but I think I can manage."

He left the house, not even noticing whether Melissa Martin was still on the porch, and ran down the street as though he had entered a Greek marathon. Springing upon the wagon, he was on his way to his own cabin at once. He was sure Cate was not the kind of man who would take the word of another man, or even his IOU, so he was going to see the scoundrel with cash in hand. Surely Cate would not be able to resist that.

If it took every cent he had, he was going to buy Madeline's indenture papers from Cate. He looked toward heaven, silently asking for help, and noticed the darkening sky. There was no way he could get home, get the money, and then reach Cate's until long after dark. He became frantic as panic once again took over.

Tondah was sitting in the doorway looking forlorn when Gavin drove up to the cabin. As soon as she saw him returning alone her face lit up with a smile. It was obvious that she had expected him to bring Madeline back with him. Well, God willing, he would, and in a very short time.

She stood up to meet him, but he dashed past her, saying, "I'm in a terrible hurry, Tondah. No time to explain." He went to the fireplace and removed two large stones from the hearth, then picked up the leather purse. In it was all the money he had. As he dashed back past Tondah again, she said, "You come back to eat?"

"I don't know," he called from the wagon. "I'm not sure what time I'll return. Go on and eat without me."

He did not see the frown that returned to her face as he drove off or hear the muttered, "He going back to her."

It was totally dark by the time he reached Cate's and there was no moon tonight. The lantern on the side of the wagon gave very little light. He left the horse and wagon beneath a tree and went quickly to the door and knocked loudly.

The door was opened instantly by Madeline rather than Cate and she murmured, "Thank God you've come. I had given up hope."

Gavin patted her hand reassuringly and went inside.

"What the devil you doing back here?" Cate growled. He was sitting at the table, sopping up soft-boiled egg with bread, and his bottom lip was yellow from the yolk. "Told you once to get off my property and I ain't going to tell you again."

"I'm glad of that because I have a business proposition for you," Gavin said amiably.

"I got no business with you and I don't want none." Cate finished his supper, then pushed his chair back and propped his feet on the table.

"You could make a handsome profit," Gavin said.

"Doing what?" Cate was interested in spite of himself.

"I would like to buy Miss Boyd's indenture papers from you, and I am prepared to pay you more than the expense money you have put out." He heard Madeline's soft gasp, but he did not take his eyes off Cate's face. The man's eyes narrowed, then he laughed.

"That good, is she?" Cate looked at Madeline. "Well, I might have gotten myself more of a bargain than I thought."

"I am serious, Cate," Gavin said. "Tell me what you have spent in passage money and other expenses and I'll . . . double it." He wasn't sure he could afford to double it, but somehow he would find the money if he had not brought enough. He could borrow from Wes.

Cate continued to laugh. "Gets better all the time. You must really be something, honey."

The way he was looking at Madeline made Gavin's fury rise again, and again he wanted to knock the man flat. Cate stared at her hungrily, as though he would not even wait for Gavin's departure before devouring her whole.

"Her papers ain't for sale, Durant, and neither is she," he said. "She belongs to me now. I put out a lot of blunt to get her here, and here she's going to stay for four years. You or nobody else can keep me from getting my money's worth."

Hold your temper, Gavin told himself. Getting angry won't help matters any. "I am willing to see that you get quite a bit more than your money's worth," he said.

"It's quite legal, you know. To sell indenture papers, I mean. It's done all the time."

Cate guffawed. "Yeah, well it's also legal *not* to sell them."

Thinking it might help his cause, Gavin said, "I was just talking to the governor and he thinks it is a good idea for me to buy Miss Boyd's papers."

"Governor, huh."

"Tom Cary. He said he remembers you."

"If he's going to stay governor, he damn well better remember everybody in the colony," Cate said. "But I don't care if you were talking to the Queen of England, you ain't going to git them indenture papers."

"Not for any amount of money?" Gavin asked. He had that sick feeling in his stomach again.

"Not any amount. Now git the hell out of here."

Gavin turned and looked at Madeline for the first time. Her face was chalk white and her gray eyes were wide, a look of both horror and revulsion in them. He wanted nothing in the world so much as to pick her up and carry her out to his wagon, then take her home where she would be safe from the advances and indignities that she surely would suffer at the hands of that animal. But he could not do it legally, and to do it illegally would only bring more trouble down upon their heads than he and she already had. Felton Cate was not one to let someone walk out with what was his. Gavin had not the first doubt that he would stop at nothing—including murder—to keep Madeline with him.

Slowly, he went to the door. He could not meet Madeline's eyes as he passed her, could not bear to see the anguish, the fear, and, yes, even the accusation there. At the door, he turned to Cate once more. "If you change your mind . . ."

Before the sentence was out, Cate had picked up his tin plate from the table and thrown it at Gavin's head. Gavin ducked and the plate hit the doorframe and clattered to the floor. He stared down at it for a moment as though it were a live thing, then he went out and softly closed the door behind him.

He went to the wagon and started back down the path to the woods though he had no intention of going back home. Out of sight of the cabin, he tied the horse to a tree, then he went back to the cabin quietly, like a stealthy, stalking Indian. He went to the right side of the cabin and peered in a window. Madeline was washing Cate's supper dishes in a wooden bucket and Cate was standing a few feet away as though waiting for her to finish her task before . . .

Again Gavin's imagination went wild, and he chided himself. Maybe Cate was all bluff and bluster and rough-mannered on the outside, but somewhere inside was a spark of kindness, a stunted bit of humanity that would show itself now that he was alone with the terrified girl.

But Gavin knew better. Cate had been alone with Madeline since late morning and she was still just that—terrified. If there had been any kindness or humanity in him, it would have manifested itself before now and Madeline would not still be cringing every time Cate looked at her.

Madeline put the tin plate, a cup and a pan into a cabinet, and for a minute or two stood still, her back to Cate. Finally, she turned and looked at him, and it was obvious that the expression on his face frightened her even more. Since Cate's back was to Gavin, he could not see.

"I am very tired," he heard Madeline say, "and I would like to retire now."

Cate gave a nasty chuckle. "I'm ready too. Been ready all day."

"Where am I to sleep?"

The chuckle turned to a laugh. "In the bed, naturally. Didn't think I'd put you out for the night like a cat, did you?"

"You mean the trundle bed, I suppose." Madeline was trying to sound casual, overlooking the insinuations in Cate's voice and words. "Would you mind pulling it to the other side of the room and then hanging a curtain between us?"

In two steps, Cate was beside her. He put his arms around her waist, drawing her to him. "I got Durant's word for it that you're a friendly sort," he said, "and you better be or you'll regret it."

Madeline struggled to free herself, but there was no way she could extricate herself from his arms. "Please, Mr. Cate," she said finally, "as your servant I will do whatever you tell me, but I thought I had made myself clear when I told you my duties end with working for you. I will not share your bed."

The man was kissing her neck now, his lips moving upward to the side of her face, and then, turning her, his lips were planted firmly on hers. Her struggles were as futile as those of a baby mouse against a starving cat. There was no longer the slightest doubt in Gavin's mind that Cate meant to rape her.

Legality or illegality be damned, this was no time to worry about the law . . . or even about the principles under which he had lived all his life. He tore around the cabin and burst into the front door and with one blow knocked the surprised Cate to the floor.

"You're coming with me," he said to Madeline. Pale and trembling, she was staring agape at the scene before her as though not quite believing anything that had happened.

Cate started to get up, but Gavin planted his foot firmly on the man's chest. "You make one move and I'll knock you senseless," Gavin told him.

Though Cate had more weight than Gavin, Gavin was taller and more fit. It was obvious that in a fight he could get the better of Cate with little or no difficulty. Raising only his head, Cate looked toward a corner of the room where his musket stood. Gavin's eyes followed his glance. "Forget it," he told Cate. "Your only weapon is words now and you're plumb out of ammunition."

"You're breaking the law," Cate said, "coming in here, in *my* house, attacking me and trying to kidnap my woman. You'll hang for this."

"I think not," Gavin replied mildly. "Since there are no constables in Bath Town, no jails, I don't think I'll even be arrested. Listen, Cate, when I let the people know how you were trying to take advantage of this helpless, indentured girl, they'll be ready to lynch you. You'll be the one who'll feel the noose around your neck."

He removed his foot and helped Cate up, then raised his arm as though to give Cate the beating of his life. It delighted him to see Cate cringe like a coward, flinching before being hit by the first blow. Taking advantage of the man's fear of physical harm, he said, "You are going to help me load Miss Boyd's belongings back on my wagon."

"She's indentured to me," Cate began weakly. "You can't . . ."

"I not only can, I will," Gavin interrupted. "You have changed your mind, and you are going to sell me her papers. Right now." He raised his arm again, making a fist.

"You'll give me double the money, you say?"

"I'll pay you exactly what you have paid out for expenses," Gavin said.

"You promised double!"

"I made you no promise," Gavin said, "I *offered* you double and you refused it. The situation has altered somewhat now. If I let it be known what you . . ."

"All right, all right. Give me the money." He named a sum which Gavin was sure was more than the actual amount paid in Madeline's behalf, but it was less than Gavin originally had intended to pay, so he took out the purse, counted the money out on the table, and said, "Now I'll take the indenture papers."

"I can't remember where they are. I don't think you gave them to me."

"I gave them to you this morning, as you very well know. Hand them over." He did not have to say it out loud; the tone of his voice implied the "or else."

Cate went to the bureau and opened a drawer. He took out the two sheets of paper and gave them to Gavin.

"You have to sign them." Gavin pointed to the place for Cate to affix his signature.

"No, wait," Gavin said. "Give me a quill."

"Ain't got one," Cate said.

"I have one," Madeline said quickly. She rummaged around in her trunk, finally coming up with a quill and an ink pot. "Here."

Beneath her signature on the indenture paper, Gavin wrote, "I hereby sell this indenture and any claim to it or to Miss Madeline Boyd's services to Gavin Durant."

"Now," Gavin said, "sign right under this."

Cate hesitated a moment, looking at Madeline, then at Gavin.

"Sign!" Gavin thundered.

Cate bent over and wrote his name slowly, as though it required a great effort to do so.

Gavin folded the papers and put them in his coat. "Now I'll get the wagon and we'll load the baggage. Madeline, come with me." He knew better than to leave her, even for a few minutes, alone in the cabin with Cate.

Outside, Madeline took a deep breath while she almost ran to keep up with Gavin's long strides.

"We'll have to hurry," he said. "I want to get away before Cate changes his mind."

"But he's already signed," she said, "and you paid."

"He could claim I made him sign under duress," Gavin said. "I'm not sure about the law on that point, but it might work for him. I'm hoping he won't think about that."

Cate refused to help load the baggage and watched the two of them with a malignant stare as they labored to get the trunk up on the wagon. Madeline, emotionally and physically exhausted, had no more strength than a small child. When, at last, the trunk and portmanteaux were in the wagon and she and Gavin were deep in the woods on the way to his cabin, Madeline took another deep breath and then began trembling uncontrollably. Now that the ordeal was finally over, she found herself giving way as she had not allowed herself to do all day. Tears of relief as well as of long pent-up fear and frustration coursed down her cheeks. "I'm free, I'm free," she whispered.

Gavin put his arm around her shoulders, holding her tightly. In an effort to help her get over the bad experience sooner, he tried to make light of it. "No, not free exactly," he said, his tone cheerful. "I bought your papers, remember?"

To Madeline, who was on the thin edge of hysteria, still in the clutches of terror, the words had only an ominous sound. She could not stop either the trembling or the tears.

"I suppose I can expect more of the same kind of treatment from you now . . . now that *you* own me," she said.

Chapter Eight

It was a long time before Madeline relaxed and was her normal self again. For the first few days that she was back at Gavin's, her nerves remained on edge. Every time she heard a horse whinny or the sound of a wagon or cart, she was sure that Cate was coming to get her. She would look up from whatever she was doing, her eyes like a frightened animal's. If Gavin happened to be nearby, he would smile at her reassuringly, not actually saying anything to her for fear of magnifying her terror. If he were out somewhere and she was alone with Tondah, there was no reassurance. Madeline was sure the Indian girl would like nothing better than to have Cate come for her and drag her off to his cabin by the quickest possible means.

She filled her days with work, helping Tondah with the household chores and the cooking, though Gavin told her she did not have to. "After all," he said, "you are doing what I am paying Tondah to do."

"After all," she came back at him, "you have bought and paid for *me*. I am your indentured servant now, and will be for the next four years. I intend to earn my keep as well as pay you back for your initial outlay."

Tight-lipped, Gavin strode away from her and went outside to hitch the horse to the wagon and go to town for supplies. He had no answer for her constant reminder that she was nothing more than a servant. He was sure she had gotten over her idea of that first night—that she would get the same treatment from him that she had gotten from Cate—but she still was like a skittish young colt. He had not touched her, had not even watched her quietly as she slept (in his bed, which he had insisted that she take again), though God knew it was all he could do to keep from getting into bed beside her and taking her in his arms. He was sick from wanting her, but he was determined he would not take her until she could be a willing partner, until she wanted him. By the end of her first week, he thought she was reasonably sure that she had nothing to worry about as far as *he* was concerned, and perhaps, with the passing of a little more time, she would stop worrying about Cate.

Madeline had another worry, however, which she did not want to confide to Gavin: Tondah.

From the night Gavin had brought Madeline back from Cate's until today, a little over a week later, Tondah had become more and more sullen and resentful. This attitude was not shown so much when Gavin was around, but he had only to leave the cabin and Tondah, her face like a raging storm, would begin pointing. She never spoke a word to Madeline, but would point to the broom, a silent order for Madeline to sweep the floor, or she would point to the wash bucket, meaning plainly, "You do the wash right now." The longer Madeline was there, the less work Tondah did herself, and the more she gave to her adversary.

Madeline did not mind the work; it gave her something to do to pass the hours, and it also made her feel that she was repaying her debt to Gavin. She was only sorry that Gavin was unaware of how much of the work around the cabin she was doing and how little Tondah did in his absence.

More than anything Madeline could think of, she wanted to send Tondah back to her people, but she did not dare suggest it to Gavin because she was still unsure about the relationship between the two. There had been nothing between them since she had been in the cabin—at least not to her knowledge—but that didn't mean that the relationship had not existed in the past and would not again in the future. Probably they were both a bit shy about it with someone else in the cabin.

The thought of Tondah and Gavin together was one Madeline tried hard to put out of her mind every time it came to her. She tried to think that she was not jealous, that what they did was their business and none of hers, yet to think of Gavin with his arms around Tondah, as they had been around her the night he had brought her back, made Madeline look at the girl with almost as much hatred as she saw reflected in Tondah's eyes.

There was another reason also—the main reason— why she did not ask Gavin to tell Tondah to leave: it was only Tondah's presence in Gavin's cabin that made her own tenancy there acceptable. If she were staying alone with him, she would be the talk of Bath Town and all the outlying area. Her reputation would become worse than it had been in London, for at least in London very few had known of her activities and those few would never have dared tell.

Gavin had been gone for nearly an hour and Madeline was just finishing hanging wash on the line strung up between the cabin and the shed where the cart and wagon were kept when she heard the sound of a horse and wagon approaching. Quickly hiding behind a bush, she parted the leaves and peered out. It was too soon for Gavin to return for he had said he was going to stop by Wes Martin's before coming home. Tondah was sitting under a tree in front of the cabin making a bright-colored beaded dress for herself. She also was staring toward the path, curious to see who was approaching.

Madeline knew that if it were Cate coming to take her back with him, and if she hid, Tondah would be only too happy to lead Cate to her. And Gavin would never know of Tondah's perfidy.

She began to tremble. Looking behind her at more woods, she thought about bolting into them, but to do so she would have to go through a small clearing and Cate would see her before she could get out of view.

She looked through the leaves again and this time she saw the horse and, instead of a wagon, a buggy carrying three people. As the buggy came nearer and she recognized the occupants, she ran from the bush out to meet them. "Jessie!" she cried. "Carrie, Con!"

Jessie stopped the buggy in front of the cabin and the three of them piled out, all trying to hug Madeline at once while she half-laughed, half-cried at the same time. Tondah, who had not budged from her seat under the tree, watched curiously.

"I'm so glad to see you!" Madeline cried.

"I just saw Gavin in town and he told me he had bought your indenture back from Cate and that you were staying here now," Jessie said. "Thank God you're not with that man any more. No one has a good word to say about him."

"There aren't any good words to say about him," Madeline said.

"Miss Boyd, it looks funny to see you in buckskins," Con said, his head cocked as though appraising her attire.

"Your skirt is just like mine," Carrie said proudly.

"Come in," Madeline said. "Come into the cabin where we can talk. It's a bit cool to stay outside."

"Is it all right if we stay outside and look around?" Con asked.

"If you don't wander off," Jessie said. "Stay right here at the cabin."

When she and Madeline were inside, she said, "Good, now we can really talk."

"How *are* you, Jessie?" Madeline began firing the questions like a round of ammunition. "What do you *really* think of Bath Town and your new home? Do the children like it here? When am I going to get a chance to meet Cyrus?"

"Whoa!" Jessie held up her hands. "One at a time. I am fine, and though it still is going to take more time to get used to them, I think I am going to like Bath Town and my new home very much. People are friendlier here. In town we're all like one big family."

"And the children?"

"It's all still a big adventure for them." Jessie laughed. "The only thing they don't like is having to go to school. I think they got it in their heads when they left England that there would be no school here."

"Is there a school house?" Madeline asked. "I don't remember seeing one."

"Lucinda Mulligan holds classes in the back of the store. She was a schoolteacher before they came here."

Jessie was looking at her assessingly. "What about you? I see the Indian girl is still here, but don't you think it would be a good idea if you stayed with us instead of out here?"

Madeline shook her head. "I have to stay here, Jessie. I am indentured to Gavin now."

Jessie smiled. "I gather you don't think that's the worst thing that ever happened to you."

"No, going to Cate's was."

"What I mean is," Jessie persisted, "you are a little sweet on Gavin now, aren't you?"

Madeline hesitated. Was she? She had not actually taken inventory of her feelings for some time now; she had been living from day to day, doing her work and trying to avoid Tondah as much as possible. She knew her pulse did beat a little faster when Gavin was near and when he smiled at her, which was often, she felt her heart would cave in, but she had been telling herself that it was all because of her gratitude to him for saving her from Cate. Now, asked the question point-blank, she looked Jessie in the eye and answered truthfully: "I think I may be."

"I *know* you are," Jessie said.

"How do you know?"

"By the look on your face when his name is mentioned. By the way your eyes light up. You are not the same person who came over on the *Sea Lion* with us."

"If I'm different," Madeline said, "it is because I have been through a lot since I arrived."

"That may be, but what you have been through has led you straight to love, if I'm any judge . . . and I am."

"I wouldn't call it that . . ." Madeline began.

"How does he feel about you?" Jessie asked.

"I don't know."

"Of course you do." Jessie waved aside the indefinite answer as if it were not worth considering. "You can always tell if a man is in love with you, and Gavin is."

"How can you say that? You don't know."

"Cyrus told me."

"How in heaven's name would Cyrus know? Except for seeing him from a distance the day we arrived, I have never been near Cyrus, let alone talked to him."

"But Gavin talked to him the day he took you to Cate's," Jessie said. "Cyrus said that he had never seen anyone so frantic. 'He's a real goner on that girl,' is what Cyrus said."

"I think Cyrus is mistaken," Madeline said wistfully. "If Gavin is a goner on any woman it's . . ." She looked toward the door.

"You mean that Indian? Uh-uh." Jessie shook her head. "I don't really know him, but Gavin strikes me as being . . . well, not the kind of man who would mess around with . . . with someone like that."

"A lot of men form . . . alliances with Indian women," Madeline said. "Some even marry them."

"I know," Jessie said, "but when Gavin marries, you will be the bride. When will the wedding be?"

Madeline laughed and reddened. This was something that even in her wildest flights of imagination had not occurred to her. She and Gavin marry? The thought sent a shiver of delight through her. Yes, she would like that; she would like that more than anything. His arms holding her close, his blue eyes looking at her with warmth and love shining in them. But it would not happen, for Gavin felt no love for her. And then there was Tondah.

"There will be no wedding, Jessie," she said sadly. Now, only now would she admit to herself that she was falling in love with her "protector," that she had begun to love him from the moment she had seen him on shore staring at her on the top deck of the ship, but at that time she had thought of her emotion as fascination, interest in a new land and new people.

"Well, anyway," Jessie said cheerfully, "unless you are honeymooning, the two of you shouldn't hide out here all the time. You should come into town and join in the merriment."

"What merriment?"

"Mercy! You don't think everyone sits at home with long faces all the time, do you? We have quite a social life. In fact, you can see for yourself if you come tomorrow. We're having a pot supper at the back of Mulligan's store."

"What's a pot supper?"

"Every family brings a pot of something and we put them all together. Like a picnic."

"I'll see if Gavin would like to."

"We'll look for you." Jessie stood up. "Now I'd better collect the children and go before Cyrus comes looking for us. He didn't like the idea of just the children and me driving out here."

"Why not?" Madeline asked. "It isn't far."

"He wouldn't give me a specific reason, but I think it has something to do with the Indians." She lowered her voice even though there was no chance of Tondah hearing.

"But I thought everything was all right, that the Indians and the settlers got along now."

"On the surface that's how it seems," Jessie said, "and the men never come out and say anything else because they don't want to frighten the women, but I think they expect trouble."

It would come as no surprise, Madeline thought, if all the Indians were as hostile as Tondah. But then, Tondah was hostile only to her. "Maybe you have exaggerated it in your mind," she said.

"I hope so." Jessie went to the door, then turned and hugged Madeline. "We'll see you tomorrow."

Madeline counted the next three weeks among the happiest of her life, at least since leaving Bath and going to London with Rufus. Bath Town, she found, was every bit as warm and friendly as Jessie had said, even more so than the English Bath. She learned a great deal about the people and about the way of life in her new world. She and Gavin went to the pot supper at Mulligan's the night after Jessie's visit, and Madeline met most of the townspeople there as well as some of the people from the surrounding area. In the back of the store, where classes were held during the day for the children, there were four long tables where the many pots were placed. A long line of people passed by each table, everyone helping himself to a variety of dishes: pork, fish, hominy, cornbread, beef, mutton, fowls, wheat-bread, honey, and almost every kind of vegetable. After the meal, the tables were pushed back and Tom Milton brought out his violin and played for dancing. Those who did not want to dance milled around the room, socializing. It was then that Madeline was introduced to most of the citizens of Bath Town. During the evening she received many invitations from the women to visit them in their homes. She wanted to reciprocate and invite them to visit her also, but she did not, thinking it would not be quite right for her to invite company to Gavin's house. Several mistook her for Gavin's wife and some of those who had come over on the ship with her were sure that Gavin was the "fiance" she had come to the Colonies to marry. Thankful that Gavin was not within earshot when the mistake was made, Madeline said only no, we are not married, and moved on to another group, leaving behind unasked and unanswered questions.

After that night, Madeline had Gavin teach her how to hitch up the dog cart, and she drove into Bath Town frequently, visiting Jessie and her family, Elizabeth Milton, and others whom she came to know and like.

It was during these early days that she absorbed a wealth of information about life in the colony. She had been surprised at that first supper to find that everyone did not wear buckskins. There were many gowns, as well as men's clothing, made from homespun, and some even wore more elegant clothing they had brought, or had sent, from England. Most of the clothing was made at home from cotton and wool raised by planters in the area. Some flax and hemp were grown also to make table and bed linen and summer clothing. In almost every house and cabin could be found spinning-wheels, flax-hackles, linen-wheels, and looms. The ladies of Bath Town obviously were an industrious lot, Madeline decided, thinking she would ask Gavin to get a spinning-wheel so she, also, could make her clothing and, possibly, his. She knew Mulligan's store carried most everything she could possibly need—cotton and linen sheets, linen shirts, window curtains, white homespun damask, caps, silk handkerchiefs, silver buckles, gowns, petticoats, laces, aprons, stays, muslins, dimity jackets, fans, ribbons, calicoes, buttons, and pins—but she did not want to be thought highfalutin by her peers.

She found there was no want of entertainment either. The pot supper had been her initiation to a new area of amusements. While the men engaged in contests of leaping, wrestling, running, and horseracing, the women enjoyed quilting parties, chinquapin hunts, informal tea parties, and old-fashioned country dances. In the cool nights of late autumn, she and Gavin joined others in partying and feasting during the time of corn-shucking.

It was in late November that the idyll ended for Madeline. She had been visiting Jessie in Bath Town one afternoon and had stopped by Mulligan's on her way home to buy some homespun out of which she was going to try to make Gavin a shirt. As she entered the store she had the feeling eyes were on her, unfriendly eyes. She turned her head slightly, almost expecting to see Tondah nearby, but what she saw was . . . Felton Cate. The man was beside the table which held seasonings and condiments, glaring at her with that malignant leer she still saw occasionally in nightmares. He did not say a word to her, but she heard him humming under his breath. She turned immediately and ran out of the store. Outside, she leapt into the cart and drove back to the cabin as fast as the horse would go, unmindful of the rough path, the horse's fragile legs, or her own neck. She knew only that she had to get back to Gavin . . . and safety.

Gavin, who was putting an armful of corn in the bin beside the shed, looked up as the galloping stallion thundered across the clearing in front of the cabin. He dropped the corn and rushed to catch the horse by the reins.

"I was afraid from the beginning it was a mistake to let you take the stallion by yourself," he said, not knowing whether to scold Madeline or just be thankful that she wasn't hurt by the wild ride with the runaway.

Madeline jumped out of the cart before he could assist her. "He was magnificent, thank God," she said. "Just any horse could not have gotten me here so quickly."

"You mean you took the whip to him?" Gavin was aghast. "Surely not!" Then, after a moment's thought, "Why were you in such a hurry?"

"I saw Felton Cate in town. He was standing as close to me as you are. In Mulligan's."

"Did he do or say anything?"

"I didn't give him the chance," she said. "I left the minute I saw him."

Gavin exhaled. "Madeline, in a place as small as Bath, you are going to see a lot of people from time to time you'd rather avoid, including Cate. You're going to have to get used to it, and you're going to have to get over your fear of him. He can't hurt you now. He no longer has any power over you."

"But you said he might try to get me back."

"I don't think he can," Gavin said. "He sold your papers to me in good faith . . ."

"Under duress, you said."

". . . and if he had thought he could get you back, he would have tried long ago."

Madeline took a deep breath. Although she had worried less and less as time passed, there still had been that tiny fear in the back of her mind bothering her. She knew now beyond any doubt that she loved Gavin, that she wanted Gavin, wanted to share the rest of her life with him, and all of her love with him. Only that small fear that Cate might come for her had kept the past few weeks from being perfect. That, and the fact that, though Gavin was always kind and attentive and pleasant, he did not love her. Even Tondah's hostility paled to insignificance beside so large an obstacle to total happiness.

She looked toward the path along which she had just come and, seeing nothing, smiled sheepishly. She had half expected to see Cate barreling down the road after her. "I think I'll go in the house and . . . have a cup of tea," she said.

Gavin wanted to leave the corn on the ground and go with her, but instead he continued piling it neatly in the bin. Ever since the night he had brought Madeline home from Cate's (and he thought of his cabin as her home now as well as his), he had played down the sinister Cate and everything concerning him, hoping that by doing so he would allay Madeline's fears sooner. Until today, he thought he had succeeded, for it had been a long time since she had mentioned Cate's name or had a look of terror in her eyes. Now he knew the fear still burned in the back of her mind and had been ignited into an explosion by seeing Cate today. Somehow, she would have to get over that fear for, as he had just told her, there was no way she could live in the vicinity of Bath Town and avoid him. Their paths were bound to cross once in a while.

Dear God, how he wished he could take her in his arms and comfort her, show her how much she meant to him and tell her she need never worry about that scoundrel again; he would protect her from Cate and anyone or anything else that threatened her. But he could not do it because, as she had the night he brought her back, she would think him no better than Cate; she would think he was also trying to take advantage of her "situation." He would never forget the tone of her voice as she said, "I suppose I can expect more of the same kind of treatment from you now . . . now that *you* own me."

And the whole sorry, troubling truth of the matter was that he wanted her in exactly the same way Cate did. Night and day she was on his mind, his thoughts as carnal as Cate's ever were. Not a night passed when she pulled the blanket across the room that he did not want to tear the blanket down, throw it in the fire, and then get in bed with her and make love to her. He could think of nothing else, and only God knew how much his restraint was costing him. His nerves were taut, like tent ropes stretched almost to the breaking point, and he found himself having to make a great effort to be pleasant, whereas before, a good disposition had been one of his natural resources. He found himself being especially short with Tondah who, for the first time since she had come to work for him, was constantly underfoot. She seemed to be staying in the cabin more, and even when she went outside, she was never far away. She almost never went out with Walking Bear for a visit, and Gavin could tell that the Indian brave was getting more and more miffed about it.

I hope to God he doesn't think it's my doing that she never goes out, Gavin thought. If Walking Bear became angry enough, he might very well go after Gavin with his tomahawk . . . not that Gavin had ever seen Walking Bear with a weapon of any kind.

It was more than apparent to him now that Tondah did not like Madeline, but he did not know what to do about it. He could not send Tondah back to her people because he knew Madeline thought of her as their "respectability."

When the last ear of corn had been placed in the bin, Gavin went to the woods behind the cabin and knelt beside the little creek which ran down to the river. He washed his face and hands in the icy water. The chill of winter already was in the air although autumn had extended longer than usual. For the past two weeks there had been a threat of snow which had caused feverish activity in the colony as everyone tried to put up enough fruit and vegetables to get through the winter. Almost all of the leaves had fallen now, making it possible to see his cabin from a much greater distance.

He walked back slowly, wondering what this winter held in store for him—and Madeline. He had been treating her as though she were the mistress of the house rather than as a servant because he had not once thought of her as being a servant. He had allowed— even encouraged—Madeline to visit her friends in town, and he had tried to discourage her from working at the house. After all, that was what he paid Tondah for. Even so, he was aware that Madeline did a tremendous amount of work. It was as though she were trying to work out her four years in half that time.

When he went in the cabin he found her sitting in front of the fireplace, a teacup in her hand. Tondah was in the back part of the room, peeling potatoes.

"Would you like a cup?" Madeline asked.

"I'll get it," he said, reaching for the kettle. Before he touched the kettle, Tondah was beside him, cup in hand, pouring the tea for him. She gave him a big, welcoming smile.

"Thank you," he said automatically.

"These teacups are lovely," Madeline said, turning hers around in her hand. "You must have brought them from England."

"I had them sent," he said. "Just because I live in the wilderness doesn't mean I have to live like a wild man."

She gave him a thin smile.

"You like what you eat tonight." Tondah injected herself into their conversation. "Your favorite."

"Vegetable stew?" Gavin asked.

Tondah nodded.

"You will have to teach me how to make it, Tondah," Madeline said, adding hastily, "though I'm sure mine would never be as good as yours."

"Yes," was Tondah's only reply. She went outside to add the potatoes she had just peeled to the pot of cooking vegetables and meat.

Later, Tondah served the stew to them in large bowls. When Gavin had first brought Madeline back from Cate's, he had insisted that Tondah eat the evening meal at the table with them, but she had refused. It was obvious to Madeline that the girl did not want to sit at the table with her, but Gavin seemed perplexed. However after several days, he dropped the issue. Madeline assumed he had finally figured out Tondah's reason.

When they finished they both complimented her on the stew. She acknowledged Gavin's words with a pretty smile and ignored Madeline.

This has gone far enough, Gavin thought. Tondah is acting like a spoiled child. Tomorrow I will have a talk with her and let her know that if she doesn't do her part, meet Madeline halfway, she must go back to the Indian village.

The last thing he wanted was a pair of warring females on his hands. To Madeline's credit, she had never acted surly toward Tondah. Except for a few frowns, which Gavin had noticed, she had been very much a lady—exactly what he would have expected of her.

After supper, Madeline got up to help Tondah with the dishes, and Gavin propped his feet up against the fireplace, looking hypnotically into the blue flames glowing from the logs. When the heavy knock sounded at the door, it surprised him so that his feet fell to the floor. Both of the women started violently.

Gavin was up and at the door instantly, flinging it open, then he took a step backward, his second surprise greater than the first.

Without saying a word or waiting to be spoken to, Felton Cate staggered into the cabin, so drunk that he threatened to lose his balance with each step he took. With his eyes on Madeline, who cringed against the logs of the wall, he lumbered toward her.

Springing across the floor, Gavin caught the man by

the scruff of the neck and whirled him around. "Just what do you think you're doing?"

"Her," Cate pointed. "I've come for her."

"You'll get out of here right now or you'll live to regret it . . . if you live at all." Gavin had never been so furious. If he had wanted to smash Cate's face in before, he was ready to do much worse now.

"I'll buy her back." Cate's tongue was thick and his words slurred. "Shouldn't have sold her."

Gavin pushed Cate toward the door. "Get out."

"Whatsha matter with you, Durant? You got one woman. What you need with two?"

Gavin opened the door and heaved Cate out. "If you come back here, I will not be responsible for your life," he called after the retreating figure. Then he turned to Madeline and Tondah. "He was too drunk to reason with."

Madeline's face was deathly white and she almost seemed to have stopped breathing. Tondah, on the other hand, looked strangely exhilarated by the intruder and, for the first time, Gavin realized the extent of her resentment of Madeline.

He also realized for the first time the extent of his own feelings for the beautiful, terrified girl. That he had been attracted to her from the first he had never denied, nor had he denied to himself his consuming desire for her. What he *had* denied from the beginning was his love for her. The thought of Cate, or anyone else, taking her away from him was absolutely unthinkable.

He went to her and took her in his arms, unmindful of Tondah's sudden intake of breath and dark scowl.

"He is not going to bother you again, Madeline," he said softly. "Tomorrow, when he is sober enough to understand what I'm saying, I'll see to it that he never comes near you again."

For a second Madeline buried her face against Gavin's shoulder, but then they both jumped at the sound of a nearby crash. Tondah had dropped one of Gavin's English teacups on the floor and broken it to fragments. Without a word, the girl stooped and began to pick up the pieces.

It was obvious to Gavin the cup had been thrown down, not merely dropped, but he said nothing. He put his arm around Madeline's waist and took her back to a chair in front of the fireplace. "He will not bother you again, my love. You have my word on that."

Outside, Felton Cate stumbled across the clearing that served as a yard for the cabin, finally losing his balance and falling into the dirt. Emitting a stream of foul words, he pushed himself up off the ground and looked back at the cabin. From the window he could see the soft glow of lamplight and the silhouettes of Gavin and Madeline as they passed between the lamp and the window. Asking both God's and the devil's damnation on Gavin, he went slowly back toward the house. That high and mighty Durant was not going to get away with this. First he, Cate, had been cheated out of the indenture papers and now cheated out of having the girl, while Durant not only had that gorgeous wench to warm his bed every night, he also had the Indian girl who didn't exactly hurt the eyes to look at. There was no justice, no justice in the whole damn world.

His horse and wagon, which he had brought so he could carry Madeline's baggage back to his cabin, were at the edge of the woods. He stared at the wagon for a moment, then headed back to the cabin. The chill night air had sobered him somewhat, and he knew better than to knock on the door again. Instead, he went to the side of the cabin and peered through the window. His anger, which had been building steadily since the night Gavin had taken Madeline away from him, had now reached volcanic proportions and was on the verge of erupting.

Nothing had turned out right for him, not since Agnes had died. Actually, not since long before he had left England. Caught pocketing the money in the livery stable where he worked, he had been instantly dismissed. For a month he had stayed home, not bothering to try to find another situation. His only companion had been a keg of ale, and he was never far away from it. Agnes had found a domestic situation in a manor house to "tide us over until you are better situated." The thing was, he was as well situated as he wanted to be. He took an instant liking to idleness. Unfortunately for him, Agnes was not quite as entranced with domesticity outside her own home and, after six months, left her position as second maid to Lady Malveran. It was up to Cate again to support the two of them so, rather than looking for another situation, he became a dip—the name for one engaged in the ancient profession of picking pockets. Again bad luck smiled its blessing upon him because his thick fingers were neither agile nor quick and he was caught with his hand in the pocket of a gentleman at a county fair during his second week of dipping. However, he did manage to break from the hold of the constable who was marching him to a nearby stock where he would be held until the end of the day when he, and others in his profession, would be transported to the gaol. He disappeared into the crowd and then left the fairgrounds and went home. All night he tossed and turned in bed, expecting the constable to show up on his doorstep and take him away. Toward morning he broke out in a sweat and felt really ill. Terrible things happened to people who were caught picking pockets. Even small children did not escape dire punishment.

By morning he had made up his mind that he and Agnes would leave at once for the place that was being called "the land of milk and honey," that Eden across the ocean. Using all the money he and Agnes had managed to save during a lifetime of menial work, he bought their passage.

Still the jinx hovered over him, for Agnes became quite ill during the voyage and survived less than a week after they reached Bath Town. Feeling sorry for the man who went into such a decline that he was unaware of where he was or even who he was for several weeks, the people of Bath Town built his cabin for him and helped him with the farming during his first season. It made him smile every time he remembered those early days in the colony, for he had known very well who he was and where he was; he had also known how to get the most out of those crackbrained, soft-hearted settlers.

In the years since, he had grown increasingly tired of the hard work and, with the little money he had managed to scrimp together, had sent for a couple to be indentured to him to take care of both the housework and the farmwork. His initial disappointment at getting only a woman vanished the minute he laid eyes upon the woman.

Now, his plans in that direction also had gone sour.

He wanted to shake his fist at heaven in his wrath, but he knew his energy would be better spent in another way. Standing at the window, looking at that beauty sitting by the fire, he decided exactly what he was going to do. He would bide his time, wait until Durant and the girl had gone to bed (the Indian already had gone into a back room), and then he would go back inside, kill Durant and take Madeline home with him. With Durant out of the way, no one would question Cate's ownership of the indenture papers because everyone in Bath Town knew that Madeline had come to the colony as his servant.

Durant was sitting in a chair opposite the girl now, looking at her as though he could eat her with a spoon, relishing every mouthful. Well, it wouldn't be long now before he, Cate, would have her all to himself. He smacked his lips in anticipation.

What Cate didn't know was that even as he watched the two inside the cabin, he himself was being watched. From behind the trunk of a tree four feet away, a pair of eyes narrowed to see through the darkness and a pair of hands were rubbed together, making ready to fit around Cate's neck.

Walking Bear, who was looking for Tondah, had also been peering in the window. He had arrived shortly after Gavin had thrown Cate out and he had seen Tondah go to her room. He had been about to go to the back of the cabin when he had heard Cate returning. Stepping behind the tree, he watched the man at the window. Whatever the white man was up to, it bore no good for anyone in the cabin. Of that, Walking Bear was sure. It made no difference to him what happened to Durant and the white woman, but he would not see Tondah put in any danger whatever. The foolish girl was living there against the wishes and advice of everyone in the tribe, her own family no longer spoke her name, as though she were now among the spirits, but he still wanted her. Like a sick animal he whined after her, and he loathed himself for doing it, but no other woman interested him. He had wanted Tondah, and no other, since the day he noticed that she had become a woman.

Long had he despised Durant. He was sure the white man had not put his hand on Tondah—she had told him as much, and he believed her—but that situation might change at any moment. No man, red or white, could live with a comely girl like Tondah month after month, year after year, without finally laying claim to her womanhood. It had been in Walking Bear's mind for months that he should kill Durant before that happened. He had hoped when Tondah first had deserted her family and tribe to work for the white man that she would soon tire of her independence and the strange ways of the strange people. He had counted on it. But it had not happened, and the longer she stayed the less likely it was to happen. She had become bewitched by the man and his ways.

Now, the only thing left for Walking Bear to do was to get rid of Durant and reclaim Tondah for himself and for her people. She would object strenuously in the beginning; it made him smile to think how she would object and how he would overcome those objections. But soon she would realize that it was for the best. Soon she would desire him even as he desired her.

At this moment, however, the most pressing problem was that bulky man known as Cate who looked at all women as though he would make them his squaw. As loathsome as Durant was, he was less so than Cate, who was not liked even among his own people.

Without a sound, Walking Bear crept up behind Cate and caught his throat between forearm and elbow, then bent the arm in a slow, strangling movement. Cate struggled wildly, kicking out at the Indian, even kicking the logs of the cabin, but he could not escape the strong arm that held him. His screams turned out to be loud gurgling noises.

Inside the cabin, Gavin froze instantly when he heard something hit beneath the window. His first thought was that Cate had returned.

Madeline, who was just beginning to regain her color and her composure after her fright when Cate had come into the cabin, now paled again as she saw Gavin go tense. "What is it?" she whispered. "He's out there, isn't he?"

His finger to his lips, Gavin went to the door, opened it quietly, then went outside.

"No!" Madeline said in a loud whisper. "Don't go out there!" But it was too late. Gavin already had disappeared into the darkness. She went to the door, looked out, but could see nothing. From the side of the cabin, though, she could hear a fierce struggle. Anxious for Gavin, yet terrified herself almost to the point of fainting, she retreated back into the cabin and, weakly, fell into a chair. "Gavin," she said softly, prayerfully, "Oh, Gavin."

In the lamplight from the window, Gavin took in the situation at once: Walking Bear with his stranglehold on Cate was just about to break the man's neck. "Hold off!" he said, and when the Indian paid him no attention, he grasped Walking Bear around the chest, forcing him to let go of Cate to defend himself. Cate fell to the ground, gasping for breath, and Walking Bear turned his full attention to Gavin.

"Wait, Walking Bear," Gavin said quickly, "we have no quarrel."

His arm in midair, ready to strike, Walking Bear slowly lowered his hard fist, unclenching his hand. He would get Durant, dispatch him to his ancestors, but not now. Not with Tondah close by. As for that other worm—he looked down at the squirming Cate trying to rise from the ground—he would finish him too, but at another time.

Even in the indistinct, dim light, Gavin could see Walking Bear's eyes, and what he saw there was murder. He knew that the Indian would much rather kill him than Cate. He also knew instinctively that he was safe . . . for the moment. "Go back to your village, Walking Bear," he said. "Tondah is asleep. Come to visit her another time."

The Indian looked from Gavin to Cate, then back at Gavin, his expression inscrutable, then he quickly disappeared into the darkness and the woods.

Cate, on his feet now, looked around wildly as

though expecting the entire Tuscarora tribe, their tomahawks at the ready, to come whooping out of the woods. Without so much as a glance at Gavin, he took off, literally scared sober, running to his horse and wagon at the edge of the clearing. Gavin stayed outside for a minute or two, listening to the rumbling wagon as it went through the woods until he could no longer hear the sound. Then he went back inside to Madeline.

Once again he had stood between her and disaster and he knew now that he always would. It was more than attraction, more than fleeting desire, even more than love that filled his whole being as he looked at her, pale and shaken, in the chair. Her hands gripped the arms so tightly that her knuckles were white, as white as her face.

"Gavin! Oh, thank God!" She half rose from the chair.

He said not a word, but held out his arms. She came to him then, to the safe enclosure of his arms, and her own arms encircled him. For a short while, they stood thus, each gaining strength and serenity from the other. Then, slowly, Gavin tilted her face up to his, gently kissing her forehead, her eyelids, and then her mouth. The pressure of her arms around him increased as she responded to his kiss. For the first time, she realized that she was loved, loved as deeply as she herself loved. Their kiss was long and deep and probing and she found her whole body arching to be closer to him, swaying as his hands caressed her body.

He had called her "my love" earlier, and it had thrilled her, but then, cautiously, she had told herself that he had said it in friendliness, not in love. But never could the emotion she felt now, and knew that he felt also, be mistaken for mere friendliness. It was love . . . adoration . . . exultation!

He pulled her toward the wooden bench at one side of the fireplace, the only place in the room, save the bed, where the two of them could sit close together. There were no words between them as they continued the embrace, another long, long kiss that sent fire through her body, causing an unfamiliar ache as she longed to give herself to him completely. That thought caused her to pull away somewhat. "Gavin . . ."

"Madeline, I want you so," he said in a hoarse whisper. "We must be married . . . at once!"

"Oh, yes. Yes!" she breathed, a long sigh of pure contentment escaping her. She had been afraid that he was going to suggest something other than marriage, and, wanting him so, she also had been afraid that she would have said yes to that as well.

He straightened suddenly, surprising her. He smiled at her, that wonderful impish grin that so enthralled her, and said, "If we are to be married, I had better show some restraint now, else you might refuse me for being too impetuous."

She wanted to tell him that could never happen, but thought better of it. Instead, she smiled back at him, saying nothing.

"I suppose you are Church of England," he said, and she nodded.

He was thoughtful. Though Quaker, he would not insist on a Quaker wedding if she would rather be married by a priest. "As you know, there are no ministers in Bath Town," he said, "but an Anglican priest comes through from time to time. I know there will be one here next month; there's always one through sometime in December."

"The Advent season is a lovely time to be married," she said.

"I don't think I can wait until Christmas," he said, drawing her to him again, finding her mouth and continuing to kiss her as though there had been no interrupting conversation.

Chapter Nine

THE FINAL DAYS OF NOVEMBER DRAGGED BY EVEN THOUGH
Madeline was happier than she had ever been. Yet
there was a certain frustration in her bliss. Though she
and Gavin embraced often, touched often, and were
seldom apart for more than a few minutes at a time, she
yearned to give herself to him completely, to love him
with every inch of her body, every fiber of her being.
She knew the restraint they were showing was as hard
on him as it was on her, perhaps even more frustrating,
for sometimes in the midst of an embrace, he would
break away for no reason at all and go to the other side
of the room, or even outdoors.

"Would you prefer I go to Bath Town and stay with
the Rolands until we are married?" she asked him
once.

"No!" he thundered, his nerves taut. Then he relaxed a little and grinned at her. "How can we prove
to each other that we are strong enough not to yield to
temptation if there is nothing or no one around to
tempt us?"

Madeline looked toward Tondah's door, but said
nothing. As soon as she and Gavin were married and
she was indisputably mistress of the house, she would
insist that Tondah go, but for now, they still needed her

presence. There were times, however, when Madeline would have been willing to forego a little respectability just to be rid of the girl. But still unsure what the relationship might have been between Gavin and Tondah before she herself arrived, she did not express her wish to him.

Madeline could hardly wait to share her happy news with Jessie and the other Rolands, but on the day she had planned to drive the cart into town a sudden snowfall caused her to hesitate.

"I might have an easier time of it walking," she said to Gavin, "unless it gets too deep."

"No need for that." He took her out to the shed and she watched as he took the wheels off the cart and put runners on. "Now we have a sleigh, or something similar," he said, "and Walt is perfectly capable of pulling it."

The stallion was named Sir Walter Raleigh, long since shortened to Walt.

Gavin drove her into town, afraid to let her go by herself the first time she tried the converted cart. On the way she marveled at the beauty of the snow in the woods, covering the barren ground and tree limbs but leaving parts of evergreens—cedars, junipers, and pines—verdant against the white. Icicles from pine branches resembled tiny chandeliers. In the new world she had found an even newer world, both inside herself and outdoors.

Knowing that she was loved as much as she herself loved was a feeling it would take her a long time to get used to—and, in a way, she hoped she never would. She was sure she would not take Gavin's love for granted, not even after years of marriage, though it might be comforting to do so. She had taken all of life for granted before her father's death, and just see how drastically her life had changed! Finally, for the better.

Gavin went to Mulligan's for provisions while she went to the Roland house, and Jessie's surprise and delight at the news was all she had hoped it would be. After commenting and carrying on like a school girl, Jessie suddenly clapped her hands and said, "Oh, Madeline, the story you told on the *Sea Lion* is true after all. You were not lying. You came to the Colonies to marry your fiancé."

"But I didn't even know Gavin then," Madeline laughed. "No, Jessie, I don't think there's any way to whitewash a black lie. But isn't it a blessing that it came true?"

"God's own mercy," Jessie said, hugging her, "and you deserve it."

"Do you have any idea when a priest will come to Bath Town?" she asked.

"No, but Cyrus says there is always one here sometime around Christmas for a service."

Madeline sighed. Christmas seemed so far away, such a long, long time.

"It will be here before you know it," Jessie said, reading her thoughts. "Meanwhile, there are preparations to keep you busy."

"I suppose," Madeline said. "I hadn't thought about that. I will have to make a wedding dress and I am the world's worst seamstress."

"With that trunk full of gorgeous gowns, why would you want to make one?"

"They aren't suitable for . . ." Madeline began, then remembered one which might be used. She had not even considered those gowns because they were the ones Rufus had insisted she buy or have made to assist him in his nefarious scheme; if not tainted in actuality, they were in her mind, and she did not want to begin her married life with Gavin with any leftovers from that other pernicious life. But there was one gown which was a distinct possibility, one she had never worn: a white silk with a lace overskirt. Wearing that, all she needed to transform herself into a bride was a veil.

She laughed happily. "Do you suppose I could find a white veil at Mulligan's?"

"If not a white veil, possibly some material that could be made into a veil," Jessie said. "I saw some window curtains that . . ."

The planning went on through the afternoon and by the time Gavin appeared to take Madeline home it had been decided that the wedding would be at the Roland house, followed by a wedding breakfast or supper, depending upon the time of day.

As they drove through the still-falling snow back to the cabin, Madeline was quiet. When Gavin asked her why, she replied, "Because I'm a little afraid."

Surprised, Gavin turned around so he could look her full in the face. "But why? Cate will never bother you again. I promise you. After what happened at the cabin, he's afraid of his own shadow now. Lester Mulligan said just this afternoon that Cate rarely even comes into town any more." He laughed. "I hear he's as afraid of me as he is of Walking Bear. My reputation of being a quiet Quaker has been ruined by rumors that I bested both Cate and an Indian brave in battle at the same time. Much exaggerated, of course, as rumors usually are."

"It isn't Cate I'm afraid of."

"Then what?"

"I'm afraid to be too happy," she admitted softly. "I think the gods do not smile for long on something as ephemeral as human happiness."

"That's silly," he scoffed, "as well as superstitious and pagan." He put his arm around her, even though she was behind him, and pulled her close enough to kiss her. "Don't ever be afraid of happiness . . . or the things that make you happy. That's the soundest advice I can give you."

He did not know that later he would be applying her statement to himself as well as wondering about the soundness of his advice.

A change in the household as well as the plans occurred early in December. The snow remained on the ground for ten days, making it impossible for Gavin to work outside except to chop firewood, not that there was much work to be done at this time of year with the crops in. Winter was the one season when the farmers could get some much-needed rest, although most of them, Gavin included, were so used to being outdoors and active from sunup to sundown that they became like caged animals during the winter, restless, pacing, wanting to be outside again.

It was on a frigidly cold afternoon that Gavin stood in front of the frosted windowpane wondering how many more days before the snow would turn to slush and then to mud in the soggy fields. Next spring he would plant more tobacco, for tobacco was turning out to be more of a money crop than anyone had thought possible. By next year this time there might be three

Durants to feed and clothe instead of two, and the more money he could save in advance, the better it would be.

With his mind on such practicalities, he almost jumped when Madeline slipped up behind him and put her arms around him. He turned immediately, all thoughts of crops or money gone from his mind. He grabbed Madeline in a bearhug, kissing her until she was breathless. "That's a sample of what you will get when you sneak up on me," he growled playfully. Then, suddenly, he was not playful any more. His mouth was burning hers in a searing kiss, making her so feverish that her legs threatened to buckle under her. With no more words between them—no time for words—he picked her up and carried her to the bed, his mouth never leaving hers while his hands pulled at her clothing. At first she lay quiescent, ready, eager for his all-consuming love, then something about the impatience with which he was trying to remove her blouse struck a familiar, and unpleasantly discordant, note in her mind. She was reminded of all the offensive men she had taken back to Wigmore Street, all the pawing and heavy breathing as they tried to bring her to bed. If she let Gavin make love to her now, it would bring them to the level of that other low experience in which both love and the men had been cheated, and Madeline most of all.

Heretofore, it had been Gavin who had called a halt before they became too carried away, but this time she must do it for it was obvious that there was no turning back for him now. She pushed at his chest and struggled beneath him trying to squirm away.

"What . . . ?" Gavin looked at her with glazed eyes,

a dazed expression on his face, while his hands still played up and down her body, causing her to squirm even more.

"No, Gavin," she said in a raspy voice. "We mustn't. Please. We must wait."

He was about to respond by closing her mouth with a kiss when a sudden change in her eyes caused him to look at what she had just seen. Standing on the other side of the room, her face contorted in indescribable rage, was Tondah.

Gavin, his own face reddening with anger, got up from the bed instantly. "What do you mean by coming in here staring at us like that?" he roared. "Get out of here!"

The girl neither answered nor budged an inch. Her eyes were upon Madeline with such naked loathing in them that it was frightening to look at her.

Gavin, his temper under control now, considered the fact that Tondah was not spying since this was her home too, and that she probably had just come into the room to warm herself by the fire. He went over to her, standing between her and her view of Madeline on the bed. "Tondah," he said, in a quieter tone, "Madeline and I are to be married this month and . . ."

"No!" Tondah hissed. "You speak untrue."

"It is true," he said, "and when Madeline becomes Mrs. Durant we will not be needing you here to help out. Madeline has said she would like to take over all the duties of the household and . . ."

"You will not wed her," Tondah interrupted again. "She is pale, sick, do-nothing. She not be good wife to you."

"Oh, yes I will!" Madeline was up now, standing

beside Gavin, giving Tondah back the same unflinching stare.

Forestalling what could turn out to be a real cat fight, Gavin said quickly, "Tondah, I think it would be best if you left now and not wait until the wedding. You have taken care of me wonderfully well all this time and you will have my gratitude and my friendship always." He went to the fireplace, removed the loose stone from the hearth, and took his leather purse, counting out money far beyond that which Tondah had earned. He pressed it into her hand. "If you let Walking Bear know you are leaving, I am sure he will help you take your belongings back to your people."

"No!" Tondah cried again. "You my people. You my man, not Walking Bear."

"No, Tondah," Gavin said, his voice gentle. "Madeline and I will soon be man and wife, and I would like to think that you will be happy with your own people again."

Her expression still heavy with hatred for Madeline, Tondah edged slowly toward the door of her little room. "I go," she said, seeing that defeat was inevitable, "but I come back. When you tired of her, I be here."

She went into her room and closed the door. Madeline listened, thinking she might hear the sound of crying but she heard no sound whatever, only a silence that seemed oppressive and ominous.

The next morning Tondah left, her few belongings in a bundle tied on her back like a papoose. She did not speak to either of them, but before going out the door she gave Gavin a long, loving look.

"Will she go back to her people?" Madeline asked.

"I hope so, but I don't know," he said. They went to the window and watched her as she tracked through the snow to the woods. At the edge of the woods, she turned briefly for one last look, then was on her way again, out of their sight.

"She may come back in the dead of the night and burn down the cabin," Madeline said, only half in jest. Though she was worried, her mind was on other things now that the one imperfection had been taken out of her otherwise perfect existence. It did not matter that the wedding wouldn't take place for another two or three weeks; she did not think it necessary that they have a chaperone in the house any longer. Tondah had served her purpose, and after this afternoon's thwarted lovemaking, it was highly unlikely that Gavin would approach her again so amorously until they were married.

Chapter Ten

THE REVEREND CHARLES ALGERNON CRESTON, CHURCH of England, arrived in Bath Town the eighteenth of December for a four-day stay, during which he would perform the rites of his church for a churchless colony. He was enroute to New Bern, a larger town and a more populous area, where he would hold the Christmas Eve and Christmas Day services and where he would remain for several months. He was a tall, gaunt man, in his early fifties, with a fringe of wispy gray hair around his otherwise bald head. He had a hawklike nose and eyes which also seemed more like those of a bird of prey than a human. Another thing he had was no liking at all for this uncivilized country to which he had agreed to come once every five years on a rotation basis with the other missionaries of the church. This was his second six-month stint in the New World and he abhorred everything about it. He had been sorely tempted after his first visit to the Colonies to renege on his agreement, but the thought of facing the unyielding bishop with this news was slightly more terrifying than the dreaded crossing of the ocean and six months in the savage land.

During his four days in Bath Town, he baptized eleven white and five Indian babies and children, performed seven marriages, and read prayers for the repose of the souls of the forty-six who had died since the last priest had passed through the area.

Because of their remoteness from town, Gavin and Madeline did not know the priest had arrived until Jessie and Cyrus rode out to the cabin to tell them. They went into town immediately to make arrangements with the Rev. Mr. Creston for their marriage. He was staying with the Martins, their guest for the time he would be in Bath Town, so it was there that Gavin and Madeline went.

Madeline had been accustomed to friendly, sometimes even jovial, churchmen, so she was unprepared for the stern man who faced them, not even a hint of a congratulatory smile in his eyes as he said, "I have never been able to understand why the church permits marriages over here without the posting of banns."

"It has been generally known for the past four weeks that Madeline and I plan to marry, sir," Gavin said, taking an instant dislike to the man. "Besides, there is no church here, therefore, nowhere to post banns."

"Any public place would suffice," he said in clipped tones.

"But the reason for the posting of banns, as I understand it, is to see if there are objections or any reason why the marriage should not take place," Gavin said, and he added, laughing, "You'll find no objections here."

His lips pursed, the priest said nothing. Finally, with a sigh, he nodded. There was no way he could ever get used to the almost pagan ways of these people, so the only thing he could do was grit his teeth and go along with them, praying nightly that God would forgive his laxity. "You will have to be the last," he said, "because I already have a full schedule. You may be married on the afternoon of the twenty-second."

"We've waited four weeks," Madeline said. "I think we can wait a few more days."

Shocked, the man of the cloth could only stare at this woman who implied such boldness and immodesty. Probably there was a reason for such unseemly haste to get married, a very good reason.

Actually, there was a good reason, but not the one Creston had in mind. Since Tondah had left, life in the cabin had become even more frustrating. So much did Madeline and Gavin want each other that they became afraid even to touch for fear they would fall into bed, all restraint gone.

"Why would it be so terrible if we did?" Gavin groaned one night, sitting across the table from Madeline, a suffering expression on his face. "Is it so important that you be virgin when you marry?"

"No, I suppose not," she said slowly, "since it is you I shall be marrying."

But obviously it was important to her, he thought; therefore, he would try to curb his desire until a priest could mumble a few words over them to make it all right. The blanket would remain over the rope and he would stay on the other side of the room at all times in an effort to lessen temptation.

From the Martin house they went to the Rolands' to discuss the wedding plans. It was agreed that Madeline would spend the night before the wedding with the Rolands so her bridegroom would not see her until the wedding, which would take place in the front room. Then the guests and wedding party would be treated to a wedding supper, cooked by Jessie with the help of others in town, and after that, the newlyweds could retire to the children's room (the children would be sent elsewhere for the night) where they would not be disturbed.

"We'll go home after supper," Gavin said as soon as Jessie revealed this part of her planning.

"But it will be dark, maybe late at night," Jessie said.

"And the ground may be covered with snow again by then," Cyrus added.

"We'll go home," Madeline repeated. "We don't want to put the children out."

"The children don't mind, but if you'd rather . . ." Cyrus winked at Gavin.

"We'd rather," Gavin said cryptically.

"Oh, Jessie, you are so good to do all this for us," Madeline said, hoping her friend would not be hurt that they were not going along with *all* her plans. "You and Cyrus both."

"It will be our first social occasion here at the house since we arrived," Jessie said. "I can't wait."

That went double for the prospective bride and groom.

At a time when she should have reached the zenith of happiness, Madeline was extremely troubled. In the three days of frantic final preparations for her wedding, her mind was never off her worries, and they were worries she could not share with Gavin. As she went about with a preoccupied look on her face or a slight frown, he attributed it to prenuptial nervousness and tried to reassure her by breaking their unspoken rule of not touching. He would take her in his arms, kiss her, hold her close, and whisper words of endearment, completely unaware that this only magnified her worries. The more remote and standoffish she became, the more affectionate and tender he became, thinking he would dispel all her nervousness before their marriage. Thus, it became a vicious circle.

Lying in bed, sleepless, two nights before the wedding, she stared through the darkness at the blanket separating them, her anxiety so great it was like another fretful person in bed with her, keeping her wide-eyed.

Whereas only a few days ago, and for weeks before that, she had wanted nothing so much as to have their love consummated, now, ever since they had almost given themselves completely—stopped only by the watching eyes of Tondah and Madeline's own bad memories—she had been afraid. As Gavin had fumbled with her clothing she had, in her mind, substituted for his face the composite face of all those avid men who had panted over her on Wigmore Street. It had ruined the moment for her and made her love for Gavin seem as tawdry as the evening spent with Robert Crawley or any of those other vulgar pleasure-seekers.

Would it happen again on their wedding night? As Gavin, whom she loved more than her own life, embraced her, ready to make her his own, would she suddenly freeze in his arms, an unwilling participant in the act of love?

She could only wonder and worry.

The afternoon before the wedding Gavin took Madeline into town, leaving her—reluctantly—at the Roland house. He prolonged his goodbye for so long that Jessie finally said, "Oh, for heaven's sake, Gavin, you are not sending her back to England. You'll see her again in less than twenty-four hours, and then for the rest of your life. Now be off with you . . . unless you want to spend the night at hard labor, which is what we will be doing."

Which meant that they spent a good part of the night decorating the front room, making it look as much like a chapel as possible. They turned a table into an altar, placing upon it a wooden cross that Cyrus had made for the occasion, two silver candlesticks that Jessie had brought with her, and two small vases of greenery. Chairs—all the Rolands had, plus some borrowed from neighbors—were placed in rows with a center aisle to the altar. The rest of the room was decorated with evergreen wreathes with red ribbons, and other fragrant greenery.

"We need something white to make it look bridal as well as Christmassy," Jessie said, "but I don't know what it would be."

Looking at the white tapers in the candlesticks and the white runner, made from sheets, down the aisle to the altar, Madeline said, "There's enough white. It looks beautiful, Jessie, absolutely beautiful." There was a catch in her voice.

Jessie went to her, putting her arm around Madeline's waist. "You're not getting a bit shaky, are you? You shouldn't. I never saw a man more in love than Gavin. You don't have a thing to worry about, now or in the future."

Madeline nodded, saying nothing. She wished she could confide her fears, tell Jessie the whole story, but she dared not. Not only would she lose Jessie's respect, she probably would lose her friendship as well.

"You *do* have a case of nerves, don't you?" Jessie went on when Madeline did not respond. "Oh, Maddie, it's going to be all right, I promise you. In fact, it's going to be much better than all right. You and Gavin will . . ."

"I know, Jessie," she interrupted, trying to give her friend a reassuring smile. "I know."

Jessie relaxed somewhat. "What I know is that you'd better get to bed and get some sleep. It's almost tomorrow, the big day." And as Madeline started up the stairs to the room she would share with Carrie tonight, she added, "Just remember, Madeline, tomorrow you will come from the shadows of love into love's full bright sunshine."

The morning rushed by. Madeline helped Jessie with last-minute preparations, last-minute cooking, arranging the buffet table and dishes—both Jessie's china and all that she could borrow—in addition to taking a leisurely bath and washing her long silvery hair. The wedding was scheduled for five o'clock, the last of the rites of the church to be performed by the Reverend Mr. Creston during his sojourn in Bath Town.

In Carrie's room where she was dressing, Madeline suddenly became breathless and had to sit down. Her heart was palpitating so hard she was afraid it was visible through her thin chemise. What if she should faint in the middle of the ceremony? What if Gavin should change his mind and not appear at the Roland house at the appointed hour? What if . . .

Jessie and Carrie entered at that moment, Jessie resplendent in blue satin and Carrie more doll-like than ever in a red Christmas dress that Jessie had made for the occasion, her honey-colored hair hanging in long curls.

"Why are you just sitting there?" Jessie asked. "It's almost time. Tom Milton has already started playing."

Madeline was well aware of that fact. It was the sound of the violin and the sudden hush of voices below that had made her breathless.

"Is Gavin here?"

"He's waiting in the back room," Carrie said, clapping her hands in excitement. "He's going to enter from there."

"Here, let me help you." Jessie reached for the white gown lying across the bed. "Magnificent!" she breathed. "You will be the most beautiful bride ever married in the Colonies."

The most terrified anyway, Madeline thought, raising her arms for Jessie to slip the underskirt over her head, followed by the overskirt of white lace. The fingertip veil was held in place by Jessie's pearls in a circlet, lent for the occasion.

"Oh, Miss Boyd!" Carrie cried, unable to say more. She stared at the bride, as wide-eyed as a marigold, obviously thinking of the day she herself would be in Madeline's place.

"She won't be Miss Boyd but a few minutes longer," Jessie said. "She will soon be Mrs. Durant."

Impulsively, Madeline hugged the child. "You and Con must stop being so formal anyway," she said. "Call me Madeline."

Carrie looked at her mother to be sure this met with

her approval and when Jessie nodded she said, "All right, Madeline. I'll go tell Con."

There was silence after she left the room. Finally, Jessie said, "I envy you, Madeline. You have so much joy ahead of you."

Madeline smiled wistfully. "I hope so . . . but you sound as if all *your* joy were behind you."

"I didn't mean to," Jessie said, "because I know it isn't. I was just thinking that you and Gavin can be happy together with no long separation to worry about. I think if I had known when I married Cyrus that he would leave me behind for two years while he settled himself in a new land, I would have had second thoughts about the marriage. Gavin is already settled, so you don't have to worry. Oh, listen! Tom has started the wedding song." She went to the door, opened it, and told the waiting Cyrus to come in. It was on his arm that Madeline would enter the front room. Jessie gave her a last hug, stood back and inspected her one more time, then went belowstairs to join the others.

Trembling slightly, Madeline put her hand on Cyrus's arm.

"Gavin is champing at the bit to get through this part of it and take you home," Cyrus said reassuringly.

The words did not reassure her. Once again, her fear of what was to come and her possible reaction to it caused a catch in her breath. Either not noticing or else thinking all brides should be that nervous, Cyrus led her down the stairs and then, before she was quite aware of it, they began walking slowly over the white runner toward the altar, the white robed Mr. Creston . . . and Gavin.

The bridegroom, in his one-dress outfit, was as well

turned out as if he were getting married in Westminster Abbey. He wore an exquisitely fitting midnight blue dress coat and satin knee-breeches of the same color. His ruffled white blouse was only partially hidden by an intricately tied neckcloth. His white silk hose showed off his muscular legs to perfection.

He did not take his eyes off Madeline as she and Cyrus progressed down the aisle, and his appreciation of the beauty he was getting was obvious to all—all but Madeline. Her first glance toward the altar took him in, all of him, and then she looked down as though afraid to stare back into those piercing blue eyes.

In front of the altar, as they stood side by side, she did look up at him, almost pleadingly, and, without waiting for Cyrus to place her hand in his, he took her hand, holding it firmly.

A sudden feeling of well-being came over Madeline then. It would be all right; she did not have to worry any more. She loved Gavin and he loved her. He was not like those other men who had cared nothing for her and wanted only the use of her body for a short while. He wanted her for always. She listened intently to the words Reverend Creston read from the Book of Common Prayer as she promised to love, honor, and obey Gavin in sickness and in health, forsaking all others, so long as they both lived.

Forsaking all others meant forsaking also the memories of those wretched men that had been haunting her, she told herself. She would never think of them again.

The vows spoken, they were pronounced man and wife and blessed by the priest. Then, to a joyous air from Tom Milton's violin, they went back up the aisle together, both faces wreathed in wide smiles, and went into the dining parlor where the wedding feast awaited them and the guests. Just through the door, before others had time to follow, Gavin took her in his arms, kissing her soundly once, and then again. "I hope we don't have to stay and be sociable too long," he said, confirming Cyrus's earlier assessment of Gavin's impatience. "I would just as soon leave now."

Almost everyone in Bath Town attended the wedding and the sumptious feast that followed: the Mulligans, the Martins, the others whom Madeline had met and many she had not, as well as all of her fellow passengers on the *Sea Lion*. Following the ceremony, Elizabeth Milton was the first into the dining parlor after the bride and groom. Hugging Madeline, she said, "Why didn't you tell us your fiancé was so handsome? We would all have been green with envy."

Quickly looking at Gavin to see if he detected anything strange about the remark, she saw that he didn't. "You have no reason to turn green, Elizabeth. Tom is quite handsome himself, and I do want to thank him for playing the violin so beautifully for us. Oh, here he comes now." She excused herself and turned to meet the inrush of guests.

Side by side, she and Gavin spoke to everyone, receiving kisses and hearty congratulations. Then, when the last of the guests had crowded around the table, they left their place beside the door and went to the head of the line to receive the first plates. Never had Madeline seen so much food, so many unexpected delicacies. Even the pot supper had not had such a variety: fish, lobster, poultry, ham, roasts of beef and pork, haunches of venison, every vegetable known to grow in new world soil that could be preserved, fresh loaves of bread and muffins, cakes and pastries and pies.

It was noted by one and all that the newlyweds ate sparingly, and much was made of it.

"Better eat heartily, Gavin," Les Mulligan called across the room. "You'll need your strength . . . later."

Amid laughter, Madeline blushed. She wished people had not become so open with their risqué remarks and insinuating glances; it was enough to make one think the whole world was undergoing a decline in morals.

From time to time Madeline noticed that Gavin kept looking toward a window. "Is someone out there?" she asked, curious.

"No, but it is dark now. Do you think we could steal away and leave the others to the revelry?"

"Jessie said there would be dancing after supper," she said. "They'll move the table and other furniture to the wall and Tom will play again."

"Do you want to stay?" He looked as though he might go into a decline if she said yes.

For an instant only, she was tempted to postpone the moment they would be alone, then, smiling, she shook her head. "I am ready whenever you are."

"I am ready *now*."

They sought out Jessie and Cyrus and poured out their gratitude for the wedding and supper, then with the Rolands' help, managed to slip out the back door to Gavin's waiting wagon.

"I thought you'd bring the cart," Madeline said as he helped her up.

"In the cart you can't sit beside me," he said simply, climbing up beside her and taking the reins in one hand, his other arm around his new wife. "Git'up, Walt!"

They talked about the wedding and the supper as they drove out of Bath Town, then for the rest of the way they were silent, though it was not an uncomfortable silence. Madeline, a heavy cloak over her wedding gown, felt both at ease and at peace and wondered why she had ever dreaded this night. It had been nothing but bridal nerves—as Jessie had said—and had had nothing at all to do with that seemingly long ago, faraway time when she had lured men back to Rufus's lair.

Back at the cabin, she felt she had been away for weeks rather than a little over twenty-four hours. "It's so good to be home," she said to Gavin as, in his arms, he lifted her from the wagon. Instead of answering, he gave her a lingering kiss. Then, without putting her down, he carried her inside the cabin.

She was astonished by the transformation as he put her on her feet again and went about lighting candles and a lamp. Like the Roland house, the cabin was decorated for Christmas with red-bowed wreaths, evergreens around the walls, and in a corner, a little cedar Christmas tree decorated with ribbons and colored paper. She sucked in her breath. It was obvious Gavin must have stayed up most of last night working to get it ready for her. "Oh, Gavin, it's lovely," she said softly. "Thank you."

And then she noticed the biggest difference in the room, a change she had overlooked because of the decorations. There was no blanket dividing the room, no blanket in sight anywhere except for the quilt on the bed. Even the rope which had held the blanket had been taken down.

Gavin, noticing where her eyes were, said, "That's an improvement, isn't it?"

She nodded, reddening.

"I'll go put Walt up and feed him while you . . . while you're getting out of your wedding finery," he said, and was out the door before she could reply.

She undressed hurriedly, not wanting him to return and catch her half in, half out of the sky blue nightdress with the lace collar and cuffs. When he did return, she was sitting on the foot of the bed, brushing her long, pale hair.

He did not go to her immediately, surprising her. Instead, he went to the hearth and removed the stone where he kept the purse. From beneath the purse, he took a paper which he brought to her.

"This is my wedding gift to you," he said. "You may tear it up and forget it ever existed."

It was her indenture paper. She looked at it for a moment, not quite sure of his intention. Then, in a rush of gratitude and love, she knew he was offering her her freedom. She would be in servitude to no man for the next four years . . . or ever.

Unless she wanted to.

She looked at him, tears glistening in her gray eyes, love in every syllable she uttered. "You may extend the date of indenture." She gave the paper back to him. "I want to be in bondage to you for as long as I live. That is my gift to you."

"Oh, my love!" he said hoarsely, and could say no

more. He pushed her back toward the head of the bed, then went about the cabin blowing out the candles and lamp he had just lit, except for two candles at bedside. He returned to her then, leaning over the bed, his hands caressing her body, his mouth slowly descending to hers.

She felt her body straining toward him as his kiss set her on fire. At the same time, his hands had gone beneath the blue nightdress and were gradually easing it up over her legs, her thighs, her hips, her breasts and then her head. Only when it was completely removed did he permit himself the luxury of taking in her whole body. She felt his eyes burning into her nakedness like hot coals; she wanted, and yet did not want, to cover herself with the quilt. Her fingers reached for it, but when she saw the pure pleasure in his eyes and knew that it was there because of her, she forgot the guilt. Taking him by the shoulders, she pressed him to her, but he pulled back, whispering, "Wait . . ."

He removed his clothing in such haste that she was almost unaware he had done so until he lay beside her and she felt his flesh, the lean hardness of him, against her softness. There was no thought in her mind now except for him, his body, her body, and the pleasure they were giving each other.

He nibbled gently at her earlobe, then trailed kisses across her face to the hollow of her throat, where the flick of his tongue again made her arch to him, wanting to feel the entire length of his body against hers. Then his mouth moved downward, kissing each of her breasts until she began to writhe. She closed her eyes, unwilling for him to see right then the effect he was having on her, and for a moment he gave her surcease, remaining still himself like a general regrouping his forces before another attack.

Then she felt his hands, again softly caressing her body, moving across her shoulders to her breasts, lingering there, stroking, stroking, the small velvety mounds. Her spine tingled and her breasts jutted to peaks as the stroking hand moved to her hips, across her abdomen, and then to that secret part of her, still stroking, caressing, sparking her need for him to a full blaze.

Fully aroused, her hands became as active as his and fluttered about his body like small butterflies lighting here and there, leaving sensations that caused Gavin to groan in urgency, his own caressing fingers becoming frenzied, causing a low moan of pleasure to escape her throat. She was feverish with desire, a feeling she had never before experienced. There was pressure on her as she felt his hard, muscular body mount hers, felt his throbbing manhood suddenly inside her. There was only a moment of discomfort, forgotten at once in the rhythm and immediacy of love that was like a storm, with elements working together slowly, wind and rain mixing and mingling stronger and stronger until the full fury of the storm was upon them in hurricane proportions, raging out of control, more and more frenzied, exploding finally in a thunderbolt of passion that left them both shivering and breathless in each other's arms where they lay silent for a long time.

"I love you, my Madeline," Gavin whispered finally.

She held him even closer, "And I you. Oh, Gavin, so much."

Involuntarily, wordlessly, the ritual began again as

his mouth covered hers, his hands traveled the distance of her from face to hips, this time a more familiar journey. Again they made love, gently, without the frantic urgency of the first time, savoring the sight and feel and taste of each other until their desire finally was slaked and sleep was upon them.

Madeline's last thought before giving in completely to her warm drowsiness was: this is perfect; I'll never be unhappy again as long as I have Gavin. It is all like a beautiful dream.

And then she was lost, to sleep and to dreams.

Chapter Eleven

THE "BEAUTIFUL DREAM" LASTED FOR THREE WEEKS and then the dream world began to give way to the world of reality.

On Christmas day and for a week thereafter Gavin and Madeline were snowed in. The light snow began falling Christmas morning and continued to fall for three days, making it impossible to go more than a few feet from the cabin, though Gavin, wearing hip boots, did make it to the shed to feed Walt and to bring back wood for the fire. Except for these mild inconveniences, they considered the snow a blessing for if they could not go to town, neither could the townspeople come to the cabin. They were blissfully alone with little to do except to revel in each other and their love.

The departure of the snow marked the departure also of their idyllic existence, though its going was so gradual as not to be noticed at first.

It was a late afternoon in the middle of January when the first stirrings—that would later bring about near cataclysm—began in a usual enough way. Madeline and Gavin were sitting before the fire discussing whether it would be worthwhile to get a loom or a spinning wheel. "If you don't like that kind of work, why bother with it?" Gavin asked. "It's very little savings, and we can buy what we need at Mulligan's."

"But all the other women make everything they need. I feel so useless!" It was almost a cry of complaint.

"Useless! You?" Gavin scoffed. "You do more work than any three of the town wives. Forget it, my sweet. I have a feeling that along with fraying cloth, your disposition could also become a bit frayed from bending over one of those contraptions."

She smiled happily. It was exactly what she had wanted to hear because she had been afraid he might think, since all the other women were so expert at sewing and spinning and weaving, that she should be also.

The sudden knock at the door startled them both. Gavin got up and opened the door, exclaiming, "Wes! Come on in. This is a surprise."

"Good afternoon, Wes. You're our first visitor." Madeline stood to greet their guest while Gavin pulled another chair up to the fire.

"Gavin, Madeline." Wes Martin bowed gravely to both as though meeting them for the first time. "I wouldn't have bothered you, but . . ."

"Bother!" Gavin said. "We have been thinking about going into town just to be sure the town is still there. Besides, we're getting low on supplies. I stocked up right before the wedding, but I hadn't counted on a snow that would last so long."

"That reminds me . . ." Wes went back outside, then returned carrying a large box. "We were all going to come pounding you after the first week. Since we couldn't, I brought some of the stuff."

Madeline looked into the huge box, marveling at what she saw: a pound of butter, a pound of cheese, a pound cake, a pound of several different vegetables, a roast, some jams and jellies and cremes. "Look, Gavin!" she cried. "We won't have to go into town for a long time." Turning to Wes, "Thank you—and everybody. But what do you mean by pounding?"

"It's customary around here to pound newlyweds and new arrivals to the colony," he explained. "That means take them a pound of as many different kinds of food as possible."

"A great custom," Gavin said. "We're doubly glad to see you."

"You may not be when you hear the news I bring," Wes said as they all sat down. "Remember the rumors back in October, Gavin, about the Lords sending another governor?"

"Yes, but when no governor appeared, I assumed it was just that, another rumor."

"Well, our rumor has arrived in person," Wes said. "A man named Edward Hyde is here claiming the governorship."

"Here in Bath Town?" Gavin asked.

"Not yet, but soon, I understand," Wes said. "He has arrived on these shores. Probably in New Bern, or maybe Virginia. The thing is, he has no official papers from the Lords Proprietor stating that he is, in fact, governor. The way we feel around here—well, we aren't going to accept him as governor. We've got no complaint with Cary; I guess he's as good as anybody. At least, with his farm right here on the Pamlico River, he's one of us. God knows what this new man is like."

Gavin nodded thoughtfully. "Maybe without papers he won't try to take over."

"Word has come that, if necessary, he'll bring a regiment in with him to establish him as governor," Wes said as sorrowfully as though he were announcing a death, and, indeed, if the events he predicted came to pass, there would be more than one death.

Madeline sighed. "I have never understood why people can't live together peaceably."

"Because some have a voracious appetite for power," Gavin said.

"Amen," Wes said. "I don't know why anybody would even *want* to be governor of this godforsaken colony."

Gavin looked surprised. "I thought you liked it here, Wes."

"I do. I like everything except the way we're governed." His face contorted in a ferocious frown. "We ought to do our own governing instead of those people over yonder." He pointed in what he assumed was the general direction of England. "Well, I've got to get back. Told the wife I'd be home before dark."

"Thank you again for this marvelous box," Madeline said. "Tell the others I'll thank them in person as soon as I get to town."

"Jessie Roland wants to know when that will be," Wes said.

"Probably next week," Gavin said. "You've saved us from having to go sooner. You'll let us know if you hear more about the new governor, won't you?"

"You can count on it."

After he left Gavin and Madeline busied themselves

putting the food he had brought into the larder, and Gavin took that which might spoil to the stream behind the house where he put it in an airtight bucket. Returning to the house, he sat contentedly watching Madeline as she prepared their supper.

During the meal they talked of Wes Martin's visit, though they did not mention the news he had brought. They also talked about friends in town and a dozen other things. Madeline wondered why Gavin did not mention the subject which must be uppermost in his mind—and she noted a tiny frown appearing on his face from time to time—but she asked him no questions, nor did she broach the subject herself. If he had some good reason for not wanting to talk about it, then she, even without knowing the reason, would respect it.

Weeks passed and the worst of the winter was over, giving way to a blustery March. Madeline and Gavin went to town occassionally, but not as often as Madeline had thought they would. The talk in Bath, among the men at least, was only about Edward Hyde and his efforts to take over the reins of government from Thomas Cary. Always, on their return home, Madeline would notice worry lines creeping into Gavin's face, and once she even ventured to ask what was wrong, though she strongly suspected that he did not want to talk about it.

"There is nothing wrong . . . yet," he replied, trying to give her a reassuring smile. "I hope cool, level heads will prevail."

That was all he would say. Silently, she agreed with him, though she was unsure what would happen if cool, level heads did not prevail. She found it impossible to believe the colonists would fight among themselves. They were too few in number, the areas of population too separated.

More time passed and when nothing untoward transpired, Madeline began to relax. Though rumors persisted, Tom Cary was still governor and it seemed likely that Hyde would not try to press his claim. After all, with no commission to back him up, how could he simply step in and take over the government of North Carolina?

The spring planting began in earnest, with both the townspeople and those of the neighboring farms and plantations giving their time and interest to the soil and the crops rather than to political rumors. Once again Gavin was busy from sunup to sundown, tilling his acreage and planting tobacco, cotton, and vegetables. Madeline worked alongside him, liking outdoor work far better than working inside the house. "We can see the results out here," she said.

Gavin laughed. "If you'd let the house get dirty enough, you would see the results when you clean. You *do* see results when you wash our filthy clothing, don't you?"

She had to admit that she did, adding that, even so, she preferred to be outside with him.

The change in their lives that had started gradually with a rumor in October and a confirmed rumor in January, now sped to a climax. Just after dawn on what promised to be a beautiful spring day, Gavin was visited by eight citizens of Bath Town, among whom were Wes Martin, Cyrus Roland, and Les Mulligan.

Gavin and Madeline were just finishing breakfast and preparing to go to the fields when they heard the approaching horses' hooves and went to the door.

Gavin stiffened suddenly when he recognized the men.

"What could it be?" Madeline asked automatically, not expecting an answer.

"War," Gavin said quietly. They both went outside to greet the men. Wes obviously had been appointed spokesman for, though they all said good morning, it was Wes who stepped forward.

"It's come, Gavin," he said. "Trouble of the worst kind."

Gavin nodded. "I've been expecting it."

This surprised Madeline for Gavin had seemed as relaxed as she, and she thought he had come to the conclusion that since there had been no trouble in these past weeks, there would be none, that Edward Hyde would go back to England, his cause a lost one.

"Hyde has declared Cary in open rebellion because he won't relinquish the governorship to him," Wes said. "He has gathered an army and says he will seize Cary by force. You know we can't allow this. Since Cary is one of us, Bath Town is like the seat of government."

Gavin nodded. He already knew what was coming, had known that it would come even before the delegation arrived. His battle would have to be fought with his conscience now, not on a battlefield later.

Cyrus Roland stepped forward and stood beside Wes. "All of us in Bath Town are going to rally to Cary's side, and we need every man who can hold a musket. They say Hyde has a whole regiment at his disposal."

There was a slight pause as though the eight men were waiting for Gavin to volunteer. When he said nothing, Cyrus continued, "You know how much the people around here respect you, Gavin. We not only want you to join us, we want you to lead us. There'll be two, possibly three different groups who will defend Cary's home on three sides, and Cary and his folks can take care of the river side."

Even before Cyrus finished, Gavin began slowly to shake his head, then he said, "Why is Cary resisting? Why must you fight?"

"Good God, man, how can you ask such a question?" Les Mulligan entered the conversation now and the other men talked softly among themselves. "Here is Hyde claiming to be governor and not one scrap of paper to prove it."

"Nor is there any way to disprove what he says," Gavin pointed out. "He says the Lords Proprietor sent him to govern. Does any one of you know for a fact that he is lying? I say we shouldn't take sides. Until we know for sure that Hyde is an imposter, we should not discredit him. After all, the real rule of the Colonies is in England."

"Are you saying you won't join us?" Wes asked. "You mean you'd just let this man come in here and take over, throwing Cary out . . . or worse?"

"Until I know who is right, I will not take sides," Gavin said, adding, "nor will I bear arms against any man."

An oath came from one of the men, a vulgarity from

another. "That Quaker stuff again," Wes said, and Cyrus said at the same time, "Tom Cary is a Quaker and you don't see him backing off from the fight."

"Cary is the keeper of his conscience and I am the keeper of mine," Gavin said.

"You're not going to do one damned thing to help, are you?" Lester Mulligan growled.

"I will do anything I can to help, short of fighting," Gavin told them.

The men, all but Cyrus Roland, turned away, mounted their horses and started back toward the woods. Madeline heard the mutterings among them as they rode away—"bloody coward," and "white-livered milksop," and "yellow streak for a backbone"—and she was seething with anger. At that moment she would gladly have fought the eight of them, borne arms against them and used whatever weapon was available. To call Gavin cowardly because his conscience forbade his wantonly killing or maiming others was enough to send her into battle, banners flying.

Cyrus said nothing for a moment, looking from one to the other of them. Then he crossed the few feet separating them, standing beside them, his slightly stooped shoulders drooping even more. For the first time, Madeline noticed that his dark, graying hair looked as though it had not been combed since he left his bed. He probably had rushed out to join the others in confronting Gavin. No, that was the wrong word, she thought, for at that point Cyrus had no way of knowing it would be a confrontation—though she supposed if he knew Gavin at all he must have guessed it.

Finally he said, "Won't you reconsider, Gavin? We need you. We need everyone we can get."

"Even if I were sure that Hyde is an imposter, I would not take up arms against another human being," Gavin said.

"You're a good shot," Cyrus said, a note of cynicism in his voice. "I've hunted with you."

"I kill animals for food," Gavin said simply.

Cyrus looked at Madeline. "Can you make him change his mind? The future of the colony may depend upon it."

"*May!*" Gavin repeated. "You don't even know if you have a just cause."

Madeline shook her head. "I would not try to make him go against his conscience."

Cyrus grunted. "Then stay here and be damned! We'll all go fight for your rights while you sit here nursing that streak of cowardice you call a conscience. I never though I'd say it, Gavin. I never thought I'd even *think* it, but you have the courage of a scared rabbit." He started toward his horse, then turned around. "Neither of you will be welcome in the Roland house again."

"But Cy . . ." Madeline began, but Gavin hushed her. "Let him go," he said.

"But he and Jessie are our *friends,* Gavin. We can't let it end like this."

Cyrus heard her and turned around again. "Will you try to convince your husband that he is wrong about this? He *is* wrong, you know."

Madeline emitted a long sigh and shook her head sadly. "No," she said at last, "I have found Gavin to be both a kind and a wise man. I will stick by his decision."

Cyrus mounted his horse. "I hope my eyes never fall on either of you again." He dug his heels into the horse's flanks and took off hell for leather in the direction of town.

On the verge of tears, Madeline looked at Gavin. She was too hurt to say anything for, next to Gavin, she felt closer to Jessie than anyone else in the colony. She could not bear the thought of not having Jessie and her family as friends any more.

Gavin did not speak either. He put his arm around her and, together, they went to the fields to resume the spring planting.

The men of the Bath Town area, with the exception of a few Quakers, were organized and ready for battle within a week. Gavin was surprised to find that some Quakers, like Cary, were willing, even eager, to do battle for their feisty Quaker governor. Although most of the people were for Cary, there were some who had not wanted him for governor from the first and they quickly joined Hyde's complement, and there were others, like Gavin, who were not sure who was in the right and preferred not to fight over a murky cause. These finally joined with Cary's men, thinking the status quo probably better for them and their families than a change. Who knew what this Edward Hyde was like or what the Lords Proprietor had told him to do once he was governor?

The fact that Hyde had declared Cary in open rebellion also riled most of the colonists who thought Cary was nothing of the sort: he had been declared the lawful governor and he was trying to govern lawfully. That was all anyone, including those old men in England, should ask.

At first the fighting was spasmodic, with few casualties, and though there were battles in the area of Bath, they never erupted within the town itself. To everyone but Hyde and Cary, it seemed to be only a half-hearted cause.

Then, in May, there was a drastic change.

Hyde, who had established a home on Salmon Creek, miles from Bath Town, assembled eighty men under arms. On May 27, he crossed the Albemarle Sound and acquired seventy more men from the territory around the Roanoke River. With this force, Hyde marched for two days to the Pamlico River home of Thomas Cary. Cary, however, had got wind of what was descending upon him, so he fled downriver to the home of his friend, Robert Daniel, a former governor of the colony. On finding Cary gone, Hyde and his men proceeded to the Daniel house, but found it too well-fortified to storm. Daniel, anticipating Hyde's move, had brought in forty armed men and five cannon to protect Cary. When Hyde saw there was no hope of getting a surrender from his enemy, he returned to the Albemarle region.

Much encouraged by this retreat, Cary's followers then began an attack on Hyde with a brigantine and several smaller vessels. Hyde, who now had only sixty men under arms and two cannon, seemed to be defeated even before the battle began when the two strong landing groups from the brigantine headed for shore. However, at that moment, a shot from one of the two cannon on shore severed the brigantine's mast, causing the Cary forces to panic. They immediately cut anchor and sailed away, only to be pursued by Hyde's best men in a sloop. When the sloop finally overtook them, the brigantine was found beached with only three men aboard, the others having fled to their homes. Seizing the brigantine with all her guns and ammunition, Hyde thus won his first decisive victory.

It did not take Cary long to regroup. He began to fortify another island in the Pamlico and amassed another large force of men. Hyde's attempts to drive Cary from the island were futile and for a while it looked as though the Hyde cause was lost.

The "self-proclaimed governor" found an unexpected friend in the governor of Virginia, however. Governor Alexander Spottswood decided to go to the aid of the Hyde faction and readied his militia to march into North Carolina. But it was never necessary for the men to cross the border. A company of royal English marines from guardships in Chesapeake Bay were sent to aid Hyde in July. Seeing them, the Cary men surrendered without firing a shot. They were unwilling to fire upon the royal standard and be charged with treason against the Queen. Cary and his lieutenants fled at once back to his home on the Pamlico where Cary was subsequently seized.

Although there was never a battle in Bath Town, the fighting had a disrupting effect upon the people and every aspect of their lives. During the long absences of the fighting men, the crops went to wrack and ruin and the supply of meat became low, meaning that some families, who expected to be well-fed from their own gardens and fields, were actually hungry. Also during these months, repairs to cabins, houses, and barns were neglected since there was no one to do the work. Cotton was white in the fields, unpicked, unbaled, and tobacco was untopped, resembling a flowering weed. In addition to the immediate emergencies and hard times, there was no hope for better times ahead with the money crops languishing in the fields.

Madeline and Gavin were not untouched by the hardships in spite of the fact that Gavin was at home and could tend his crops, repair his buildings, and hunt for meat. One night in May as they both lay sleepless on the rope bed, Madeline said, "As hard as you have worked today, you should have been asleep an hour ago. Why do you keep turning and tossing?"

"Sorry to disturb you," Gavin said without answering her question. "It seems you can't sleep either."

"I know. I keep wondering how long the fighting will last, how it will all come out."

"Nothing good ever comes out of fighting," Gavin said, "not even when you are victorious. Just look about you. Even if the Cary forces come home in glorious triumph, they are coming home to hungry families, ruined crops, leaking roofs, dilapidated barns. It will be as though they just landed on these shores. They will have to begin all over."

"I wish we could do something to help," Madeline said.

"Do you mean that?"

"Of course. Why else would I have said it?"

The sigh which came from Gavin was one of relief. "It has been bothering me for a long time," he said. "I want to help where I can, but I wasn't sure how you would feel about it since we have been ostracized."

"I want to help too," she said quickly. "I have been feeling guilty every time I look at our fields, every time I pick vegetables or cook a stew or a roast."

"Would you be willing to work with me in others' fields?" he asked. "It will be back-breaking, trying to do our own work as well as take care of as many others as possible."

"Of course I'd be willing," she said. "More than willing."

"Tomorrow we'll begin," Gavin said. He turned over one more time and then was asleep.

The following day Gavin visited those Quakers in the area who had elected not to fight and solicited their help in taking care of the families of the fighting men. All agreed, but with their own businesses to run or farms to tend, there was only so much time they could allow for others.

With the help of fewer than a dozen others, Gavin and Madeline worked daily to do what they could to aid their neighbors in salvaging crops and making necessary repairs, and Gavin went on frequent hunting expeditions to keep meat on most of the tables of Bath Town. Sometimes they found themselves in their own fields after dark, working by lanternlight, and there were many nights when the two of them got less than three hours sleep.

Even wearing thick gloves, Madeline's hands became red and sore from blisters, and her skin, after burning and peeling, finally became as brown as Gavin's. At the same time, her pale hair became even lighter, a tremendous contrast—though not an unbecoming one—to her darkened complexion.

There was no time for anything but work. Even lovemaking, which until now had seemed the core of their existence, was postponed because of extreme fatigue.

"I may not be fighting, but I feel battle-scarred and

battle-weary," Gavin said one night in June as he lay beside Madeline, his hand resting lightly across her breasts. All day he had thought about her as he gathered vegetables and distributed them, thought about her soft lips, the feel of her breasts as his hand stroked them, her eager responses to him and to love. Tonight he would see that they retired earlier than usual, tonight would be for them. They deserved one night for themselves, didn't they? But it had been after midnight before they had finished in their own vegetable garden and even as they undressed and put on their nightclothes, they were preoccupied with what was to be done the next day.

"I think I should put up some of the corn and beans tomorrow," Madeline said. "We may need them worse this winter than we do right now."

"I need to go out tomorrow and try to get a deer or two," Gavin said. "The meat supply is low again in town."

Now, with his hand lying quiet on Madeline's breast, it was all he could do to muster the energy to kiss her goodnight. He was asleep almost before his head was back on his own pillow.

Spring turned to hot, humid summer and still the fighting went on. When they were in town helping with repairs or gardens or taking food to Mulligan's store to be distributed, Madeline and Gavin heard the latest news from wherever the battle happened to be raging at that time. Though there had been casualties from Bath Town, so far none of their friends had been among them.

"We talk as though we still have friends here,"

Madeline said bitterly when they were remarking on the subject. Even though she and Gavin worked themselves into a state of total exhaustion daily for the people of the area, they remained, if no longer completely ostracized, at least out of favor. Only Lucinda Mulligan, who was aware of how much the Durants were doing for others, was civil to them. It was from her that they heard the news of the battles and kept in touch with the homefront as well.

One afternoon when Gavin had returned from hunting and had dressed the deer he brought back, Madeline went with him in the wagon to take the meat to Mulligan's where it would be divided and given to those most in need. As they were leaving the store after depositing the last of the meat in the huge larder, they met Jessie and Carrie going into the store.

It was the first time Madeline had seen her friend since Cyrus had told the Durants they were no longer welcome in the Roland home. Madeline assumed that Cyrus had forbidden his wife to go to their cabin as well, so she had made no effort to get in touch with Jessie, but she could not believe that Jessie felt the hostility for her that Cyrus did.

"Jessie! Carrie!" she cried, ready to hug them both, but waited just a split second to be sure such effusiveness was wanted.

It was not. Jessie stared at her coldly, then nodded slightly. Carrie, however, flung herself at Madeline, saying "Why haven't you been to see us, Madeline? We've missed you. We miss my father, too. He's off fighting."

Madeline hugged the child and stroked her hair, "I know, sweet. We hope he'll be home soon . . . and all the others." She looked at Jessie. "How are you getting along?"

"Not as well as *some* people," Jessie said coldly. "Not nearly as well as those whose husbands were too cowardly to fight."

Madeline drew back as though she had been struck in the face. She could have imagined remoteness from Jessie, but never viciousness, never those icy tones or that frigid look.

"Come, Carrie, we haven't time to dawdle." Jessie took the child's hand and all but pulled her into the store.

"Oh, Gavin," Madeline said, tears in her eyes.

He helped her into the wagon. "Nothing comes of war but death, destruction, ruin, and bitterness," he said. "Maybe some day people will learn. Maybe some day they will be too rational, too clear thinking to allow war . . . but I doubt it."

The effects of the Cary Rebellion on the people of Bath County continued to worsen as June turned into July and a long drought began. The crops that had not already been lost began to wither and dry up in the fields. Gavin, Madeline, and their handful of helpers worked even more frantically, but it was impossible for a few to do what had been done before by many, and the crop losses were staggering.

"Will it never end?" Madeline asked perfunctorily, not expecting an answer. "I'm even beyond caring now who wins as long as it is soon over. What difference does it make in the long run whether Cary or Hyde is governor?"

"As in most wars, it is a principle they are fighting

over," Gavin said, "not positive action or misdeed. I imagine it matters less and less to the men who are fighting who is governor also."

"No matter which man wins, he will only be a puppet in the hands of the Lords Proprietor," she said. "The real rule will always be in England."

Gavin smiled ruefully. "Not always, I think . . . and that will lead to a bigger war and even more devastation."

Their never-ending fatigue kept them in the depths of depression most of the time. Though each tried to put on a cheerful face for the other, they both knew that until things were back to normal, their bodies, their dispositions, their marriage, their very lives would suffer. And buried deep in both was the sure knowledge that nothing would ever be "back to normal" again.

It was in mid-July, a scorching day, when Madeline and Gavin were leaving Mulligan's Store that they heard horse hooves galloping over the sunbaked earth. Standing on the steps of the store, they waited, afraid to step into the street lest they be run over.

The horseman was James Buncomb, one of the eight men who had gone to the Durant cabin that long-ago day to ask Gavin to join them in the fight. The horse was in a lather and Buncomb, hoarse from yelling, was crying something unintelligible at the top of his fast-fading voice.

Gavin stepped out into the street and caught the horse's reins. "Stop!" he said. "What is it?"

"Out of my way, scum!" Buncomb attempted to spur the horse on, but Gavin would not relinquish his hold.

"Tell me!" he said. "Tell me what has happened."

"It's over," Buncomb said, suddenly slumping in the saddle. "It's all over."

Gavin stared at him, unbelieving. "How? Where?"

"Shouldn't you ask 'who?' instead?" Buncomb said sarcastically. "But no, I suppose it makes no difference to you whether Cary lives or dies."

"Tell me, man!" Gavin had grabbed Buncomb by the leg and was about to pull him off the horse.

"We were met by a company of royal marines," Buncomb said, "and no one would fire on them. The whole thing ended just like that, as quiet as death. No cannon, not a gunshot."

"What happened to our men?" Gavin asked.

"Ha! Some nerve you've got, Durant, calling them 'our men'. They aren't *your* men."

By this time a sizable crowd of women and children had gathered around and were divided in giving dirty looks to Gavin and Madeline and looks of acute curiosity to Buncomb.

"Please," Madeline said, trying to remain calm and unperturbed, at least outwardly, "please tell us what happened."

"Our men turned tail and ran," Buncomb said. "There was nothing else they could do. But don't get the wrong idea, Durant. There wasn't a coward among them. They simply knew better than to fire on the flag and get charged with treason."

"What about Cary?" someone in the crowd asked. "Where is he now?"

"He and some of his lieutenants went to his plantation, but Hyde's men went right after them," Buncomb said. "They seized Cary and I heard that Hyde said he was going to see that Cary was sent back to England where he wouldn't bother anybody anymore."

"So Hyde is governor now," Gavin murmured. "I wonder if we'll know the difference?"

There was no answer to the question. Buncomb rode on, telling his news about the countryside, and the crowd disbanded, some to go home and give thanks that the lengthy confrontation was over, others to weep that so much havoc had been wrought for nothing.

Gavin and Madeline returned to their cabin in a pensive mood. They neither felt like celebrating nor weeping; they only felt like being quiet and being together—since neither was quite sure that, for them, the unpleasantness was really over.

"Now that Cary has been seized, the rebellion is over . . . to all intents and purposes," Gavin said, "but the aftermath could still be bitter, especially for us."

And they were not long in finding that the people of Bath Town, though civil to them because of their unstinting help, still were not overly friendly.

Chapter Twelve

THE CHANGES THAT HAD BEGUN IN THEIR LIVES MONTHS earlier continued in August, and it seemed to Madeline (and she supposed to Gavin too, though, for some reason, she was reluctant to bring up the subject to him) that a great deal of the quality of their daily living that they had taken for granted before was missing now.

Their crops, while not a loss, had suffered from less than total care. In spite of their frantic efforts, it had been impossible to get good yields from their own fields as well as dozens of others throughout the county in which they had worked during the Cary Rebellion. With luck, they could just make it through the winter with the money the cotton and tobacco would bring in.

Madeline spent the entire month of August putting up fruits and vegetables. At least, if they did not have enough money for some necessities, they would be able to eat. And, of course, Gavin could go on regular hunting expeditions to keep meat on the table. Somehow, they would manage . . . probably better than many others in the area whose crops had been total losses and who had suffered the most severe loss of all, that of having a husband or father die in the Rebellion.

The biggest change—as well as the most depressing one—was in their social life. Before the Rebellion, Madeline and Gavin had often gone into town for visits and socials. After the Rebellion, they were no longer welcome. Some of the residents of Bath County openly snubbed them, others spoke civilly—but just barely. In order to save themselves the embarrassment, they only went to town when necessary to pick up supplies from Mulligan's store. Lucinda Mulligan was polite to them, though she made it obvious that there was a limit to her courtesy. Lester, on the other hand, would leave the store part of the house any time the Durants entered. Having fought in the Rebellion from the first day to the last, he could not forgive Gavin his "cowardice." No matter that Gavin had worked the Mulligan garden and had helped Lucinda tremendously with distribution of food, any man worthy of being called a man would have fought for Tom Cary and his right to continue as governor of North Carolina.

Madeline found it no less than astonishing that Gavin could take the snubs, the cutting remarks, and the malevolent looks with the good grace that he did. Whereas she wanted to complain to him (though she never did) or to answer back to some of his detractors, he acted as though nothing were amiss, as though life were going on exactly as he wanted it to.

"How can you be so patient, so persevering all the time?" she asked one day, slightly annoyed that he had not even glanced up when a man they didn't know passed them on Water Street and muttered something about "that Quaker."

"Would you have me knock him down?" Gavin asked. "I've never seen him before in my life."

"All the more reason," she replied, disgruntled. "What right has a stranger to judge you?"

"As much right as I have to judge him—and knocking him down would certainly be a form of judgment."

"Are you trying for canonization?" she asked, really becoming miffed now.

He laughed. "I've never heard of any Quaker saints."

"You can be the first," she said, and then she laughed at her own ill humor in view of his even temper. "I'm sorry, Gavin. It's just that these people make me so mad sometimes, the way they treat you."

He took her hand. "I am only sorry that you have to bear the brunt of their anger with me when it is not your fault. But most memories are short, and I predict that we'll be back in their good graces before too long."

"How long?"

"Oh—a few months at most."

"We'll see." She was not as optimistic as he, but then he had not seen Jessie and Cyrus the last time they were in Mulligan's. The Rolands had started into the store, spotted Madeline and Gavin near the rear, and had instantly turned around and gone out again. Gavin had been helping Lucinda make up their order, so he had missed the snub, but Madeline had seen and had been left with tears in her eyes, not knowing which she felt more—angry or hurt.

The only aspect of their life that had undergone no change whatever was their all-consuming love for each other. To Gavin, Madeline was still as beautiful (in spite of sun-bronzed skin, a few freckles, and an even reedier look due to her hard work during the Rebellion), and he knew she always would be. There was a quality to her beauty that was unchanging, eternal. At eighty, she would still fascinate him, still keep him bewitched. No matter how tired he was after a day of picking cotton or curing tobacco in the hellishly hot little shed he had built in the field, he was always ready to take her in his arms, feel the softness of her against him, look at the glory of her womanhood, triumph in her trembling passion which matched his own as they reached ever new plateaus of ecstasy. He was sure the wonder of having her with him, of loving her for the rest of his life, would never end.

For Madeline it was much the same. She would always be thankful for her good fortune in finding Gavin and knowing his love. It had taken much heart-ache, revulsion, disgust, the crossing of an ocean to a new world, fear, resignation, and, finally, hope to bring her to this point in her life. But she knew now that as long as she had Gavin beside her, nothing in her life could ever be as bad as it had been before. Her love for him was so great that it sometimes frightened her. In the midst of cleaning the cabin she would stop suddenly and wonder if he was all right. The temperature in the little tobacco barn was often well over one hundred degrees. What if he should have a heatstroke? She would put down her broom or mop and go to the field to check. Or, if he went hunting, she was miserable until he returned. What if he should trip over roots or vines and accidentally shoot himself? Or what if some other hunter should mistake him for game and shoot him? She insisted that his expeditions last only one day for she couldn't stand the thought of having to worry all night. Also, she couldn't stand the thought of not having him beside her at night, not being able to feel the warmth of his body, the strength of his arms, the power and tingling excitement of his love. If anything should happen to Gavin, she would want to die also for she knew she could not live without him. She might survive him, but that would not be living. A world without Gavin would be a much lesser world, a world not worth living in.

Though she was sorry for the loss of her friends in Bath Town, though it grieved her to think they could turn against her, she did not despair. As long as she had Gavin and his love, she could not be unhappy.

Neither of them knew on the afternoon in late August when they went into town in the wagon that there were more devastating changes to come.

A ship, The *Good Faith*, had docked the afternoon before and Madeline was eager to get to Mulligan's to see the new fashions that had come in. She had heard Luncinda say during the summer that she had ordered two dozen gowns from a London modiste, and she wanted to see them before the other women bought them. Also, she and Gavin had sent for bed linens, towels, and a few pieces of furniture which were expected on the *Good Faith*.

They tied Walt in front of the store and went inside. Lester was standing behind one of the counters showing piece goods to two women whom Madeline recognized by sight but not by name. Gavin nodded to them, said, "Afternoon, Les," and waited behind the women for his turn at the counter. There was no response from Lester other than raising his eyebrows as the Durants came in the store.

Madeline went to the back of the store where Lucinda was folding ribbons onto a large card. "Afternoon, Lucinda. Did the gowns you were expecting come in on the *Good Faith?*"

Lucinda nodded. "Some did. The modiste only sent eight. I guess they think over there that there aren't a dozen women in the colony interested in the latest styles. I suppose they think we've all turned savage over here." It was obviously a sore point with her.

Madeline laughed. "If the modiste could see us in our buckskins and homespuns, they'd have no doubt left. May I see the gowns?"

"They're in the other room." Lucinda left the store part of the building.

Madeline looked across the room at Gavin who was still waiting for Les to finish with the women customers. Another man, wearing the uniform of the British marines, had come in and was standing beside Gavin. He must have been one of the marines who quelled the Rebellion, she thought. She had heard that some of them had remained in the area to be sure there were no more uprisings. There was something about the man that looked familiar, but since she knew none of the marines, she supposed she was imagining it.

Gavin, growing impatient, turned to the man beside him, saying in a low voice, "It may take those women the rest of the afternoon to make up their minds."

The man did not reply. He was staring at Madeline as though he had just seen someone rise up from the dead. His mouth was agape, his face pale, his eyes wide open in surprise. "God's blood, it can't be!"

"Is something wrong?" Gavin asked. The marine swayed slightly forward as though about to faint.

The man pointed to Madeline. "That woman almost got me killed one night in London, the devil take her."

His own eyes equally wide in surprise, Gavin said, "You had better explain yourself, sir."

"I was in a tavern one night in London when I saw her and she looked to be decent enough," he said. "God knows she's a looker, decent or indecent. Well, she asked me to find a hackney carriage for her because it was quite late, and I volunteered to take her home. She invited me to go in the house with her, and like the most demented of Bedlamites, I went." He gave a long sigh as though he wished he could change that whole regrettable evening, then he continued. "Just as we were settling down in her bedchamber for a good night's entertainment, her husband burst in the door and threatened me, life and limb. I had no idea the trollop was married."

Gavin, his fists clenched at his sides, growled, "You are grossly mistaken, sir, or else you are a liar. That woman you are defaming is my wife."

"She may be your wife now, but in London she was the wife of Mr. Rufus Delong. That's a name I will never forget." He did not take his eyes off Madeline as he talked, therefore he did not see the color leave Gavin's face. "I'll never forget the woman, either. There can't be two in the world who look like that."

Gavin also remembered the name of Rufus Delong. It was the name of the man Madeline had said was her guardian. He had been about to grasp the marine by the throat and demand satisfaction, but the name of Rufus Delong stopped him. Obviously there was a terrible mistake, but whose?

"A real sweet little rig the two of them were running," the man continued. "Delong told me if I wanted to get out of there with life, limb, and reputation intact,

I'd better be prepared to pay whatever I thought my life was worth. Took me for everything I had." He looked down at his uniform. "That's why I'm in the service of Her Majesty today, why I am in this land of Lucifer."

Madeline, waiting for Lucinda to return with the gowns, saw Gavin talking with the marine and went to see if there was news that they, living out of town, had not yet heard. The minute she was at Gavin's side, she regretted having gone one step nearer the "stranger." She recognized him instantly and she could tell by his expression of disgust that he also recognized her.

He was Robert Crawley, the last of the men she was forced by Rufus to take home for fleecing.

Gavin, incredulous and yet knowing he must believe what he saw, stared at his wife in abject horror. It was all too apparent that she knew the marine and that she wished she did not. And if she knew him, then it followed that what the man had said must be . . . Oh, my God, could it possibly be true? Before she came to Bath Town had Madeline . . .

Gavin could not even bear to think the words, let alone say them. "You two have met, I take it," he finally managed to say.

"I believe not," Madeline said, though it was obvious to Gavin how flustered she was.

"Oh, yes, we've met," Crawley said, "and I would prefer not to meet Mrs. Delong again."

"I am *not* Mrs. Delong," Madeline said emphatically. "I am Mrs. Durant."

"You change your name as often as I change my clothing," Crawley said. "In London you told me you were Madeline Boyd, then I found out you were Madeline Delong. Well, whoever you are now, I don't want to get involved with the likes of you again. Good day." He gave a half-salute to Gavin, more a gesture of sympathy than respect, and hastily left the store.

For a minute or two Gavin remained absolutely still, so stunned that he could not move a muscle. His mind, however, was moving like a runaway horse. There was not the slightest doubt now that the marine had been telling the truth. He knew Madeline's first name, her maiden name—if Boyd had been her maiden name—and he knew the name of Rufus Delong.

Madeline, his wife, his love . . . Madeline had been a . . . what? An extortioner? A criminal? A whore? God, in heaven, he could not believe it! And yet it was true; he *had* to believe it. He had just seen the proof with his own eyes; it was irrefutable.

He looked at her, standing rigidly beside him, and could see that she knew he was aware the marine spoke the truth. Would she be so foolish as to deny it?

He did not want to hear anything she had to say, so before she could open her mouth, he muttered, "Shut up," took her by the arm, and propelled her out of the store.

As they were going out the door, Lucinda returned and called, "Here are the gowns, Madeline, Sorry I took so long to . . ."

The last words were lost as Gavin pushed her toward the wagon, but did not help her in. "Get in!" He commanded in a tone of voice Madeline had never heard before. His face was as red as the red glints in his hair, and his mouth was compressed in a straight line. She had never seen, nor felt, such anger in a human being before.

She climbed into the wagon and sat quietly beside him. The truth was, she was afraid to speak. She knew he was not a violent man, but at this moment he looked as though he could do murder without giving it a second thought.

As the wagon rumbled out of town and down the path through the woods which led to the cabin, she finally said in a low voice, "I can explain."

When he made no reply whatever, did not even glance sideways at her, she said, "Will you let me explain? Will you listen?"

But Gavin could hardly hear the sound of her voice because of the loud voice arguing in his mind. She is not what you are thinking, one voice said. You know her too well, have loved her too long; every instinct tells you that Madeline could not have done those things. Then he heard the other voice in rebuttal: you have gone soft in the head if you try to refute what you have just seen and heard. She knew the marine and he knew her, called her by name . . . by all of her names.

Madeline Boyd, Madeline Delong . . . and now Madeline Durant. But was she really his wife? Were they legally wed? Or did she have another husband—possibly more than one—somewhere else?

"Gavin, please let me tell you about it." She spoke now as though to one hard of hearing. "Please *listen* to me."

He looked at her, suddenly remembering her presence beside him. "I've already heard too much," he said in a hurt tone. "I want no more lies, no more pretense from you."

"I have never lied to you . . . and I never will," she said. "I can imagine what you are thinking and . . ."

"You couldn't possibly. And I prefer to be left to my thoughts." He shut out the sound of her voice again with those leaden thoughts that weighed his mind down. He was remembering now the way it had been when she had first left the *Sea Lion* and gone with him home. He had wondered about her status then: a beautiful, unattached young girl who had come to a land where she knew not one living soul except her fellow passengers on the ship. And, worst of all, she had come indentured to an unattached male with whom she expected to live. That fact should have told him all he needed to know about Madeline Boyd, or whatever her name was. But because she was so beautiful and had seemed like a gracious lady who had come upon hard times, he had wanted to believe that she was exactly as she had represented herself. Probably she had taken one look at Cate and his cabin and decided that her fortune would fare better with Gavin, then had done everything in her power to get Gavin to want her back. She had succeeded, too, for he had risked his own reputation, even his life, to get her back from Cate.

What an idiot he had been! She had played him for a fool exactly the way she had those men in London. Certainly the marine was not the only man she had lured, like a poisonous spider, into her web.

He wondered how many others there had been, then decided he did not really want to know. What an actress she was! She had acted innocent and uninitiated at lovemaking, and he had fallen for her act, hook, line, sinker, pole, and boat.

His disgust with himself at that moment was almost as great as his disgust with her. He, who had at one time prided himself on his knowledge of and experience with women, had been completely taken in by her.

He stopped the wagon in front of the cabin to let her out. She gave him a long, imploring look, but when he said nothing, she climbed out and went inside. He took the horse and wagon to the shed, then went for a long walk in the woods behind the cabin, not returning until well after dark.

She did not question him as to where he had been when he went in. She merely nodded toward the table and said, "Supper is ready."

There were ham biscuits and beans and corn and a blueberry pie, but neither of them ate enough for her to have bothered preparing the meal. He would not look at her across the table, but stared down either at his plate or at the hearth. He knew she wanted to talk, but he was not ready to listen to any more of her lies; for that matter, he would never be ready.

If only the marine had not been so sure of her identity. If only he had not called her name. If only Madeline had not come up at that time and recognized the man. If only . . .

God, would he be in torment the rest of his life because of this woman?

Probably. He had loved her too much, too completely, to put it all out of his mind now. Until the day he died, she would haunt him—but he could not continue to live with her, have her mocking smile across the table from him every day, have her close to him in bed every night. With how many other men had she shared her bed? And he had thought her virginal, modest, sensitive! No, she would have to go; he would not have her staying here, making a fool of him time after time. How many other men might pass through Bath County and point an accusing finger at her?

But, dear Lord, how he would miss her! Miss her loveliness, her humor, and at night . . . He could not bear to think what the nights would be like without her—but she must go! He kept telling himself that over and over.

He continued to sit at the table while she cleared it and washed the dishes. When she finished, she came to him and stood beside his chair. "Please, Gavin, can we talk now?"

"No!" The one word was loud and clipped and split the air like a gunshot.

She said nothing else but went to the bed, turned it down, and began undressing. He got up from the table then and went to the large chest where the linens and blankets were stored. By the time she was in bed, he had made a pallet on the floor, put a rope from wall to wall across the room, and once again they were separated by a blanket.

He knew he would not sleep at all during the night, and it gave him some satisfaction to hear her turning restlessly in the bed. One time, he thought he heard her crying, but, of course, he was mistaken because women like her were too hard, too manipulative, to cry.

He did not know how long he had been lying there when he heard her bare feet padding across the room. In the moonlight through the window, he saw the blanket move, and then felt her kneeling on the pallet beside him.

Without a word, she began to rain kisses upon his

face: his forehead, his brow, his cheeks, and then his mouth. It was all he could do to lie as still as death. It was second nature with him to reach for her, respond to her. But he knew if he allowed himself to respond now, it would be even harder to do what must be done tomorrow.

Her hands went over his chest, down his body. She would know now. There was no way he could hide the fact that she had succeeded in arousing him.

Gruffly, he said, "Go back to bed." He almost added, When I need a whore, I'll go find one, but something kept him from saying the painful words. Even knowing what game she played, what she was, he could not bring himself to say it out loud.

She hesitated only a moment, then rose from the pallet and, with a sob, flung herself back in the bed. Now there was no doubt in his mind that she was crying, but that, too, was part of her act, part of the shenanigans she was going through to make him feel sorry for her, to make him keep her on and continue providing for her.

She could always go back to Felton Cate. There was no question that he would take her in. Gavin wanted to say that also, but he couldn't bring himself to utter the words because he couldn't stand the thought of Cate putting his hands on that creamy skin, or holding that soft body . . .

He groaned inwardly. Would morning never come? He wanted, yet dreaded, to see dawn streak the sky for he had decided what he was going to do.

He was up before she was and prepared their breakfast. Apparently she had finally gone to sleep and was sleeping deeply. He called her several times before he heard her stirring.

"Gavin?" she said, coming from the other side of the blanket, her nightdress clinging to her body, outlining every curve, every angle. He looked away.

"Breakfast is ready," he said.

She looked at him questioningly, then sat down at the table. She did not begin to eat the eggs and fried ham he had cooked, but said, "I made up my mind during the night that you are going to talk to me, listen to me. There is a perfectly logical explanation for what happened yesterday and you are going to hear it if I have to hogtie you and force you to listen."

He laughed mirthlessly. "You? Hogtie me?"

She sighed. "Let me tell you how it was in London. How it was after my father died . . ."

"Up against it, were you?" he said. "Many women come upon hard times, but they don't all do what you did."

She lowered her eyes and a blush stole over her face.

"I see my shot hit the mark."

"I never, Gavin, never in my life . . ." she began.

"Spare me any more histrionics," he said. "I have seen so much playacting over the past thirty-six hours that I doubt I'll even want to go to the theatre next time I'm in London."

"Won't you let me tell you what happened in London?"

"No." He looked away as he said, being completely honest with her, "I don't want you to cheapen yourself in my eyes any more than you already have."

He got up from the table, the sight and smell of food

making him sick. "I want you to pack your things now," he said. "Everything."

"You are . . . sending me away?" Her voice broke.

"I am taking you into Bath this morning."

"T-to stay? Where?"

"You can stay with anyone who will give you house-space until the next ship comes in to take you away."

Chapter Thirteen

GAVIN WENT OUTSIDE WHILE SHE PACKED. IT WAS OBVIous to her that he could not bear the sight of her. Like one drugged, she went about her task automatically, dropping clothing and personal objects into her trunk and two portmanteaux haphazardly, neither noticing nor caring what would be wrinkled and what would be broken when she unpacked later.

Where would she unpack? Where would he take her? She had no friends in Bath Town any more. Lucinda Mulligan treated her with more civility than anyone else, but that was in business. The last thing Lucinda wanted was to see Madeline come into the house, bag and baggage, and as for Lester, he would sooner welcome a water moccasin.

One by one she emptied the drawers of the stand Gavin had made for her to use until a proper bureau could be obtained from England. She grimaced as she thought that the bureau had probably come in on the ship day before yesterday and was in the back of Mulligan's now, waiting for them.

Unaware that she was crying again, hot tears coursed down her cheeks. She realized now that Gavin would never listen to her explanation. And even if he would, could she convince him that she had been forced by Rufus to do what she had done? Could she make him believe that he was the only man with whom she had made love, the only man she had truly loved and would love for the rest of her life? Even though she knew he would not listen, she would have to try one more time.

She finished the packing quickly, still not quite believing that she was about to leave the cabin, that she was seeing this room in which she had known so much happiness for the last time. Months ago she had been afraid to be too happy, afraid the gods might envy her and take her newfound joy. They had done just that.

She closed the trunk and bags and walked slowly around the room, touching objects that were dear to her: the back of the chair in which Gavin always sat, the homespun shirt he had worn yesterday that she had planned to wash today (Who would take care of him now? Would Tondah come back, gloating in victory?), the head of the bed where she would never lie with him again. It was too much for her; she turned away, blinded now by her tears.

She heard the wagon being brought to the front door for the baggage. Without even glancing at Gavin as he took the two bags out, she climbed into the wagon. She did not offer to help with the trunk. If he was so anxious to get rid of her, he could manage by himself.

He did, grunting as he finally hoisted the trunk onto the back of the wagon. When he sat down beside her and took up the reins, his only words were to Walt, "Git'up!"

She waited a moment or two, then said, "Gavin, I love you with all my heart. You are the only man I have ever loved, the only one I ever will love."

He was not unaffected by her words. She could see the muscle in his temple twitching.

"What Robert Crawley said yesterday . . ."

"Why didn't you introduce us since you remember his name so well?"

She ignored the sarcasm and went on, "What he said was . . ."

"Are you going to tell me he was lying? That you didn't lure him home with you, take him to your bedchamber, and . . ."

"That much was true." She bowed her head, unable to look at him now. "But there was a reason I did what I did. I have to tell you why . . ."

"If there was something that needed explaining, the time to have done it was *before* we were married," he said. "I want nothing from you now but your promise to stay out of my sight forever."

"That is a promise I cannot give," she said.

They did not speak again until they were in town. Gavin, apparently, had decided exactly what he was going to do with her, for he drove unhesitatingly to the Roland house and stopped the wagon. He got out and unloaded her baggage in the yard. "I imagine they will put you up until the next ship comes in," he said. "Tell Cyrus I will pay him for your board and room. I'll also pay your passage back to England, of course. After that, you are on your own." He gave a dispirited laugh. "You'll manage very well, I'm sure. You did before."

She sat as though comatose, not even blinking her eyes.

"Are you going to get out or am I going to have to pull you out?" His voice was harsh.

"You are making a mistake," she said quietly.

"You are the one who made a mistake, quite a few of them. My only mistake was in taking you home with me in the first place."

Those words got her out of the wagon as though they had lifted her out and set her hastily upon the ground. As soon as she was out, Gavin got in again, clucked to Walt, and started down Water Street as though he were an ancient charioteer in a race.

Madeline stood at the edge of the Roland yard watching him go. She wanted to run down the street after the wagon, as she had when he had left her at Cate's, but she knew it would do no good this time. She could talk to him until halfway through forever, but she would never be able to make him understand that, although she was guilty of Crawley's accusations, there were extenuating circumstances. She knew him well enough to know that even after his anger, and yes, his hurt (for she could look beyond the anger and see the hurt that caused it), had diminished somewhat, he could never forgive her wrongdoing no matter what the circumstances. And probably the worst thing of all was not telling him the whole story before they were married.

Yes, she should have told him as soon as he took her home with him. She could see that now, but at the time all she had wanted was to forget the whole wretched experience and to live among people who did not know about her past. Was it so terrible of her to want to start anew?

Slowly she walked up to the Roland's porch. Had there been any alternative, she would not even be on their property, but she had nowhere else to go. She went up the steps, then hesitated at the door. Finally, she knocked timidly, having no idea whether the door would be opened to her.

After what seemed a very long while, the door was opened just a crack. She could not see who was on the other side. "Jessie?" she asked, "Is that you?"

The door was opened another few inches and she saw part of Cyrus's face. "What are *you* doing here?" His voice was as cold as a winter blizzard.

"Please, may I come in?"

"You may not." He closed the door firmly.

"Cyrus," she called. "Gavin has . . . has put me out and I have nowhere else to go." If only the world would open up and swallow her completely as she was trying to swallow her pride, she would not feel so mortified.

Once more the door was opened, but only a couple of inches. "Jessie and both children are sick with the fever and . . ." The door opened wide as Cyrus clutched at the frame to keep from falling.

She reached for him, supporting him as she helped him inside to a chair in the front room. Touching him, she realized that he was deathly ill, burning with fever.

"What is it, Cyrus?"

"Yellow fever," he said, his voice hardly a whisper. "Jessie, the children . . ." He gestured toward the stairs. "An epidemic . . . all over . . . county . . . everywhere . . ."

She knew she could never get him up the stairs to bed, so she said, "Stay right here, Cyrus. Don't move. I'm going to see about the others. I'll be right back."

She hurried abovestairs to one of the bedrooms and found Carrie and Con in their beds, both asleep. Both with a jaundiced look. She tiptoed to the next room and found Jessie weakly trying to get out of bed. She also looked yellow and feverish.

"Get back into bed," Madeline said at once. "You should not think of getting up."

"The children . . . must see about the children."

"They are both asleep."

"Cyrus . . ."

"He's downstairs."

"You," Jessie pointed as though suddenly remembering something. "Get out. We are all sick."

"I know. I am going to take care of you."

Jessie shook her head. "Don't want you. Get out before you catch it."

"I am a doctor's daughter," Madeline said. "I am not afraid of illness."

"Go away," Jessie repeated. "It is the yellow fever."

"I am not going to leave you," Madeline told her. "You nursed me through my illness on the ship; I will do the same for you."

"May not get through it." Jessie lay back down, too exhausted to sit up any longer.

"How long have you and the others been ill?" Madeline asked.

"Don't know. Can't remember. Think this is the third or fourth day. Con . . . he's bad, the worst."

"Has a doctor been here?"

"No . . . too much sickness. Doctor needed everywhere."

She could see it was too much of an effort for Jessie to talk. "Stay quiet," she said. "Rest. I am going to see about Cyrus, then I'll be back up here."

She hunted through chests and wardrobes until she found linens and a coverlet to make a pallet for Cyrus belowstairs. In his weakened condition, she would never be able to get him to bed. It probably was better if he and Jessie did not share the same bed now anyway, she thought.

He was sitting where she left him, but he was mumbling deliriously. She put her hand to his forehead, then jerked it away. He was so hot that her hand felt scorched. Quickly, she made up the pallet, then almost lifting Cyrus out of the chair, she got him to the floor and got his clothes off, leaving him covered with only a sheet while she went to the kitchen for cold water. There was no water at all in any of the water jugs or jars. Apparently Jessie had used it all and had not had the strength to bring in more.

Taking the largest of the jugs, she went out the back door to the well. Though she knew little or nothing about yellow fever, it stood to reason that the first thing to be done was to bring down the high fever. Back inside, she removed the sheet from Cyrus' burning body, soaked it in the cool water, then replaced it over him, tucking it around and under him so it touched all of his body. Next, she brought him a glass of the water and tried to get him to drink it. Holding his head up, she managed to get him to take a swallow or two but no more.

She went back abovestairs then to see what could be done for Jessie and the children. Carrie was awake now and seemed glad to see her though the child said nothing. Con, still asleep, was turning from side to side restlessly and murmuring gibberish. Madeline quickly stripped the sheets from his bed and gave him the same treatment that she had his father, and then she did the same with Carrie.

When she got back to Jessie's room, it seemed that Jessie's fever also had gone up in the past few minutes. Her face was flushed, a combination of dark red and yellow. Once again, Madeline applied a cold, wet sheet.

That done, she looked at her patient. Dear Lord, suppose what she had done was exactly the wrong thing! Just being the daughter of a physician certainly did not give her any expertise in the field. Her father had not even allowed her in his laboratory. What if, in her ineptitude, she killed the Roland family?

After a silent prayer for guidance, she said to Jessie, "When have you eaten?"

"Don't . . . know. Can't . . . remember."

She tried to get her three patients abovestairs to take water, and was no more successful than she had been belowstairs, then she returned to the backroom and looked in the larder. It was filled with food—vegetables that Jessie had put up, meat in airtight containers (which probably would spoil within a day or two)—and she wondered if the family had eaten at all during the past few days.

She set about preparing a thick soup for them, using the meat and vegetables, but only Carrie ate an appreciable amount. Jessie, at Madeline's insistence, took a few spoonfuls, then was instantly nauseated, and neither Cyrus nor Con would take any. Perhaps it was just as well; the food was hot. If they had anything at all, it should be cold.

The house itself was stifling in the August heat. She herself was almost gasping for breath. She went from room to room, raising every window as high as it would go, then she opened the front door wide. It was then that she saw her baggage in the front yard, exactly where Gavin had left it.

Strange. She had been with the Rolands for several hours now and had not once thought of Gavin. The immediacy of the situation had sent everything else out of her mind.

She made two trips outside to bring in her portmanteaux. The trunk would have to stay there until she could find someone to help her bring it in.

By nightfall she was so exhausted that she felt she could have fallen in bed beside Jessie and remained there for at least twenty-four hours without moving. She had spent the afternoon going from one to the other, keeping the sheets as cool as possible by continuing to soak them in cold water. After dark, there was a slight breeze which blew through the house, and for that she was thankful.

Before making a pallet for herself on the floor of the back room, she went once again to the four fever-ridden people whose lives were in her hands. Cyrus seemed a little cooler and he was no longer delirious, and Carrie even managed a small smile. But Con had not responded to any of her efforts and kept holding his head as though in great pain, and Jessie still suffered wave after wave of nausea. She sat beside Jessie until Jessie finally dropped off to sleep, then she went belowstairs to the pallet and was asleep almost before she stretched out on the scratchy blanket.

The following morning Madeline left the Rolands long enough to go to Mulligan's to see if Lucinda or

Lester knew where she could find a doctor who would go to the Roland house.

"I knew they were ailing, some of them," Lucinda said, "but I didn't know they all had it. Lord God, what is to become of us?" She threw up her hands. "Don't get close to me if you've been in it. If Lester and I get sick, we don't have anybody to tend to us." She looked at Madeline with new respect.

"There must be a doctor somewhere in the vicinity," Madeline said. "I don't know if I'm doing the right things. They need a doctor."

"So do most of the other people in the county, even further." Lester came from the back of the store. "I hear the epidemic is all the way to New Bern now." He shook his head, as though in disbelief. "I guess you heard that Elizabeth Milton and her baby died last week."

"No!" Madeline cried. "Oh, no." Tears welled into her eyes as she remembered the happy little family on the ship, Tom's violin at her wedding . . .

"They aren't the only ones in Bath to go," Lucinda said. "They've been dropping like flies. Look, there's only one doctor in these environs and he's running thither and yon day and night. If we see him, we'll tell him to go to the Rolands', but it's not likely we'll see him."

"I don't know what I'll do," Madeline said completely discouraged now.

"It's nice of you to stay with them," Les ventured, his first kind words to her since before the Cary Rebellion. "Surprised your husband would let you."

She had no answer for that, not wanting to get into

her own personal tragedy. "My trunk has been in the front yard since yesterday," she told them. "I can't get it in the house by myself."

They both stared at her for a minute, then looked at each other. There was obviously more going on here than met the ear when Madeline talked. Finally, Les said, "I'll get Wes Martin and we'll carry it in for you. I reckon we don't hold it against you, your husband's ways."

"I would appreciate it," she said, and left the store before the barrage of questions she feared would begin.

The trunk was moved into the house that afternoon while she was wrapping Con in a freshly soaked sheet.

For a week she continued her treatments and no doctor appeared to tell her that she was doing right or wrong. For a day or two, there was no change, and then suddenly Carrie and Cyrus seemed much better. Their fever dropped considerably, and they began to eat. Con, however, remained in a state close to unconsciousness, when he wasn't wide-eyed and delirious. And Jessie's fierce headache and nausea continued.

Another week passed and Madeline, who was doing everything she could think of to keep from getting the disease herself, began to suspect that she was far from well. She was so busy going from patient to patient that she seldom had time to think of her own health. She noticed, however, that she was always tired, and lately she, too, had been having headaches. It was just fatigue, she told herself. She was worn out with the hard work, the long hours of tending the four Rolands.

By the end of the second week she was elated to think that three of them had passed the crisis and were now, to all appearances, out of danger. Only Con remained grievously ill. Once again she went back to the store to inquire if the doctor would be in the area soon only to find that the store was closed, the door locked. Puzzled, she started back to the Roland house and met Tom Milton on the street.

"Oh, Tom, I'm so sorry," she said. "So terribly sorry."

Tom bowed his head, unable to speak. When he trusted his voice, he said, "She was so good, so kind . . . and the baby, a little angel. Why would God want to take them? They were all I had."

She patted his arm sympathetically. "It's hard to understand sometimes."

"I'll never understand. Why couldn't it have been me?" He looked toward the store. "I guess you know Les Mulligan has it now and Lucinda's probably going to get it, taking care of him."

"I hope . . . she'll be careful," Madeline said, wondering just how contagious the disease was.

When she got back to the house she found Jessie not only out of bed but belowstairs as well.

"What are you doing down here?" she asked, slightly exasperated that Jessie would risk a relapse. "You're still weak as a kitten, you know."

"A little weak," Jessie admitted, "but regaining strength every day, thanks to you. You've saved our lives, Madeline. There aren't even words to thank you for that."

"I only did what I could to help and Con is still . . ."

"He's better, thank God," Jessie said. "I just looked in on him. His fever is down, finally, and he's resting comfortably for a change. I think he's going to pull through."

Madeline gave a huge sigh of relief.

"It was good of Gavin to let you come to us," Jessie went on, "especially after the way we've treated him. Can you—and he—ever forgive us?"

"There's nothing to forgive. You seem to have forgotten how you nursed me on the *Sea Lion.*"

"A little seasickness is nothing compared with the yellow fever," Jessie said. "Anyway, I think by tomorrow Carrie and I will be able to take care of everything, with some help from Cyrus, of course. You can go on back to Gavin. I'll wager he's been champing at the bit, waiting for you."

What could she say to Jessie? No, he's not champing at anything. He left me here because he didn't want to see me ever again. He thinks I am a harlot . . .

No, she couldn't say those things, not now anyway. What she did say was, "I'll stay on a little longer, if you don't mind. I think you could use a bit of help around here."

"Yes, but I hate to ask it of you," Jessie said. "You've done far too much already, but look, since we're all so much better now, why don't you at least visit Gavin for a while tomorrow? He must be down in the dumps at having you away so long. A visit would cheer him."

Madeline hesitated, then said, "We'll see how everybody is getting along tomorrow."

"We'll all be fine," Jessie said. "Certainly well enough to spare you for a few hours."

"We'll see," Madeline said again.

There is a point in continuing fatigue when one becomes too exhausted to rest, and Madeline had reached that point. That night she lay on her pallet, too tired even to think, and yet sleep would not come. She tried to bring it on by imagining that she was lying in Gavin's rope bed, his arms tightly around her, but the hard floor of the back room, softened only by a blanket, was no substitute. Her imagination could not take her that far.

It had been two weeks now—two weeks and two days by tomorrow—since Gavin had left her here. Had his attitude toward her softened any in that time . . . at least enough so that he might listen to her explanation now? Surely his anger and disgust, his hurt, could not have been maintained at such a peak all this time. Perhaps Jessie was right: she should visit him.

The fact was, she so yearned to see him that she would have decided on the visit with even less of an excuse, or no excuse at all.

After preparing breakfast for the Rolands the next morning, she started walking to the cabin. Cyrus offered his horse, but she was not a good rider and she didn't want to risk taking a strange horse. Besides, it was only a mile and a half and she could walk it in twenty to thirty minutes.

As she went through the woods, she thought of the first time Gavin had brought her this way, the day she had arrived in Bath Town. If only she could go back to that day and tell him everything! We are not given second chances, she thought, at least not in that respect. Besides, she was not so sure that Gavin would have taken her in at all had he known about her past. He had seemed so horrified . . .

The clearing and the cabin were in view now. She stopped. Never had a dwelling seemed so dear to her, not even her father's house in Bath, England, and she had thought she was heartbroken when she left there.

She had not even known what heartbreak was!

She began walking again, more slowly, looking toward the field beside the house for Gavin. By this time of day he usually had been working for two hours. There was no sign of him, however, and only a thin curl of smoke from the chimney told her he was home. Obviously he was cooking at the fireplace; the heat already was too intense for a fire. Early September was turning out to be as hot and dry as August had been.

She hesitated again when she reached the door. Should she knock, call Gavin . . . or turn around go back? Could she stand it if he came out and told her again that he couldn't bear the sight of her?

She took a few steps backward, as though the door were a live thing that was about to harm her. Her hands were trembling slightly. She looked back toward the woods, then again at the door.

She had come this far, she might as well go the rest of the way, and though it was only a step or two to the door again, it seemed an insurmountable distance.

But it was a compulsion with her now. She knew she could not go on with her life unless she could just look at him, hear his voice even if what he said to her was harsh, hurtful.

She went back to the door and knocked softly, and then a little louder.

The door was opened at once . . . by Tondah.

The Indian girl looked surprised at first, staring at Madeline as though she had dropped out of the sky, and then a grin spread slowly across her face and she said, "You see who real woman is he wants."

So stunned that for several minutes she could only stare at that grinning face, Madeline looked beyond Tondah finally, but she did not see Gavin.

"You go now," Tondah said. "He no want you. He want me."

Madeline turned and fled, running across the clearing as though chased by the demons of hell. Only when she had the woods to screen her from sight of the cabin did she stop, gasping for breath. She was stunned, and more deeply hurt than she thought it was possible to be. How long after dumping her in the Rolands' front yard had Gavin waited before bringing Tondah back? Probably he had gone for her that very day. It was unlikely that he had given so much as a thought to Madeline now that he had his Indian woman back.

She walked slowly back to Bath Town, too devastated even to cry. By the time she reached the town, she was feeling lightheaded, somewhat dizzy, and at the edge of the Rolands' yard, she fell, collapsing unconscious on the grass.

Chapter Fourteen

TONDAH CLOSED THE CABIN DOOR WHEN MADELINE began running across the clearing. She had seen the stricken look on her face, and she almost felt sorry for the white girl, except that she had been the one who'd tried to take Tondah's rightful place. The silver-haired one had tried to take Gavin away from her, had caused him to send Tondah back to her people who, except for Walking Bear, no longer wanted her. "You have touch of white man on you," her father had told her. "You no longer daughter of Fleet Foot and Little Moon." She did not dare tell him that the white man had not touched her, for then he would think that she was unwomanly. If she had lived with Gavin for all that time without arousing his lust, the fault must be hers. Better to be thought a white man's woman than to be thought unwomanly and unfulfilling of her purpose on earth.

Chief Hancock, the father of Walking Bear, also had made it clear that he did not want her in the tribe, for he had another woman in mind for his son now, so Tondah left the Indian village of Catechna and made her home in a cave near Catnip Point on Bath Creek. The cave was not far from Bath Town and only a little further from Gavin's cabin. For food she foraged in the forest like animals, living on wild berries and fruits, until it occurred to her that it was not necessary. In Bath Town and the immediate vicinity were nearly a hundred gardens where, at night, she could pick vegetables to take back to her cave.

She began with Gavin's garden, thinking she had the right to be there since, when she had been with him, she had helped him in the garden. True, the silver-haired one had helped with this year's garden, but still . . .

She took only a little from each garden, not enough to be missed by the owners. Now, if only she could think of some way to get meat, for she grew tired of the fish she caught in the river. But since she had no gun—and would not know how to shoot one anyway—and no bow or arrows, she had no way to bring down a stag, or even smaller game.

Finally, it occurred to her during the latter part of August that it would be extremely hard, if not impossible for her to make it through the winter in the cave unless she had help. The vegetables would be gone and there would be nothing but what fish she could catch. It was then that she thought of Walking Bear. He would help her if he knew of her need and if he could do so without his father learning of his betrayal, for that was how Chief Hancock would view the situation.

She went through the woods, staying well hidden lest some Indian hunter spot her, and approached the village of Catechna. She did not go into the village, but kept to the woods, hoping to see Walking Bear and signal to him. When, after several hours of waiting, she still had not seen him, she went back through the woods, more slowly this time. It was possible that he was out hunting.

She went the way she thought he would most likely go, through the thickest part of the forest away from settlements of people. But she did not find Walking Bear, nor any Indian hunters.

What she found was Gavin.

He was lying across a downed tree trunk, his gun at his feet. It was apparent to her that he had been out hunting and had been struck suddenly by . . . what?

With a cry, she ran to him, calling his name. She flung her arms around his unconscious body saying, "You sick? You hurt? Tondah take care of you. Silver Hair no good for you, no good to you."

When she pressed her lips to his face, she knew what was wrong. The fever. He was burning up with it. Somehow she had to get him to . . . Where could she take him? She could not possibly get him to her cave, not without help anyway, and she did not want to take him to his cabin and give him back to Silver Hair.

"Where?" she kept repeating the word out loud as though she expected him to regain consciousness and tell her what to do. She knew, however, that there was no chance of that, and every minute she delayed in helping him brought him that much closer to death. She had seen the fever before among her own people, and she knew it was an even deadlier enemy than the guns of the whites.

Finally, she put her arms under his arms, clasping her hands together, and began dragging him in the direction of his cabin. In the final analysis, she had decided it would be better to give him back to Silver Hair than to let him die in the forest.

It took a long time, for she had to stop every few yards to rest. Gavin was heavy, too heavy for one of her slight frame to pull any distance. When she was in sight of the cabin, she left him lying on the edge of the tobacco field and went to get Silver Hair to help her carry him the rest of the way.

When there was no answer to her knock, she opened the door and went inside. There was no sign of the white woman and, on looking around, Tondah saw that it was as if Silver Hair had never been there. Only Gavin's clothes, only his personal belongings, were in the cabin. Had he not been, at that moment, lying in the field near death, Tondah would have done a dance of joy, of victory, in the front yard. Perhaps Silver Hair had died of the fever. No, if she had, there would have been something of hers in the cabin. Gavin would not have thrown out everything.

Hastily, she made her way back across the field and began dragging Gavin the rest of the way to the cabin. She found new strength in the fact that he was once again hers, that she would not have to abandon him to the ministrations of the white woman. This beautiful man whom she loved more than her family, more than her tribe, more than the world and everything in it was hers once more!

She got him on the bed with some difficulty, then, while she caught her breath, she ran her hand lovingly through his sandy red hair. "Tondah make you well," she whispered. "When you well, you look at me the way you look at her."

She left him long enough to get what she needed. Hurrying back to the woods, she went to the spot she had seen the women of her tribe go when the fever had borken out in Catechna. On hands and knees, she looked for the little yellow-and-green herbal plants the women had picked. It seemed forever before she found a few scattered plants almost hidden by moss. Gathering those in sight, she then hurried back and started a fire under the pot behind the cabin. She boiled the herbs until they disintegrated in the water, then, with a dipper, she put the liquid into a jug.

Back inside the cabin, she bathed Gavin in the icy water from the spring that ran near the cabin, then forced a cup of the liquid down him. By night his fever had gone down some, though he was still unnaturally hot.

She lit the lamps in the room and continued the icy baths and the herbal medicine through the night. At one point, Gavin sat up in bed, a wild look in his eyes, and cried out, "Madeline! Where are you, Madeline?"

"Hush," Tondah said gently, pushing him back to the pillow. "Things better now, better without her."

"Come back! Come back!" He was yelling and, with uncanny strength, was trying to push Tondah aside.

"Hush," she said again. "Be still. Rest."

Some of the wildness went out of his eyes then as he looked at her and he lay down of his own accord. "Madeline. My Madeline." He took Tondah's hand. "Stay with me, my love, Stay . . ." He pulled her hand to his lips, kissing it.

"I stay," Tondah promised.

He looked at her again, looked at the hand he held, then flung it aside. "Madeline!" he cried. "Go away, you're not Madeline."

"I stay anyway," Tondah said resolutely. Not for anything on earth would she leave him now. Not his request, nor even being mistaken for the hated Silver Hair could make her leave his side. Once again she swabbed his body with the cold water and gave him the strange-smelling liquid to drink.

By morning the fever had broken and he slept naturally. When he awoke he was so weak that he did not try to sit up or talk, but his eyes followed Tondah as she went about the cabin. She had no idea what he was thinking or even if he was rational, but at least he was not calling for Silver Hair. During the afternoon he slept, and he slept again through the night. That was to be expected from the herbal liquid, she knew, though she had no idea why it should be so.

It was the following day that Silver Hair appeared at the door. Tondah was thankful that Gavin was asleep then or, even in his weakened condition, he might have tried to get out of bed and go to her. Since the bed was not visible from outside, she doubted if the white woman had seen him. She knew Silver Hair would not be back—the expression on the stricken face had told her that much—and her heart was glad. Now she would have Gavin for her own, for always.

He would recover from the fever; she could tell the worst of it was over. But he would be weak, possibly nauseous, for a while yet. She would bring him back to his full, robust health. He would be a man again, strong and lusty. Her man.

She would take care of him in every way that woman was meant to take care of man.

The first thing he was aware of was the terrible, unrelenting pain in his head. A dozen hammers beat against his temples and the pain shot through his skull, going down to the base of his neck. He knew he was groaning and he knew it did no good, but he could not stop. He also knew he was calling out something, calling for someone. Then, as though in a dream or from a great distance, he heard Madeline being called. Why didn't she answer? Madeline, where are you? Answer when someone calls your name.

It was a long time before he realized that it was he who was calling for her. He stopped calling then. And that was when she came to him, placing her cool hand on his hot forehead. He took her hand, held it for a minute, then kissed it.

Something was wrong. It was not Madeline's hand. Someone was beside him, impersonating Madeline. He told that person to go away, after which he vowed to himself that he would not speak again. If he could not speak to Madeline, there was no point in speaking at all.

Where was she? Why wasn't she here with him? Had something happened to her?

Felton Cate, he thought. The scoundrel has come and taken her away again.

He raised up on one elbow, looking around. No, she was not here. Tentatively, he put one leg off the bed, then the other. He could not sit up, but he could slide off the bed that way. He would crawl, if necessary, to the shed and get on Walt and go bring Madeline back where she belonged.

His other leg went off the bed and then someone came into the cabin and shoved both legs back on the bed.

"Stay still. Rest," a disembodied voice came at him sternly, disembodied because he had his eyes closed and refused to look. If he could not see Madeline, he did not want to see anyone else.

He slipped into sleep again and dreamed strange, misshapen dreams about trollops in London who took a ship to the new world, formed an army and took over every settlement in Carolina. They all looked alike with grotesquely painted faces and long white hair trailing on the ground behind them like wedding trains. As they marched toward Bath Town they chanted something about finding men to marry them. He was trying to get away from them, but they caught him and forced him to marry one of them.

He awoke then, drenched in sweat. Half lucid, half delirious, he called over and over for Madeline, but only in his mind. He would not say her name out loud. Why, he wondered, could he not say her name?

Someone was bathing him in freezing water, but it felt good. A soft and gentle touch. It must be Madeline.

Then someone was forcing him to drink a foul-tasting mess. He wanted to spit it out, but his mouth was held together so he couldn't.

Leave me alone, he wanted to yell. But he couldn't speak unless he could speak to Madeline.

Madeline, Madeline. Her name went through his mind like a litany.

Finally, he slept again, this time peacefully, with no dreams, and when he awoke he knew that he was rational and that it had been some time since he had been. He looked around and he was in bed in his cabin. How did he get here? He could not remember going to bed, certainly not in broad daylight.

What he could remember was . . . sending Madeline away. And everything that had led up to her leaving.

The front door opened and Tondah came in, a bucket of vegetables in each hand. She had been out picking . . .

Wait a minute . . . had it all been a dream, part of his delirium? Did Madeline really exist? Was she here for nearly a year, blessing his life, taking his love and giving him love in return?

Apparently he had undergone a long and debilitating illness which had affected him, his mind as well as his body, in strange ways. For everything was just as it was, as it had been for a long, long time. Tondah was here, going about her work as usual, and, yes, there was Walking Bear at the window beckoning to her to come outside. Nothing in his life had changed, not really.

Tondah was snapping the green beans when Walking Bear's head appeared at the window. She put the pan of beans hastily aside and went out. She did not need him now, now that she was back with Gavin, but she could not forget that she had needed him and had gone looking for him. If she had not, she would not have found Gavin.

He grasped her by her upper arms as soon as she was outside, telling her in their language that he had been looking for her for many moons, but had not expected her to come back to their white foe.

"He sick," she said in English, knowing it would anger him, but doing it anyway because he had just killed the kindly feeling she had felt for him by shaking and chastising her. "I take care of him."

Walking Bear looked toward the cabin, then back at Tondah. He was quiet for several minutes as though trying to decide something. When he decided, he told her. As she listened, she began to tremble and tears came to her eyes. She wiped her eyes on the back of her hand. She had never cried in front of Walking Bear before, she would not do so now. When he finished speaking, she said, using their tongue this time, "It must be stopped. Not here, Walking Bear. Please, not here."

Walking Bear shook his head. "It is too late."

He left as quickly and as silently as he had come.

Tondah watched him disappear into the woods and stood watching the spot where he had entered the woods for quite a while. At last, convinced that he would not return, she went to the garden and began to pick all of the remaining vegetables regardless of whether they were ripe. Then she hitched Walt to a wagon and took all of the food and the vegetables on the premises to her cave.

Gavin sat in his chair by the hearth watching the tiny blue flames play over the two thin sticks of wood. The weather was cool now in the waning days of September, but not yet cool enough for a roaring fire. Where had the summer gone? At some time during his long illness, it had slipped away, unnoticed and unmourned.

He was still quite weak—still ill, according to Tondah —but, except for not having the strength to do his necessary chores, he felt rather well. Physically. He knew he would never feel well in his mind again; he would always be sad, dejected. There was no longer any confusion in his thinking as to what had happened to Madeline. By now, she was probably aboard a ship, on her way back to England. He would never cease to miss her.

He had had a chance to find out what had happened to her. On learning of his illness, Cyrus Roland, Wes Martin, and some of the other men from Bath Town had come out to pick his cotton for him. He had wanted to go out to thank them, but when he tried, he found he could hardly walk across the yard, let alone into the fields. And Tondah was furious with him for trying.

"You stay." She gestured around the room. "You stay till you well, all well."

"But I must thank them," he told her. "They are doing my work for me." He did not add that he wanted to get Cyrus aside and ask about Madeline. Also, he owed the man money for putting her up and for her passage back to England.

"They thank you when you work for them?" Tondah asked innocently.

"That was different," he said.

"No different." She was firm and unyielding.

So he stayed in the cabin, obediently following her orders in everything to get his health back. She had nursed him through yellow fever, undoubtedly saved his life, so there was no reason not to go along with her wishes now.

Besides, it made no difference to him what he did or didn't do anymore. His life was worth nothing to him, not without Madeline. In his more depressed moments, he was even sorry that Tondah had found him, had brought him home, and tended him during the illness.

He had been a fool—he knew that now; why couldn't he have known it at the time?—for only a fool would have sent Madeline away. He missed her during every waking moment, and even at night he found himself reaching for her and waking on touching the empty side of the bed. Oh God, how he wanted her! How he wanted to feel her arms around him, her kisses hot upon his lips. He could die a happy man if only once more he could be submerged in the velvety softness of her, lose himself in their overwhelming love.

But it would never be, for he had been a fool. Did it really matter in the long run what she had been in England? England was an ocean away in distance, an eternity away in time. Whatever she was there, whatever she had done, it was all in the past and should not have affected their perfect present. He himself had been a veritable bounder when he had lived in England, cavorting about the countryside with any lass over the age of puberty who did not look away when he winked at her. Who was he to judge Madeline?

There were extenuating circumstances, she had said. Perhaps there were . . . but even if there were not, it made no difference to him now. All he wanted was to have her back.

It occurred to him that he should go to England after her, bring her back. But he discarded that thought almost as soon as it had formed. After the way he had treated her, she would not speak to him, much less come back to Carolina with him. What had he to offer her anyway? A tiny cabin for a home, hard work from dawn to dusk, life in a settlement that was civilized, but just barely. And his complete, never-ending love. But that had not been enough to sustain their life together before, why should he think it would be now? Certainly not after the way he had treated her.

The shadows were lengthening outside and the blue flames in the fireplace were now faint, pink embers. He had gotten through another day. Would the rest of his life be like this? Instead of living, just getting through?

The door burst open, startling him, and Tondah came in.

"I was wondering where you were," he said. "You are usually cooking our supper by now."

"We go for supper." She pointed outside. "You come with me now. I take you another place."

"What are you talking about?" The girl was making no sense.

"You weak like baby here," she said. "We go stay night and day, maybe two day, in place where air different. You get well fast."

"Where is that?"

"You see. Come now." While talking she was turning about the room, gathering up some of his clothing as well as her own few possessions from the little room.

He owed his life to the girl, so if she wanted to take him somewhere else, he at least owed her that much. It made no difference to him anyway whether he stayed here or went with her to some Indian place where she probably would try to bring about a miraculous cure for his weakness.

Outside, she hitched Walt to the wagon, loaded the things they were taking into the back of the wagon, then told him to get in. "I take reins," she said.

They started on the path toward Bath Town, then

veered to the right, going along Bath Creek, which, in England, would have been called a river. They stopped near Catnip Point and she got out of the wagon and unloaded everything on the ground. Then she took the horse and wagon into a nearby dense thicket, unhitched and tied Walt in a clump of bushes. "They be all right there," she told him when she returned. "Now we go here."

To his amazement, she parted another clump of bushes, revealing the mouth of a cave. Then she began carrying their belongings inside.

"Your wits have gone a-wandering, Tondah," he said. "What are you doing?" He followed her into the cave where she was lighting a lamp.

"We stay here night, day, maybe more."

"Whatever for? Why should we stay here when we have a perfectly comfortable cabin . . ."

"We stay here!" she said sharply. "Air be better."

That was debatable. The cave was small and dank. But that was not what caught his attention as the lamp flickered into full flame. He was amazed to see that the cave had been stocked with food and water, enough to last many days, and on the ground were two pallets, made of straw and covered with blankets.

"Why, Tondah?" he asked. "Why have you done this?"

"To make you well, keep you well," she said, and would say no more.

Because it made no difference to him where he was without Madeline, he sat down on the floor of the cave, and, by doing so, tacitly agreed to stay.

While Tondah set about preparing their meal, he watched her, seeing her only in outline for in the front of his mind he saw Madeline. No matter where he was he would see only Madeline, think about only her, so what difference did it make if he humored Tondah by staying a day or two in a cave? If she thought it would give him back his strength, why bother to argue with her? Maybe she knew what she was doing.

Chapter Fifteen

SHE DID NOT KNOW HOW LONG SHE HAD BEEN LYING IN the Rolands' front yard. Madeline opened her eyes, looking about her, not remembering at first how she came to be where she was. The street was deserted, as had been the case since the outbreak of yellow fever, so there had been no passersby to come to her aid.

Then she remembered everything: the trip to Gavin's cabin, Tondah and her cruel words . . .

She made two attempts to get up before she finally succeeded. Her body seemed almost too heavy to move, nor did it seem to be obeying the impulses sent to it by her mind. She made her way into the house slowly, each step an ordeal.

"Madeline!" Jessie cried when she went inside. "Oh, dear Lord, you have caught it from us!"

"No." Madeline sank down heavily into the nearest chair. "I am just so tired. So tired . . ." She was too tired to continue talking.

"I'm going to get you to bed," Jessie said, unconvinced that Madeline did not have the fever. She felt her forehead, which was cool. No, it wasn't the fever—but what could it be? Madeline was obviously ill.

Madeline struggled to her feet. Jessie was in no

condition to act as nurse to anyone. "I'll just go lie down for a while. I'll be all right after I rest."

Jessie helped her, feebly, to her pallet in the back room where she all but collapsed again. "Don't worry about anything," Jessie told her. "I'll take care of the others."

"You're . . . not . . . able . . ." Madeline began, but was asleep before she finished the sentence.

When she awoke the sky was gray with just a streak of red. She had slept all day; it was sunset. She got up instantly, feeling much better, but very hungry. She looked around her, trying to decide what to prepare for the family's supper. Realizing then that the house was much too quiet for that time of day, she went to the front room. Cyrus was snoring on his pallet. Tiptoeing abovestairs, she found the other three also asleep. As she went back belowstairs she noticed that the sky was getting lighter, not darker.

She not only had slept through the day, but also the night.

Apparently, the sleep was what she had needed for she no longer felt light-headed and dizzy. She felt better than she had for some time, except for the torment in her heart. She could still see Tondah's smiling face and hear her words: *"You see who real woman is he wants."*

She found some cold chicken in the larder and made a sandwich, and got a glass of milk. She was too hungry to wait for the Rolands to wake up for breakfast.

She finished the sandwich and continued to sit at the small table, staring unseeingly at the brilliant sunrise through the window.

She had planned to stay with the Rolands for a long time—at least as long as they would let her—and wait, hoping that Gavin would change his mind, hear her explanation of the rig she had been forced to run in London and, God willing, forgive her and take her back.

She knew now that it had been only a pipe dream. When he said he wanted her out of his sight forever, he had meant it. He had his Indian woman back to cook his meals, clean his cabin, help in the fields, and warm his bed. He had no need of, no use for Madeline. What they had had together for those few months had been an illusion on her part. Because she had loved him so much, so very much, she had thought he returned that ardent and profound devotion. All wishful thinking on her part!

We see what we want to see, she thought. We close our eyes to what we do not want to see.

She had closed her eyes to the fact that Gavin had not loved her as she had loved him. He may have desired her for a time, but it had not been a durable emotion. His "love" had withered and died when the first test—in the form of Robert Crawley—had come along. Why could he not have . . .

"You're awake."

She started. Jessie was standing in the doorway, dressed in her nightrobe. "You slept for a long time," she said.

"Almost twenty-four hours," Madeline said. "I didn't realize how tired I was."

"I—we were all afraid you had caught the fever from us," Jessie said. "I kept feeling your forehead all during the day to be sure you didn't have a high temperature."

"I'm all right," Madeline assured her. "I feel fine."

"You don't look fine. You look miserable." Jessie sat down across the table, continuing to stare at Madeline as though diagnosing an illness. "Did you and Gavin quarrel? Maddie, if you quarreled because you are staying away too long, please go home. We can manage now, I wouldn't for anything want to be the cause of a spat between you two."

Madeline was thoughtful for a long time. Then she decided she had better tell Jessie at least part of the problem. She would find out soon enough anyway.

"Jessie, Gavin and I . . . we are not . . . that is . . ." It was more difficult than she had imagined. It was almost impossible to say the words.

"What?" Jessie asked after a long pause. "What are you saying?"

"Gavin brought me here to stay," she said. "That is why my trunk, everything, is here. I am to go back to England on the first ship in."

"What are you saying?" Jessie repeated incredulously.

"The marriage is over. I am going back to England."

"I don't believe it!" She had a stunned expression. "But you wouldn't jest about something like that, would you? I still can't believe it. If ever I saw two people in love . . . Why, you and Gavin are perfect for each other. You can't . . ."

"I am going back to England," she repeated stolidly. "Please, I'd rather not talk about it any more."

Jessie sighed. "And just what do you propose to do once you're there? Go back to your tyrant of a guardian?"

Madeline had not thought that far ahead. "No," she

said slowly, "I will never go back to him. And I'll have all those weeks aboard ship to decide what I am going to do."

"You're welcome to stay with us as long as you like," Jessie said. "Forever, if you want to. We can never repay you for what you've done for us."

Madeline reached across the table and squeezed Jessie's hand. "You are a dear friend, and I thank you. But there is no reason for me to stay on here. No reason at all. Now, go see if the others are awake yet. I'll have breakfast ready in a little while."

Jessie worried about her friend's plight for several days before she mentioned it to Cyrus. Ordinarily, she would have told him at once, but with everyone in the household still in a weakened condition from the fever, she didn't want to give him anything else to worry about.

Finally, on the night that Cyrus gave up the pallet in the front room and rejoined Jessie in bed abovestairs, she told him what Madeline had said about leaving Gavin and going back to England.

"Something terrible must have happened," she said when she had finished, "because I know Gavin would never put Madeline out, and I know she would never leave of her own accord. We've got to do something, Cyrus, but what?"

"Maybe we shouldn't interfere," Cyrus said. "It's their business, their personal business."

"How can you say that when all you have to do is look at Madeline to see how miserable she is?" Jessie was indignant. "After what she has done for us, all of us, we've got to do something for her. She may not have the fever, but she's suffering as much—maybe more—than if she did."

"All right." Cyrus gave in. "I'll think about it."

"I hope you'll do more than think about it," she said.

Two days later, Cyrus hitched up the buggy and drove out to Gavin's cabin. He was more than a little surprised when the Indian girl answered his knock. For a moment, he said nothing, his inclination being to go home and tell Jessie that there was nothing they could do, that Gavin apparently preferred the Indian to Madeline. However, he did ask to see Gavin.

"He sick," the girl said. "He sick with fever." She pointed behind her. "In bed. No talk."

Cyrus stuck his head in the door far enough to see Gavin's fever-ridden, jaundiced face on the pillow.

He nodded to Tondah. "Does he need anything? Anything I can get him?"

She shook her head. "I take care of him. I take care of him always."

Cyrus went home and told Jessie what he had found at the cabin. They decided they would say nothing to Madeline. There was no particular reason why she should know that Gavin had yellow fever and certainly no reason for her to know the Indian girl was back—if she didn't know already.

Jessie could not help but wonder if the girl was the reason Madeline had left.

Ten days later, Cyrus, who was much recovered, got Wes Martin and two others to go with him to work in Gavin's cotton field. "I don't have much use for him," he said, "but he did save our gardens for us while we were fighting. Maybe we owe him that much."

Although he glimpsed the Indian girl several times

during the days they worked, he never saw Gavin. It was just as well, he thought, because he had no idea what he would say to Gavin if he saw him. Any man who would swap Madeline for the Indian had to have more wrong with him than just yellow fever.

On the night before Walking Bear had given Tondah the information that had frightened her so, he had attended a war council. Even though his father was chief of the Tuscaroras, he would be killed instantly if it were known to his people that he had revealed to any living soul what had transpired at the council meeting. Tondah was a Tuscarora, but she was no longer acknowledged as such by the others of the tribe. But Walking Bear could not knowingly let her be in danger. He loathed the white man she lived with—as he did all white people—and at times he even hated her (or told himself he did) for betraying her people, yet he could not stay away from her. No other woman would ever attract him as Tondah did. No matter how many others his father chose for him, he would have none but Tondah. Someday she would realize her mistake and come back to him.

Therefore, he had to tell her what was going to happen or she would meet the same fate that was planned for every white man, woman, and child in the entire area.

Chief Hancock had told his son days in advance that he was going to call a war council, but he told him nothing else. Only at the council meeting did Walking Bear find out what was on his father's mind.

Some dressed in buckskins, some in no more than

loincloths, all with bright bands with feathers around their heads, all with their faces streaked grotesquely with war paint, the warriors from every tribe in the area came. There were those of the Bay River Tribe, the Machopunga, Neusick, Coree, Woccon, and Pampticough Tribes, about five hundred warriors in all who, to a man, agreed with Chief Hancock as he addressed them beside the open fire.

The warriors made a circle around the fire, actually five circles, and raised their hands in silent agreement when Hancock made a point.

"We grow weary," the chief cried, "of the white man. He has taken our lands and is still taking them, forcing us to abandon our ancestral homes. He has taken our people, kidnapping and enslaving them, and still it is not safe for us to go singly to any place where the white man is for fear of being taken."

A low murmur went through the throng. All knew well of the appalling ignominies perpetrated by the whites.

"They are stricken by disease now," Hancock went on. "They are down with the fever which, unfortunately, will not take them all away. Those who are not sick have their minds on other things, like making war among themselves over who will rule them. Now is the time for us to strike!" He paused as hands went heavenward again, and this time the murmur became a loud cry: "Strike them now! Strike them now!"

The chief raised both hands for silence. "Daily has our resentment grown. White traders cheat us out of our furs, which we have hunted and trapped, and sell them for their own. They get us drunk with their strong medicine water and take all we have." He hesitated but a moment before saying, "Some have even taken our women for their own."

Walking Bear's hand was the first to be raised at that remark. Others followed.

"There is only one way to stop their tricks and their deception and their forked-tongues from lying words." The chief's voice was raised at that point and he nodded his head, as though agreeing with himself, causing his large feather headdress to quiver in the slight breeze. He repeated, "There is only one way to stop our enemy."

"Say it! Say it!" five hundred voices commanded.

"We will kill every settler—man, woman, and child —in what they call the county of Bath. We will burn every house, every crop in every field. There will be no plantation left. We will take back our land."

A roar of approval went up and the circles within circles began to move around the fire, their feet nimble as they moved faster and faster. Chief Hancock watched them for a few minutes, then raised his hands and they stopped.

"I want the chiefs of every tribe to meet with me now to plan the attack."

Six chiefs, dressed in the full regalia as was Chief Hancock, stepped forward, then sat in a small circle with Hancock. After some discussion they decided that the attack would take place, without warning of any kind, at dawn on September twenty-second. Each chief got up then and placed his hands on the open palms of Chief Hancock and then on each other. Separately, they gathered together the warriors of their tribes and left.

Walking Bear had mixed emotions. He was jubilant at the prospects of killing Gavin Durant—and he would see to it that that particular white man was left for him—but he worried lest Tondah be injured, or killed, in the forthcoming massacre.

All night he walked the woods, thinking of his dilemma. Finally, after the sun was long in the sky, he made his decision. He would risk his own life to save Tondah's. He would tell her of the planned attack. But first he would have to find her.

He looked in every place that he imagined she might be, and when he had not found her, he went at last to the cabin of Durant. He did not expect her to be there for it was known that the man had taken a white woman and after being sent away, it was not likely that Tondah would go back.

That was where he found her, however.

When he told her of the planned attack, she began to tremble and tears came to her eyes. It angered him for he knew it was the white man for whom she cried. She looked toward the cabin where she said Durant lay sick. "It must be stopped," she said. "Not here, Walking Bear. Please, not here."

He shook his head, already feeling the pleasure it would give him to dispatch Durant to his ancestors. "It is too late," he told her.

Now, on the eve of Day They Would Take Back Their Land, Walking Bear sat at his father's campfire in the woods near Bath Town where the five hundred warriors would congregate to wait for dawn. They would meet here first, then disperse in smaller groups to various points about the county. Walking Bear would stay right here because it was nearer the cabins of the two white men he hated most.

He grinned, not thinking so much about tomorrow as the day after. He would have his Tondah back even sooner than he thought, for after tomorrow there would be no one to stand in his way.

Chapter Sixteen

FELTON CATE LAY SPRAWLED ON THE FLOOR BESIDE HIS bed and could have been taken for dead had not his snores been loud enough to be heard far outside his cabin. He was on the floor because he had not made it to the bed before passing out. Beside him was an overturned bucket of whiskey, most of its contents already consumed, only a few drops spilled.

Since his luck had gone bad—thanks to Gavin Durant—he had taken to drink. Late every afternoon, he would leave his fields and head for the cabin where, with a dipper, he would methodically lower the level of the bucket. When the bucket was empty, he would refill it from a large keg in the corner. Some nights he made it to bed, other nights he got no more than a few feet from the chair in which he sat.

Last night had been a particularly "liquid" one. He had had to go into Bath Town for supplies and, from a distance, he had seen his indentured servant at the well in the Rolands' backyard. He would never think of her as Durant's wife. She was, and always would be, his. Had he not paid her way here? (He never remembered these days that he had been repaid, and then some, by Gavin.)

He wondered why she was at the Rolands' and when

he went to Mulligan's he asked Lucinda. He was told that Madeline had come to stay with the Rolands to help out because they had all been sick with the fever.

"How's Lester?" Cate remembered to ask.

"Better, thank the Lord," Lucinda said. "He's going to make it."

Cate went into town only when necessary. He would not admit even to himself that he was afraid of Gavin's threats to tell everyone how he had tried to take advantage of Madeline, but he did admit, nightly beside his bucket, that it would not surprise him if the townspeople turned against him. He could not afford to make any more enemies, especially among the whites, when he had so many of the redskins against him. For several years he had been stealing pelts from Tuscarora traps and selling them. Then there was the Indian who had attacked him while he had been looking in Durant's window. God, he'd like to bust that bastard up one side of the river and down the other. But he was afraid of Walking Bear. He had stolen from his traps as well as others'.

It was on those things that he pondered when he got home from Bath Town. He took his first dipper of whiskey long before sunset, and the more he drank, the more he thought of Madeline, how beautiful she had looked crossing the yard with a jug. He remembered having seen, when he was little more than a child, a biblical picture of a woman standing beside a well, a jug on her shoulder. Madeline reminded him of that long-forgotten picture . . . only Madeline was more beautiful than the woman in the picture. She was more beautiful than anybody, and he wanted her.

He dipped into the bucket again and began to think

how he could get rid of Durant and get Madeline back. She was his by rights and he was going to have her!

As the evening wore on and the level of the bucket was lowered, it began to seem possible. Since Madeline was staying in town now, Durant would be alone. He could go to Durant's cabin, put a bullet through the man's head and return home and nobody would have the slightest idea who had killed him.

He began to plan his foray and the more thought he gave to it, the more possible it seemed. He would go in the early morning, before Durant was up. He would shoot him as he lay in bed, and not even Durant would know who had done it. Not that that mattered anyway. Then he would go to Madeline, who would be a widow with a lot of land and no knowledge of what to do with it, and offer her a solution to all her troubles. He would marry her. Yes, he would even go that far.

He dipped into the bucket again, his imagination going wild at the thought of taking Madeline to bed, the things he would do to her.

Then in his drunken flights of fancy one sober thought somehow found its way through. If he was going to shoot Durant early tomorrow, he had better get some rest now. There would be the devil to pay if he aimed at Durant . . . and missed.

He stood up, headed for the bed, stumbled over the bucket and went down on the floor. Within two minutes, the snoring began.

. . . noise . . . what was that noise? Either someone had called loudly or screamed. Cate pulled himself up to a sitting position. There was thin gray light coming through the window. It was almost dawn.

He stood up slowly, his joints protesting their night spent on the floor. Then he went to the window. There was no one outside so he must have dreamed the noise.

A sudden crash against the door caused him almost to jump out of his skin. It sounded as though someone had tried to get in by knocking the door down.

"Wait a minute, I'm coming," he yelled. "You don't have to break down the door. I was asleep and didn't hear you knock."

He opened the door. "God Almighty, what . . ."

They were his last words. Walking Bear, his face painted in the multicolored streaks that were the sign of a warrior at war, planted his tomahawk firmly in Cate's head.

Stepping over the fallen body, the Indian went inside the cabin and looked around. There was nothing there he wanted, nothing worth saving except . . . His eyes fell upon the keg in the corner. Looking for containers to hold the contents, he found a large jug as well as Cate's bucket. He filled both and carried them outside, this time stepping upon Cate's body as he went by. Then he went back inside and started fires in three places so there would be no possibility that the cabin would not burn to the ground.

That done, he went out again, picked up the whiskey, and headed back through the woods toward the cabin he most looked forward to burning, the man he most wanted to kill . . . Gavin Durant.

That same scene was repeated many times that morning throughout Bath County. The secret of the attack had been kept so well—even by those Indians friendly to the whites and those who worked for and were slaves of whites—that not one soul in the colony suspected anything was afoot.

The war-whoops of the savages, arousing the plantation owners from sleep at daybreak, were their first intimation of the massacre to come. From forests all over the county, painted warriors poured out, and two hours after sunrise, one hundred and thirty colonists had been murdered. Men, women, and children fell indiscriminately beneath the bloody tomahawks and were left lying in the hot September sun. Those few who were fortunate enough to get away hid until the Indians had finished their dreadful work—burning the houses and cabins and ruining the crops in the fields—and then fled toward Bath Town, having no idea what they would find once they got there, not knowing whether the town would be a scene of ashes, blood, and desolation, like the rest of the region.

Madeline awoke slowly these mornings, as though something in her subconscious told her not to be in such a hurry to return to reality. When she was fully awake, her first thought was always of Gavin. Her next thought was to try to get rid of her first thought. She would have to get used to the idea that she would never see him again, that he was living happily with Tondah. Sometimes her hurt was forced into the background by bitterness; at other times the hurt took over all of her existence. Trying not to think about it at all was as futile as telling the sun not to rise tomorrow morning. She would never stop thinking about Gavin, missing him, and she would never get over the hurt of losing him and his love. She hoped that perhaps with time—a great deal of time—she might become less bitter.

On this morning as she finally roused herself enough to leave her pallet, she heard someone else stirring in the house. Since their illness, all of the Rolands except Cyrus slept much later than usual in the mornings. Cyrus, who now was completely recovered, had for the past few days been going back to his blacksmith shop. Before that, he had been out somewhere for four days, but he had not mentioned where he was going when he left the house. If Jessie had known, she had said nothing to Madeline.

After dressing, Madeline went to the well to fill the buckets before preparing breakfast. Jessie had said she was perfectly capable of taking over the running of the household again, but when Madeline insisted on continuing to manage things for her, Jessie had given in. Madeline knew Jessie was aware that she felt she must do something to earn her board and keep. Only yesterday Jessie had repeated her offer to let Madeline stay on as long as she liked, even forever, but Madeline had told her she would be leaving within a month.

"I found out at Mulligan's that a ship is expected sometime near the middle of next month," she said. "By coincidence, it is the *Sea Lion.*"

"Oh, Maddie," Jessie said sympathetically. "Wait for another. It would be too, too . . . I don't know . . . to have to return on that one."

"I don't mind," Madeline had said. "It seems right that I go back the way I came." She had not added "with uncertain future," but she knew Jessie was aware of that also, and that she would leave in October, the same month they had both arrived.

Cyrus was at the well, splashing water on his face

from the bucket. "You're up earlier than usual," she greeted him.

"Trying to get back to my old schedule," he said. "Sometimes the people from the plantations bring their horses in by sunup. I've missed out on a lot of business."

"I doubt that," she said. "From what I've heard, the fever was worse on the plantations than in Bath. I doubt if anyone had shoeing horses on their minds during the worst of the outbreak."

Cyrus looked at her strangely for a minute or two, then said, "I've been trying to decide if I should tell you something . . ."

"What?" By the tone of his voice, she knew it was something serious.

"Gavin has had yellow fever."

Her hand flew to her mouth as though to stop a scream.

"He's over it now, except for being weak," Cyrus said quickly. She looked as though she would faint at his feet. "At least that's what the Ind—What I was told."

"You don't have to try to keep it from me, Cyrus," she said, in control once more. "I know that Tondah is there."

Cyrus nodded. "I thought you probably did. Jessie and I thought she might be . . ." He broke off again, sure that he had gone too far this time.

She probably would tell Cyrus and Jessie the whole story before she went back to England, Madeline thought, but she did not want to talk about it now. "Are you sure he is all right now?" she asked.

He nodded. "Some of us have been out picking his cotton for him."

"So that's where you were for those four days. I should have been suspicious when you wouldn't say. It was nice of you, Cyrus, you and the others. I know how you feel about Gavin and . . ."

"I feel better about him now," Cyrus interrupted. "I guess he was only doing what he thought he had to when he wouldn't fight. Only thing I hold against him now is the way he's treated you."

She would soon be gone, but Gavin would be living among these people for the rest of his life. "He didn't mistreat me," she said softly. "What came between us . . . was something that happened a long time ago in London. It was my fault."

"I don't think he is blameless, whatever the reason, and . . ." He broke off again, this time shading his eyes with his hand as he looked toward the side street which ran beside the backyard.

Madeline also looked toward the street. "What is it?" she asked. There was something . . . or someone . . . moving along close to the ground.

"My God!" Cyrus breathed. "It's a man crawling on all fours. He's been hurt."

They both ran toward the street.

His clothing ragged and bloody, the man had stopped crawling by the time they reached him. He was on his knees, panting for breath.

"It's Harley Cruper. His plantation is near town," Cyrus said, trying to help the man to his feet. There was a wound on the side of his head and his right arm was mangled. He could not stand up without aid.

Giving up, Cyrus eased him back down to the ground, letting him sit.

"What is it, Harley? What happened to you?" Cyrus asked.

Cruper's voice was scarcely above a whisper as he said, "Attacked . . . the Indians, this morning. Everywhere. They are all over the countryside . . . killing . . . killing." Cruper then lay down as though he were going to take a short nap.

"Can't we get him inside?" Madeline asked, overcoming her horror long enough to speak. "He needs attention."

Cyrus shook his head. "Not any more. He's gone."

Cruper's last words hit Madeline and Cyrus at the same time. "Attack! All over the countryside!" Cyrus repeated. "My God, they must be butchering up the whole colony . . . everyone who doesn't live right in Bath Town!"

Madeline, standing as still as death herself, stopped breathing for at least a minute. She felt faint, as though she would fall to the ground beside Harley Cruper. Gavin! What had happened to Gavin? Was he alive or dead? Was he lying in his cabin, hanging between life and death, needing help? Would Tondah help him, or had she, too, been a victim of the attack? She was aware that Tondah was out of favor with her tribe for living with Gavin the first time; going to him the second time certainly could not have increased their regard for her.

Regaining control of herself, Madeline took a deep breath, then she began running toward Water Street.

"Madeline, what . . ." Cyrus began, then when she

continued to run, paying him not the slightest attention, he knew where she was going. "Wait, Madeline. Stop! Don't go out there. There's no point. You'll only get yourself killed . . ." There was also no point in his continuing to holler after her. She was going and nothing could stop her. She was already running down Water Street toward the path that led to Gavin's cabin.

Cyrus, leaving Cruper's body where it was for the moment, also began running then. He could do nothing about Madeline, but he could sound the warning, let the people of Bath Town know the Indians were attacking, that when they finished in the outlying areas, they probably would come into town.

She was out of breath before she had gone half way through the woods. Only when she had to slow to a fast walk did she think of her own safety. *They are all over the countryside . . . killing . . . killing.* Cruper's words went through her mind, chilling her. She looked around her, expecting to see a savage hidden behind every tree, every bush, but the woods were abnormally quiet. There was not even a bird call, a sign that strangers were around. That much she had learned about life in "semicivilized" places.

Regaining her second wind, she began to run again. It didn't matter about her safety, after all, if Gavin lay dead in his cabin.

She stopped when she reached the clearing, almost expecting to see Indians milling around outside. She saw nothing . . . except the cabin itself, looking peaceful and bucolic against the woodsy background. There was no sign of life.

That thought left her frozen where she was for

several minutes. Then she tore across the clearing and burst into the cabin. She was almost afraid to look around her, afraid of what she would find. But there was nothing. The cabin was untouched. It looked exactly as it had when she had left. Obviously, the Indians had not been here . . . yet.

But where was Gavin? Where was Tondah?

It was then that the paralyzing thought hit her. Gavin no doubt had been out in the field working when the savages struck—Tondah with him—and had been killed there.

She started out the door but was stopped instantly.

Walking Bear, terrifying in war paint, loomed before her, grinning. She stifled a scream, but was too petrified to speak.

The Indian had no such problem. Still grinning evilly, he said, "He take my woman now I take his," and he grabbed Madeline by her long, pale hair.

Chapter Seventeen

IT SEEMED TO GAVIN THAT HE HAD BEEN IN THE CAVE forever, though, in fact, it had only been four days since Tondah had brought him there to receive the beneficial air. He knew now that her talk had all been a ruse to get him to the cave. He did not know why, nor did he care particularly. As he had thought from the beginning, one place was as good as another without Madeline.

However, he was growing more restless and bored now. He should be at home, picking the last of the cotton, curing the last of the tobacco, and Tondah should be putting up the vegetables for the winter . . . finishing the job that Madeline had begun. His curiosity was becoming more and more piqued now as to why Tondah had brought him here in the first place, why she insisted that he stay here, why she would not let him go farther than to the mouth of the cave (and even then she had warned him not to part the bushes covering the mouth: "It no good for your health out there," she kept saying).

Only last night they had come the closest to an argument that they had since she had first come to work for him.

"I am feeling fine now," he had told her, "completely recovered. I am ready to go home."

"No!" she cried instantly. "You still weak. We stay longer."

"Tondah, I'm tired of this place. You know as well as I that there are things that need attention at home. I can't just sit here day after day, night after night, and think about . . ." He broke off.

She looked at him shrewdly. "You still think of her." She said it matter-of-factly, but he could see the hurt in her eyes.

He might as well let her know the truth, no matter how brutal. It might save her from a bigger hurt later. "I will always think of her," he said. He watched her to see if she would cringe, but she showed no outward sign of emotion.

"No." She shook her head. "You forget her. Tondah help you forget." Then she turned away from him and busied herself with their dinner. While they were eating, she said, "Tell me you stay here longer, just a little longer."

He sighed. "All right, a little longer . . . but not *much* longer."

Now, with a tiny light of morning showing through the bushes at the mouth of the cave, he knew he could not stand the confining situation any longer, not another day. He looked over at Tondah, still asleep on her pallet, and he stood up, his head touching the top of the cave. He took a few steps and looked back at Tondah. She had not stirred.

Being extremely quiet now, he stooped to get through the mouth, then parted the bushes, and went on the other side. Freedom! He took a deep breath, sucking the warm, fresh air into his lungs. Only now did he realize how confined, how like a prisoner, he had felt in the cave. He had stayed only to please Tondah because she had saved his life, but he would not go back in there no matter what. If she, for whatever reason, wanted to stay, that was all right with him, but she would stay alone.

He was closer to Bath Town than to his cabin, so he decided to go there first to pick up a few supplies. Tondah apparently had taken most of the food they had on hand to the cave.

Just as he reached the end of Water Street, he stopped in astonishment. Cyrus Roland was running down the street, waving his arms and shouting, "Attack! Attack! The Indians are on the attack!"

Doors along the street were opening and people were coming outside, demanding to know what was going on, why Cyrus was raving so.

Gavin began to run. He caught up with Cyrus and grabbed him by the arm, stopping him. "What is it?" he said. "Where are they attacking? How do you know?"

Out of breath, Cyrus panted, "A little earlier . . . Harley Cruper crawled into town . . . wounded . . . died. Said Indians all over countryside . . . killing . . . burning. Got to warn people."

"Tell the men to be ready, though I doubt the Indians will come into town," Gavin said. He had thought for a long time that the Indians were getting ready for an attack and, certainly, they had chosen the best time . . . from their point of view. The settlers were divided politically and battle weary, those who were not weakened or dead from disease.

He stopped suddenly in his tracks. Tondah had known the attack was coming; that was why she had taken him to the cave. For the second time, she had saved his life.

As Cyrus continued up Front Street crying his warning, Gavin went to the Roland house where Jessie and Carrie stood on the porch, their arms around each other.

"Oh, Gavin!" Jessie cried in surprise. "I was sure you were dead. The Indians are attacking every plantation and farm outside of Bath. Cyrus said . . ."

"Where is Madeline?" he interrupted. All he wanted at this minute was to see her, take her in his arms, and tell her he was sorry he had been such a fool. Then he would worry about the Indians.

"Dear Lord, didn't Cyrus tell you?" Jessie's face went even whiter than it already was.

"Tell me what?" Tentacles of panic clutched at his heart, constricting his breath.

"She was with him earlier this morning when he saw Harley Cruper and she . . . she tore off in the direction of your cabin. There was no stopping her, Cyrus said."

For an instant, Gavin felt as though he would faint, then he clutched at Jessie's hand. "Are you sure? Did she . . . did she go through the woods?"

"Yes, Cyrus said he could not make her stop. She was worried about you. I suppose she wanted to warn you about the Indians, or be sure you were not . . . were not . . ."

"Oh, my God!" He turned toward the steps, but Jessie grabbed him by the arm and tried to hold him.

"Stay here, stay here!" Carrie screamed, then began crying.

"Don't go out there, Gavin," Jessie pleaded. "It is too late to save Madeline. You will only be killed also."

"If Madeline is dead, then I do not want to live either," Gavin said, and left on the run.

Tondah awoke, feeling stiff and unrefreshed by sleep. The inactivity of the past few days had caused restless nights and a depressed, sluggish feeling during the days. She had left the cave for short periods during the past four days to look and listen for unusual sounds in the woods and along the river. It was just possible that Walking Bear had been guessing when he had given her an exact date, or it was also possible that Chief Hancock had changed the date . . . or even decided to call off the massacre, but that was not likely.

Hearing no sound from the other pallet, she lay on her side, facing the wall. She would do nothing to awaken Gavin. This morning, of all mornings he should sleep. This was the day, the day the rest of the white people would meet their fate.

Suddenly, she turned over and sat bolt upright. The cave was *too* quiet; there was not even the sound of breathing, except her own.

Gavin's pallet was empty. She looked toward the clump of bushes at the mouth, thinking Gavin had gone to relieve himself, but he was not there either.

She was up and out of the cave in a flash, knowing instinctively that Gavin had gone back to his cabin. She also knew that he would be killed going through the woods if he should meet a band of murderous Indians, and if he got as far as his cabin, he would surely be killed there. There was absolutely nothing she could do to save him, unless she could get to him before her people did.

Why, oh why, could he not have stayed with her in the cave one more day?

Gavin ran through the woods as though chased by the hounds of hell. If there were any weakness left from the fever, he forgot about it. Fear for Madeline all but gave him wings. He did stop once, at the halfway point, not to catch his breath, but because it occurred to him that he was making too much noise in his haste. Twigs were snapping beneath his feet and displaced stones hit upon each other. If there were even one Indian lurking in the vicinity, Gavin was already as good as dead.

He grimaced at his choice of words . . . as good as dead . . . and continued running. There was no way to be fast and silent at the same time. He could only hope that he was out of arrow range.

He paused once again when he reached the clearing. The cabin was there; it had not been burned. Pray God Madeline was inside, alone and safe.

He opened the door gently, making as little noise as possible. He had no idea what he would see on the other side. What he saw was . . . nothing. The room was empty.

He went to the little room that had been used by Tondah and found it empty also. If Madeline was not here, where was she? Had the Indians stopped her before she reached the cabin? Was she, even now, lying murdered in the woods?

His eyes fell on something he had missed in his haste to see Madeline. Lying near the door was something purple, a little heap of material. He picked it up, then lovingly held it against his face. Madeline's lilac shawl. She had been there . . . and no doubt had been taken away suddenly by Indians or the shawl would not have been left on the floor.

He groaned out loud, actually in physical pain at the thoughts that came to him as he imagined what the savages would do to Madeline. They had always been fascinated by that silver hair of hers and now . . . He groaned again.

He looked at the wall beside the fireplace where two firearms hung: the gun which he used for hunting, and a musket. He hesitated only a fraction of a second, then took down the musket. For Madeline he would bear arms, kill, do whatever was necessary to save her life . . . if he were not already too late.

It was different this time, not like the fighting and killing the men of Bath Town had wanted him to do. This time there was no murky cause, no undecided principles, no nameless and faceless enemy. This time he would be fighting—and possibly killing—to save a life. This time the enemy was a murderous savage bent on killing and destroying everything and everybody in sight.

He rushed out of the cabin into the woods beyond his fields, walking fast but quietly, stopping every now and then to listen for noises. There was no sound, and the abnormal quiet only added to his fear. On leaving Bath Town, he had been uncertain where the Indians were, but he knew now that he was getting close. The unnatural stillness was an indication that there were some nearby, otherwise he would have heard the normal forest noises.

Sure now that he was headed in the right direction, even though he had little of the Indian knowledge of tracking, he slowed his steps so he could be quieter. It would not do Madeline, or himself, any good if an Indian saw him before he spotted the Indian.

Suddenly a war-whoop rent the air, causing Gavin to stop dead still. God in heaven, he thought, he was right upon them. He heard voices now, several voices, in the forest just ahead of him. They were laughing . . . and was that singing, or chanting, that he heard?

Cautiously, slipping from treetrunk to treetrunk, he forged on. Then he stopped. There was a small clearing just ahead where several trees had been felled. Sitting on the ground, leaning against the trunk of one of the fallen trees, were five Indians, their faces bearing the unmistakeable war paint. In front of the Indians were three large jugs, one already empty and overturned. A fourth jug was being passed back and forth.

Gavin stared, unbelieving. They were not making war, attacking, or burning. They were drunk as billy goats and getting drunker. Undoubtedly, they were drinking the whiskey they had stolen from some hapless settler's farm . . . after killing the farmer and his family and just before burning their dwelling.

Gavin went around the small clearing, giving the Indians wide berth. Drunk, they could be almost as deadly as sober. And the fact that five were drunk did not mean the rest of the warring bands were in the same state. He had to push on until he found Madeline. He did not allow himself to think in what condition he might find her.

He walked for what seemed like a long time, passing clearings where plantations and smaller farms had been and were now piles of smoking ashes. In some cases a solitary chimney stood like a sentinel guarding the ruins. He knew there were bodies in the ashes, but he did not take the time to survey the damage or casualties. At a greater risk to his own safety, he went faster, giving little thought to how much noise he made. By being quiet and safer, he was losing time. It would do him no good to find Madeline if he were too late.

He knew he was getting closer to the Indian village of Catechna, home of Chief Hancock. Was it possible that Madeline had been taken there?

He stopped, just outside the village. It was surrounded by fields of corn, tobacco, and pumpkins. He could go between the rows of tall corn and be hidden until he was right at the village.

He came out at what appeared to be a street with approximately two dozen log and straw huts on either side. There were women and children in the street and around the huts, but there were no males in sight. He watched for a while, finally deciding that every male over twelve was out on the rampage against the whites. It was clear to him that Madeline was not here.

For a moment, he wondered what to do next, where to go. There was no point in going back through the woods the way he had come. The only alternative was to circle wide through the forest and come out on the other side of his cabin.

The woods were thicker by this route, and there was an undergrowth of thorny bushes and moss. Several times he stopped, hiding in the nearest clump of bushes as Indians passed. He hardly dared to breathe until they were well beyond him. Some, like the five on the other trail, were drunk; others, bow and arrow at the ready, looked as though they were stalking game, only now the game was man rather than animal.

The distance was greater by this route and it seemed that he had been walking for hours when, suddenly, he heard a faint scream up ahead. He stopped to be sure of the direction, then walked faster toward the sound. It was Madeline; he was sure of it! So great was his haste now that he stumbled twice over tree roots that were aboveground.

He came upon them all at once, stopping in his tracks, then hiding behind a tree before he was seen. Madeline was tied to a tree (still alive, thank God, still alive!), and Walking Bear, a grin on his evilly painted face, was prodding her with his fingers, pinching her breasts through the homespun material of her gown and then rubbing his hands down her sides.

It was all Gavin could do to keep himself in check. He wanted to dash from behind the tree and either shoot Walking Bear or beat him to death. But if he shot from this angle, the chances were very good of hitting Madeline also. And, in his still somewhat weakened condition, it would be folly to try hand-to-hand combat with the Indian.

Walking Bear's tomahawk lay on the ground at his feet. Spotting it, Gavin realized that the Indian was going to kill Madeline, but probably not before he raped her.

Gavin appraised the situation and decided the only thing he could do was to try to get the tomahawk before Walking Bear realized he was there. Inching in the direction of the weapon, he hoped that Madeline, if she saw him, would give no sign that she did.

Then, just when he was only a few feet from the

tomahawk, Walking Bear sensed a presence and turned quickly. "Gavin!" Madeline screamed. "Look out! Run!"

Like lightning, Walking Bear had the tomahawk in his hand, undeterred by Madeline's scream. In a split second he aimed and threw the tomahawk straight for Gavin's skull and, just as quickly, Gavin ducked. Behind him, he heard the weapon strike something, heard a low groan and the sound of something, or someone, falling. Afraid to take his eyes off his adversary, he did not look around, and was unprepared for what Walking Bear did next.

"Tondah!" the Indian screamed, running past Gavin as though he were not there and bending over the fallen girl. The tomahawk was buried deep in her chest, as though she had run right into it's path. Walking Bear bent over her, tears streaming down his face. He squatted and rocked back and forth on his heels murmuring something incoherent in his own tongue.

The scene in front of them had stunned both Gavin and Madeline into silence. Had Tondah knowingly or accidentally run into the path of the tomahawk? Gavin wondered. Poor lovesick girl, she could not have been more than seventeen, eighteen at the most. And for the third time, she had saved his life. This time at the expense of her own.

Walking Bear stopped rocking as suddenly as he had begun and looked at Gavin. "She dead," he muttered, murder in his voice. "She dead because of you. You the one to be dead, not her." With that, he took the tomahawk from Tondah's chest and raised it as he ran toward Gavin. Just as quickly, Gavin put the musket to his shoulder and, without taking time to aim, fired.

The noise of the shot echoed and reechoed through the woods. Walking Bear stopped in his tracks and looked first at Gavin and then at Madeline, still tied to the tree. Then he fell to the ground dead, an expression of complete surprise on his painted face.

Chapter Eighteen

GAVIN WAITED ONLY LONG ENOUGH TO ASCERTAIN THAT Walking Bear was dead before rushing to Madeline. The ropes that bound her to the tree were so securely tied that he had to take the tomahawk to cut them loose, feeling faintly ill as he picked up the Indian's weapon. Madeline, who was straining against the ropes, fell into his arms, sobbing wildly, as the ropes dropped to the ground.

He held her close, his arms tightly around her. "Hush, my love," he said softly. "We must lose no time. We must get out of the woods before more of the marauding Indians come by here."

She could not stop crying. She had held up fairly well during most of the dreadful experience, but now that the worst was over (God willing!), she could not seem to get herself under control. Gavin, also, was shaken to the core, but he knew he could not let down now; he had to be strong enough for both of them. He had killed a man, but he had had no choice. Even so, he would have to learn to live with the fact of murder. Knowing that it was Madeline's life he had saved (as well as his own) by taking Walking Bear's life would help.

"Hush, love," he said again. "We have to get out of

the woods as fast as we can." With his arm around her waist, he half led, half pulled her. Had he felt stronger, he would have picked her up and carried her.

"Gavin . . ." she began, after a few minutes of struggling to control her near hysteria.

He put his finger to his lips and whispered, "We can talk later . . . when we are safe. We mustn't make any noise at all now."

They continued walking, slowly, quietly, through the dense woods. At one point, Gavin suddenly pushed her into a cluster of bushes, causing her face and arms to be scratched by the prickly little branches. They both dropped to their knees and then lay flat as a group of Indians, apparently in a tremendous hurry, went running by.

"They were sober and still on the warpath," Gavin murmured once they were gone.

"Sober?" she asked.

"I have seen several drunk ones," he said. "I don't know whether that bodes good or ill."

They continued walking in silence. Several times Madeline's tears threatened to spill over again, but resolutely she told herself she could not cry now. Gavin was with her again. No matter what happened now, she could be comforted by the fact that they were together . . . even if only for a short time.

"I don't know where we are," she said in a low voice after they had been walking for what seemed an eternity.

"We are less than a mile from our cabin," he said, "but we can't go there."

"Why not?" A thrill went through her. He had said "our" cabin. Did that mean he was taking her back?

"The Indians are attacking every farm and plantation in the area," he said. "We would not be safe there. We have to get to Bath." Then as an afterthought, "And that may not be safe by now."

"Do you think the Indians would go into town?"

"They may. We can only hope that the people are ready for them. Cyrus was sounding the warning this morning."

It seemed eons ago since he had left the cave, left Tondah asleep, and gone into Bath Town. Now he was leaving Tondah again, deserting her in death. He vowed to himself that once this terrible ordeal was over—if he and Madeline survived—he would go back for Tondah and see that she was decently buried.

The next group of Indians to come their way were not as quiet as the last. They were given plenty of warning and this time they hid behind a giant tree stump.

There were six of them, their faces looking even more grotesque as perspiration caused the paint to run in crazy patterns. They were singing, pushing each other about, laughing, drunk now on their victories as well as on stolen whiskey.

All at once, without any warning, two of the Indians sat down less than ten feet from where Gavin and Madeline were lying. The other four, turning and seeing their comrades taking their ease, flopped down also. Then they began to pass a jug among themselves, each swigging down several swallows of whiskey. When the jug was empty, the last one to drink threw it toward the bushes and it landed no more than an inch from Madeline's face. At the same time, Gavin put his hand over her mouth to keep her from crying out.

With no more whiskey to detain them, the Indians

got up and staggered away, singing loudly, calling war-whoops, and screeching like owls.

Gavin took a deep breath. "That was close. Too close."

After another few minutes of walking, Madeline knew where she was. She recognized the woods behind their cabin. Just a little way ahead was the spring where they got water . . .

Would she ever live in the cabin again, get water from the spring, sleep with her body molded into Gavin's? He had said our cabin and he had called her "love" twice, but did that mean he had forgiven her for deceiving him and was willing to have her back as his wife? They were questions she could not answer, and she was afraid of what his answer would be if she asked him.

"We must veer around the spring," he whispered. "We dare not go that close to the cabin."

Turning to the right in the middle of the woods, she was soon lost again, then she realized that they were nearing Bath Creek. "Isn't there a nearer way into town, or are you afraid the Indians may be on all the paths?" she asked.

"I've changed my mind about going into town," he said. "We'll go, but later. I'm not sure that it is safe now."

"Then where are we going?"

"To a place I know is safe, a place the Indians won't find us."

"I . . . I don't . . . think I can . . . make it any . . . farther." Her knees seemed about to buckle under her. It was as though everything she had been through had caught up with her, physically and emotionally, and was pushing her to the ground. Tears coursed down her face again. "Go on, Gavin. Save yourself. Leave me here."

In answer, he picked her up and she could tell from his red, strained face what an effort it was for him to try to carry her. "Put me down," she said. "Neither of us will make it this way."

"We'll . . . make it." It was a struggle even to talk. "It isn't far."

He was almost beside the creek when he put her down by a large clump of bushes. "Go on. Please Gavin. I'll rest here."

"We'll both rest here," he said, pulling the bushes apart and revealing the mouth of a cave. "Welcome to our temporary home, my Madeline."

A sudden surge of relief and happiness gave her strength to go inside the cave without his help. Once there, she was amazed at what she saw in the small enclosure: two pallets, a lamp, and several boxes containing bread, fruit, meat, and jugs of water.

She turned to Gavin for an explanation, but he was busy pulling the two pallets together. When he had made them into one bed, he lay down and motioned for her to come to him. She lay down beside him, as exhausted as he. With their arms wound tightly around each other, they were soon asleep. The long, long day had finally ended.

Madeline awoke with a start. She had been having a terrible dream in which Walking Bear had been applying a burning torch to her face and arms. She was afraid to open her eyes, afraid of what she would see. Slowly, it came to her that Walking Bear was dead . . . and that she was with Gavin. She opened her eyes to find him still beside her, but propped on an elbow, looking down at her.

He smiled at her. "I thought you would sleep all day."

"Day?" she said, looking toward the mouth of the cave. Yes, the light from outside was bright. "How long did I sleep?"

"We both slept all night and half a day," he said. "It must be nearly noon for the sun is almost directly above."

"You've been outside?"

"Yes, but not very far. I wanted to be sure there were no Indians in the immediate vicinity. Are you hungry?"

"Ravenous."

He turned over one of the boxes and used it as a table—as Tondah had when she was there—and spread out all the food over it. "We'd better not eat it all at once," he warned. "I'm not sure how long we'll be here."

She looked around her, puzzled, her curiosity growing more every minute. "How did you know to have this cave ready for us?" she asked. "How did you know where I was? Or were you looking for someone else when you found me? I don't understand any of it, Gavin."

He was quiet until they had finished eating, and what otherwise might have been an awkward silence did not bother her for she was as eager as he to satisfy her hunger. She could not even remember when she had eaten last.

Finally, hunger and thirst quenched, she leaned back against the wall of the cave. He was only a few seconds behind her. "That pan," he pointed, "is for washing. You can use the water in this bucket. I'll get some more from the creek when we need it."

"Are we drinking creek water?" she asked. The water from the river and creek, without being boiled first, could be dangerous to drink. That was one of the first things she had learned from him.

"No, there is a spring on the other side of the cave that runs into the creek."

It seemed that now the time for explanations had come, they were both hesitant—afraid?—about beginning. Like boiling river water before drinking it, it also seemed safer to talk only of trivialities.

After another short silence, Gavin said, "This cave—I did not know of its existence until five days ago. Tondah brought me here. She had heard of the coming attack—probably from Walking Bear—and she knew if I stayed in the cabin, I would be killed."

"She saved your life," Madeline said softly, her animosity toward the Indian girl fading.

"Three times," he said. "I had yellow fever and she found me in the woods and took me home and nursed me through it."

"Then . . . you did not get Tondah back as soon as you left me in Bath Town?"

He looked at her in astonishment. "Of course not! Had she not found me in the woods, ill, she probably never would have come back."

"Oh." Her spirits were brightening, but there were still unanswered questions. "How is it she let you leave the cave on the very day of the attack?"

"I became restless, bored. Yesterday morning I decided I couldn't stand being cooped up here another minute—you see, I did not know why she wanted me to stay here—and I left before she was awake. I was going home by way of Bath Town to pick up some supplies and I met Cyrus. He told me about the attack and that you had gone running off in the direction of the cabin."

"So you came looking for me," she finished the story. She bowed her head and said softly, "I didn't think you cared enough about me to be concerned what happened to me."

"Oh, Madeline." He moved over beside her and took her in his arms. "Can you ever forgive me for being such a fool, such a damned stupid fool? It doesn't matter about your past. That's over and done with. What matters is *our* present and *our* future. I had to lose you before I could get my values and priorities straight."

"You never lost me, Gavin. Not really. But I wish you had let me explain about my past. That might have made some difference. I don't know . . ." She ended on an indefinite note.

"Tell me now," he said. "And then we'll never speak of it again."

There, with his arms around her comfortingly, she told him what her life had been from the time of her father's death until she boarded the *Sea Lion* to take her to the New World and her new life. She explained that Rufus DeLong had forced her to lure men home so that he could fleece them, and that it was he who had made the men think that she was married to him. "I was telling you the truth," she finished, "when I told you that you are the only man I have ever loved, the only man I have ever made love to."

He was silent for a moment only, then said. "I can

only repeat what I said before. Can you ever forgive me for being such a damned, stupid fool?"

"I love you," she said simply, adding with a smile, "No matter what kind of fool you are." Her arms went around his neck and for a while they were content just holding each other close again.

Finally, when the silence seemed about to go on for a long time, he asked, "What are you thinking?"

"I am thinking about Tondah," she said. "How I disliked the girl . . . and she saved both our lives. Now I can't even resent her, knowing that for a long time she was your 'woman'."

"She was never my 'woman', as you put it," he said. "I knew that she was in love with me—or thought she was—but I never made love to her. I thought it would be taking unfair advantage of her and of the way she felt about me."

"I should have known," Madeline said. "I should have known you well enough to know that was how you would feel about it. I guess I have been something of a fool also."

"You have no reason ever to be jealous, not of anyone," he said, taking his arms from around her and cupping her face in his hands. "There will never be another love in my life."

And then his mouth was upon hers. He took deep, swollen kisses from her which went on and on, his hands moving about her body at the same time. Until now, their driving desire for each other had been reined in by fatigue, hunger, fear, suspicions, and, to some degree, hard feelings. Now, nothing stood between them and their need for each other. Their appetites assuaged, their differences settled, they could give themselves up to pleasure and passion, abandon all to their consuming love.

At his touch, she thrust her body against him fiercely, every fiber of her being screaming for his possession. It had been so long, so long . . .

"My love, my love," he murmured, unbuttoning her blouse and then removing it, followed by her skirt, petticoats and chemise. When she was naked, he pushed her gently back to the joined pallets and then removed his own clothing. He lay down beside her again, pulling her body so close to his that they seemed of one flesh. The tips of her breasts felt seared where they touched his chest.

"You are so beautiful," he whispered, his hand going down her side, over a rounded hip and then to her thigh, "and I have wanted you so."

She could not speak. Her only answer was a soft moan as the gently stroking hand made her senses whirl. How she had missed him! How she had wanted him! And now they were together again, their love like a conflagration, devouring them totally.

Her arms wrapped around his neck, pulling him closer, ever closer, returning his kiss so unrestrainedly that he trembled slightly. But he was determined to make their pleasure last as long as possible. Moving back an inch or two from her, his kiss went from her lips to her throat, savoring with his tongue the hollow there, and then going to her breasts where he nuzzled each rosy peak until a tiny gasp escaped her and she began to writhe on the pallet. Slipping an arm beneath her hips, he held her firmly while, with his other hand, he caressed the flawless silken skin of her body, moving down to the center of her desire.

Her fingernails bit into his back as ripples of pleasure went through her, and her teeth nipped lovingly at his earlobe. She moved against him, more than ready to receive his throbbing manhood, but still he prolonged their excitement, teasing her body with his hands and with his tongue until she thought she would scream out.

He pulled away from her just enough to make her arch toward him. Her hands grasped his massive shoulders to bring him back to her, and then began to stroke the hard contours of his body, causing him to groan in need.

Unable to postpone the moment any longer, he mounted her as she shuddered convulsively, ready to experience the exquisite feeling of release. The tension built to an unbearable point in the crescendo of torrid thrusting until, finally, an explosion of pleasure left them weak and panting for breath.

Still he remained atop her, planting kisses, more gentle now, on her forehead, her eyelids, her cheeks, and her mouth, and then he was still.

For a long time they lay that way, neither wanting to break apart, both wanting to stay as close to the other as possible. All of the fear and frustration of the past weeks was gone. There was nothing between them now but love. Finally, they moved apart, but only a few inches.

With her finger she began to trace a pattern through the coarse hair on his chest. "Gavin," she said softly, "I thought we would never make love again. I thought I would go back to England and never see you again."

Without answering, he pulled her to him, clasping her against him for a minute only before starting anew his tender explorations of her body. He would never get enough of her, the look, the feel, the taste of her honeyed sweetness.

Thrill after thrill began to go through her once more, like ripples circling outward from a stone thrown into a lake, increasing and widening until the circle was all-encompassing. Her breasts responded with jutting peaks to his teasing tongue and her straining thighs lifted automatically to his touch, ready to receive him. Again they were soaring, upward, upward, to the final plateau of sharp, intense feeling that annihilates all but rapturous gratification.

The war of the Tuscaroras could be raging all around outside, but in the little cave near Catnip Point only love held forth like a cool, healing rain after an arid season of broiling heat and deadly drought.

Chapter Nineteen

THE FOLLOWING MORNING, TWO DAWNS AFTER THE BEGIN-
ning of the Indian massacre, Gavin awoke before
Madeline. Cautiously, he disengaged himself from the
cover and got up from the pallet. As much as he wanted
to, he could not, in good conscience, stay in the cave
any longer. It had been necessary for him to bring
Madeline there to safety, and necessary for him to
regain his strength after the debilitating day of seeking
and finding his wife. Also, he had told himself yesterday, it had been essential for the two of them to remain
quietly together for a time to be sure all differences
were settled and to renew their life together.

Now, he had to try to get into Bath Town to see how
the people had fared, to see if he could be of any
assistance to them. He had no idea whether the riotous
Indians had been quelled or had been victorious over
the settlers.

He poured water into the pan and washed his face,
feeling the prickly stubble of the two-day growth. Then
he dressed, hoping the time would not be long before
he could take a real bath and put on clean clothing. He
looked for a moment at his musket, lying against the
wall of the cave, hesitated briefly, then picked it up. He

did not think he would use it again, did not think he *could* use it again (unless circumstances were like those of the day before yesterday), but it was possible he might be able to frighten Indians with it.

Just as he was about to slip quietly out of the cave, Madeline stirred and sat up. "Where are you going?" she said instantly, noting the musket.

"I am going . . . to see what the situation is outside," he said. "Go back to sleep."

"Indeed not! If you are going out, I am too."

"Indeed not!" He repeated her words with the same inflection. "You are going to stay here where it's safe."

She was already pulling on her clothes when she answered. "If you're not safe, I don't want to be either. I'm going with you."

"Madeline, I'd rather . . ."

"Do you think that if I had awakened to find you gone I would have stayed here?" she asked. "I would have gone out looking for you."

He gave in. "All right, but we will have to be extremely careful. We don't know what we'll find out there."

"Are we going home?"

"Not yet. We're going to try to get to Bath Town—at least close enough to see what has happened there."

She gave him an apple and took one for herself, the last of the food left in the box Tondah had prepared. "Let's not start out on an empty stomach," she said.

Parting the bushes at the mouth of the cave, he looked all around before holding the bushes back for her to follow him. The woods were quiet, but it did not seem to be the unnatural quiet of the other day. The fluttering wings of birds could be heard, as well as the little stream beside the cave which ran down to Bath Creek.

"Surely the Indians are not still on the rampage," she whispered.

"They may be," he said. "There was more than one tribe involved. The Tuscaroras had help, probably from every tribe in this area."

They progressed through the woods much as they had before, going from tree to tree in order to have something to hide behind should they spot Indians. They also tried to keep a lookout in all directions at once.

Gavin, who was one step ahead of Madeline, stopped suddenly and she, having been looking to the side, ran into him. She all but screamed when she saw what had stopped him. Lying on the ground, not more than three feet from them, was an Indian. He was flat on his back, one arm across his stomach, the other flung out to his side.

"He's not dead," Gavin whispered, pointing to a jug near the Indian. "He's dead drunk."

They walked around the Indian and continued without further incident to the path into town. "We'd better stay beside the path, further in the woods," Gavin said. "We're too visible this way."

They emerged from the woods directly behind Mulligan's Store. "Stay here," Gavin cautioned. "I am going to look in the window to see if they . . ." He did not finish the sentence.

"And I am going to look in the window with you," Madeline said, staying in step with him.

"You are the stubbornest, most . . ."

"I know," she interrupted, "and you're going to have to learn to live with it."

Or die with it, was his grim, unspoken thought. The back windows of the Mulligans' looked in on their living quarters, not the store. There was no sign of life inside, but neither was there sign that anything had been disturbed. Gavin had said nothing to Madeline, but he had been afraid that, by now, the entire town of Bath might have been put to the torch.

"It's still not much past dawn," Madeline said. "Maybe they are not up yet. I think their bedchamber is abovestairs."

Gavin, so sure that he would find death and disaster, had scarcely considered the possibility that all might be well in town. "I hope you are right," he said. He took her hand and led her slowly around to the front of the building and to the street.

Wes Martin, a gun in his hand and one at his feet was standing at the end of the street, while another man whom they could not recognize, was at the other end of the street, similarly armed.

Gavin let his breath out as though he had been holding it for hours. The cabins and houses still stood; nothing had been burned. Still holding hands, he and Madeline rushed toward Wes, only to have him raise the gun, take aim, then suddenly lower the weapon.

"My God," he said when they reached him, "I was ready to shoot you. I thought you were Indians." Then even more surprise was in his voice as he asked, "Where did you come from? I heard you had both been murdered by those red devils."

"We managed to escape," Gavin said. "Tell us what has happened."

"It's still going on," Wes said. "They're still out there killing and burning. Every now and then one of the planters, usually wounded, manages to get into town. The few who have made it have brought terrible stories . . ." Out of deference to Madeline, he did not continue.

"Do you think they'll come into town?" Gavin asked.

"I don't know," Wes said. "We're standing guard, and if they attack we're ready to fight, but how long could we hold them off?"

Gavin nodded. He knew the ammunition would only hold out for so long and then the people in town could be trapped by the Indians on two sides of land, and even on the other two sides, the river and the creek, when the Indians were ready to take the town.

"The Rolands," Madeline asked, "are they all right?"

"As all right as anybody else, I guess," Wes said. "Cyrus takes his turn standing guard. It was Cyrus who first found out about the attack."

"I know," Madeline said. "I was with him." It seemed another lifetime ago instead of only two days. "Gavin, could we go to them?"

"Of course," he said. "Wes, I'll do whatever I can to help. Stand guard, or . . . whatever."

Wes looked at the musket hanging from the strap on Gavin's shoulder. He said nothing, merely nodded.

The four Rolands were at breakfast when Madeline and Gavin went in. Jessie, facing the door, rose from her chair screaming when she saw them and Cyrus, without even looking, grabbed the gun beside his chair and was up ready to protect his family.

"Oh, my God." He slumped back to his chair, weak with relief when he saw who it was. Jessie, however, was crying as she tried to hug Madeline and Gavin at once, and Con and Carrie were also adding to the confusion, Con by clapping his hands and Carrie by jumping up and down saying, "I knew they weren't dead. I told you the Indians didn't get them."

Getting over his shock, Cyrus stood up and shook Gavin's hand. "It's God's mercy you're both alive," he said. "Madeline, I tried to stop you . . ."

Gavin laughed for the first time in what seemed a very long time. "You should have saved your breath, Cyrus. My wife has a mind of her own . . . which she uses from time to time."

Madeline took an affectionate swipe at him. "We're almost as surprised to see you as you are to see us," she said. "We didn't know what we'd find here."

They were all solemn again, knowing that the worst still could happen. "You can't go back to your cabin," Cyrus said. "The latest word we had here is that it's still going on out there."

"You'll stay here with us, of course," Jessie said matter-of-factly.

Gavin looked from one to the other. He did not want to stir up old animosities, but neither did he want to accept hospitality from those reluctant to give it. "Are you sure?" he asked finally.

"Yes! Yes!" Con and Carrie cried simultaneously, while Jessie and Cyrus nodded.

"You're the closest thing we have to family in this part of the world," Jessie said.

"Gavin . . ." Cyrus began, then hesitated as though not quite sure how to go on. "That time . . . when we . . . well, I'm sorry for the things I said, the way I acted."

Gavin smiled at him. "I am sorry I could not live up to what you expected of me, Cyrus."

"You helped out with what you did," Cyrus said. "I know that now. Someone had to stay here and take care of things, and it was good that you did, you and Madeline."

"While we're on the subject," Gavin said, "you helped out quite a bit yourself, Cyrus, you and the others. You saved my crops for me while I was sick."

"Saved them for the Indians, most likely," Cyrus said.

Jessie, anxious to change the subject back to something more pleasant, said, "Sit down and eat breakfast. I don't know where you came from but I know you haven't eaten. Sit down and tell us where you've been for the past two days."

"Then I would like to have a bath," Madeline said, "and some clean clothes."

"And Cyrus," Gavin said, "may I borrow your razor?"

In all, the terrible carnage lasted for three days throughout Bath County with the Indians committing acts of inconceivable cruelty and horror. Only a few of the settlers managed to make it into Bath to the relative safety of the town. The last ones to come in on the day that Gavin and Madeline returned brought hope that the shocking bloodletting and burning would soon be over, for they told of seeing drunken Indians who passed out and others who were drinking instead of fighting.

On the fifth day after the beginning of the attack, Gavin volunteered to be the one to go outside of town and survey the countryside to see what the situation was. "There is something I want to do," he said, "something I have to do, so I should be the one to go. No, Madeline, you positively are not going with me this time."

She knew from the tone in his voice that there was no point in arguing. She also knew what it was he had to do when she heard him ask Cyrus if he could borrow a shovel to take with him and then ask Jessie if she would contribute a sheet.

He left at mid-morning, driving Cyrus's buggy.

"He'll certainly be an easy target for the Indians," Madeline said, not understanding why he was not going on foot.

"Unless they are mounted, which is unlikely, he can get away from them easier," Cyrus pointed out.

That fact did not keep her from worrying. All day she sat at the front window, leaving only when Jessie demanded that she eat. "I should have gone with him," she said over and over, even though she knew that there was no way she could have persuaded Gavin to let her go.

Finally, after four in the afternoon, she saw the buggy coming down the street and she ran out of the house to the yard. But she could not get to Gavin at once because he was having to stop every few feet to tell people what he had found outside the town.

Madeline grabbed him before he was all the way out of the buggy. "I thought you'd never get back," she said, kissing him. "I've been so worried."

"I wish there had been some way to let you know

that everything was all right," he said. "The Indians are not fighting any more. They have gone back to wherever they came from. I didn't even see any Tuscaroras except . . ." He stopped abruptly.

"You buried Tondah and Walking Bear." It was a statement rather than a question.

"I buried Tondah," he said. "Walking Bear's body had been moved. Since Chief Hancock is his father, I suppose he was taken back to Catechna by whoever found him in the woods."

"And Tondah wasn't? Why?"

"She was an outcast because of me. That was why I had to see that she was decently buried."

Madeline bowed her head as a tear slid down her cheek. There was one more question she was almost afraid to ask, but she had to know. "Did you come back by . . . by our home?"

"No," he said. "I wanted to be sure first that there were no Indians still lurking around, that it would be safe. We will go together tomorrow."

"Why not now? Oh, Gavin, I want to go home!"

"Not today," he said. "I have to call a meeting of all the men to report on the situation outside of town." He did not tell her of the horrors he had seen as he went from what had been one prosperous plantation or farm to another, now nothing more than rubble and ashes. He could not burden her with the picture of death and destruction that he would carry with him as long as he lived. He knew that in her mind she had already formed her own picture of what it was like, but at least he could protect her from the grisly, hideous reality of it. "We'll go tomorrow morning," he promised. "First thing."

* * *

They were up with the sun the next morning, slipping quietly out of the house, hitching up the buggy, and heading for home.

"I should have packed," Madeline said. "We could have saved ourselves a trip if we'd brought my things now."

Gavin made no reply. As he had yesterday, he continually looked from side to side as well as in front and behind them. Although not likely, there still was a possibility that an Indian or two, perhaps coming to from whiskey-sodden sleep, remained in the vicinity, waiting to attack.

As they approached the clearing, he took her hand. Remembering what he had seen yesterday, he thought he should prepare her, just in case . . .

"Madeline, the Indians have left very little standing. At some of the places I went yesterday, even the crops were burned in the fields. Our cabin may not be there."

"I know."

She said nothing else, but in those words he detected more strength than he had realized she had. She had already prepared herself; she was ready to face whatever must be faced.

She, however, was not thinking of how she would feel if the cabin were gone; she was worried about Gavin. The cabin had been his home, built with his own hands on his own land. And the land was the symbol of months, years, of hard work. It was his life, all he had. How would it affect him to see all he had worked for gone? Past, present, and future gone in a puff of smoke.

She noticed him pulling on the reins slightly, trying to slow the pace of the horse without her seeing, trying to postpone what might be a tragic sight.

But the inevitable could not be delayed for long. They had reached the edge of the woods, rounded the last curve . . . and were at the clearing.

She sucked in her breath. "Oh, no!"

There was no cabin.

There was the chimney, eerie looking against the rising sun, and there was a mess of ashes and several thick logs that had not burned.

Slowly, they made their way in the buggy to what had been the front yard. There was nothing that could be salvaged, not one stick of furniture. Only the iron pot which had hung in the fireplace remained as it was.

She started to get out of the buggy, but he put his arm around her, holding her. "There's no need," he said. "There's nothing we can do here. Nothing we can take back."

"Oh, Gavin!" She searched his face, trying to see if his own devastation showed there. But he looked amazingly calm.

He gave her a little smile and, just for an instant, she thought she saw that impish look that she so adored in his eyes. "At least my sending you away had one good side to it," he said. "Nothing of yours was burned because you had everything at the Rolands'."

She nodded, her heart breaking for him. "But you lost everything. Your whole life was here. You lost everything you had."

"Not by a long shot." He tilted her face to his and kissed her. "When I lost you, I lost everything. Now I have you back and," he gestured toward what had been his home, "this is only a minor setback. I have my whole life with me."

She returned his kiss, her body straining toward his.

When they finally broke apart, she asked, "What will we do now, Gavin?"

"We will rebuild, of course. A big house this time, not a cabin. And we'll build in town so we can see and be near our friends. I'm sure some of them will help me." He looked toward the fields. "The crops may have been hurt, but they were not completely destroyed as so many were."

"A big house," she repeated. "We'll need it, because we are going to fill it with little Durants. I want six boys—at least six—every one a replica of his father."

He nodded. "They'll be a big help on the farm," he said. "And we'd better order another six from the female department to help you with that big house."

She laughed. Suddenly what she had thought would be a catastrophe had turned out to be an opportunity . . . an opportunity to build something much better. But one part of the project seemed somewhat askew. "If we are living in town, how can you take care of the crops?"

"I can farm the land just as well from there as I can living here," he said. "The distance is very short."

She nodded, satisfied. "Yes, it is. Especially when you think of how far we have already come."

"And there's still quite a way to go before we are done traveling," he said, drawing her to him once more.

There, in the ashes of their past, they planned their new life.

Tapestry
HISTORICAL ROMANCES

Breathtaking New Tales
of love and adventure set against history's most exciting time and places. Featuring two novels by the finest authors in the field of romantic fiction—<u>every month</u>.

Next Month From
Tapestry Romances

LADY RAINE
by Carol Jerina
LAND OF GOLD
by Mary Ann Hammond